TEXAS RISING

The minutes passed by at a crawl, first ten and then fifteen. With their nerves on edge, both men held their M-16s at the ready, expecting an attack that became more eminent with the passing of each excruciatingly slow minute. Suddenly the stillness of the dark night was broken by the sound of a heavy object crashing into the pine tops and landing on the ground with a thud.

"What the…?" Rodriguez spun to cover whatever had made the noise while Jeb covered the rim of the butte with his rifle.

A low laugh came from the darkness above their heads.

"Well, you told me to toss something down as a signal to climb," Leonard called down in a loud whisper.

"I said a stick Leonard, a stick!" Jeb whispered back up, "What did you throw?"

"That was the co-pilot sir. The pilot is up here," Leonard answered.

TEXAS RISING

By

W.W. BROCK

W.W. Brock

DEDICATION

v

I would like to dedicate this book to my wife, the love of my life. Without her support and encouragement, I would not have started writing.

PROLOGUE

Three months before the national elections, large scale rioting and looting, brought on by the nationwide police crackdown on black activists associated with a growing anti-police movement, and what appeared to be orchestrated attacks on police nationwide, broke out in New York City, Baltimore, Ferguson, Los Angeles, Atlanta, Georgia, and Dallas. These riots were quickly co-opted by thousands of radical Muslim infiltrators that had been given refugee status by a government that was increasingly aligning itself with Islam.

Violence against Christian groups intensified and was seemly ignored by Washington, until multiple armed rioters were shot in Dallas, Texas by a group of local business owners, followed quickly by incidents in several states where rioting thugs were dispatched unceremoniously by law abiding citizens, acting in defense of their property and their lives. When the various state police and local police departments refused to arrest those that had been defending themselves, and the body count was reaching into the hundreds, martial law was declared by President Adi Onbekend, and the order was given to confiscate all firearms from the civilian population. In the wake of the large-scale resistance that followed, the November presidential election was cancelled until order could be restored.

Tennessee, in addition to several states west of the Mississippi, including Arizona, New Mexico, Wyoming, Idaho, Montana, Louisiana, Oklahoma, and Texas refused to enforce the executive order declaring martial law, and a standoff ensued for the next three months, leading to the President declaring a state of emergency. After an all night meeting with the Joint Chiefs, the military was called on to enforce his edict, but a majority of commanders, including two four star generals and a rear admiral of the Joint Chiefs refused the order, stepping down from their command. The word of this insubordination passed quickly through the ranks and many active duty servicemen and women also refused any orders that would have them fire on American civilians. Not all of course, but enough to seriously weaken any attempt at a military action against the states that were leading the insurrection. In addition, none of the several states National Guard troops or their commanders obeyed orders to enforce the martial law within their respective states or deployment to neighboring states. With tens of thousands of armed militia members from all over the country standing ready to oppose any force that he would try to deploy on American soil, the President then requested that the United Nations send troops. This action was quickly met with declarations from the Governors of the western states stating defiantly that should U.N. troops set foot in their states, it would be perceived as an act of war.

With this gauntlet being tossed into the face of tyranny, men and women of all ages, and veterans from all branches of the armed services flocked to militia sites in their respective states and prepared to fight. In the first few days, those conservatives that resided in states that sided with the Marxist policies of the President, packed their belongings and headed for Texas, where it was perceived that the government would strike first, but these were stopped at military checkpoints that had been set up at every freeway interchange in every major city. Only a very few made it to the Red River and the relative freedom that Texas offered. Most were detained, charged with violating martial law, and imprisoned in hastily constructed camps under heavy guard, while those brave few that chose to fight rather than surrender their arms and property were simply gunned down.

Possibly because the recent disappearance and presumed death of their beloved governor, Harold Kincaid, was viewed with suspicion by most of the citizens of Texas, recruitment numbers for the Texas Guard were also setting records. Arms sales, already at record levels, shot through the roof, and AR platform rifles were being built in many backyard shops to try and satisfy the demand for the conflict that everyone felt was coming.

With the disappearance of his predecessor the Lieutenant Governor of Texas, Jebediah Atkins, stepped into the Governor's chair amid speculation that his term would be short lived as a federal occupation seemed imminent. What happened next took almost everyone by surprise. In a bold and secretive move, the Texas legislature voted with a strong majority to move the capitol of Texas from Austin to Fort Worth. The move was in anticipation of the local left wing citizenry of Austin violently revolting against the desire of most Texans to secede from the Union, and had been planned with precision for almost a year, since the previous Governor had recalled the Texas gold reserves back into the state treasury from New York. Governor Atkins signed the bill into law, and then boarded the executive helicopter for a quick flight to the new capitol-building complex, which had been built under a cloak of tight security.

When news that the largest and most self sufficient state in the union had executed plans for secession reached Washington, DC, President Onbekend cancelled his golf outing and returned to the White House, hoping to implement a strategy that would make an example out of the Lone Star State, ensuring that the others in rebellion would come back into the fold out of fear.

Acting on the advice of his Pakistani born Senior Advisor, Durrah Jowles, a long time member of the Muslim Brotherhood, he sent a Carrier Strike Group led by the Nimitz class Super Carrier CVN77 George H. W. Bush into the Gulf of Mexico to blockade any attempts by Texas to ship crude oil from Galveston to offshore markets, and to stop any cargo containers from being received from China with supplies for the rebel states. The President took this action knowing that using a carrier named after a Texas president would be a slap in the face to Most Texians, as they now called themselves, excluding most of those that lived in the metropolitan areas of the larger cities where the most liberal of the left wing crowd seemed to gather.

All Texas Army bases were placed on REDCON 2 alert in preparation for the ground conflict, which seemed imminent.

Immediately upon receiving the REDCON 2 status order, the commandants of Fort Bliss and Fort Hood, acting on a prearranged plan, mustered all of the personnel that were either professing the Muslim faith or suspected of involvement in the faith, along with those that had not passed a psychological screening that included questions related to whether they would fire on United States citizens or not, and loaded them into transports for immediate transfer to Fort Devens in Deven, Massachusetts.

The match that would ignite the powder keg of a national revolution was about to be struck.

CHAPTER 1

"I'm telling ya Luke, I've been down here in Odessa for most of my life and I've never seen the tension between Washington and our folks up in Fort Worth any thicker. I believe that Governor Atkins is setting us up for secession!" The old man slapped his hand on the table, jostling everyone's coffee, in a manner of punctuating his remark.

As was their custom, several of the old cowboys and oil field hands tried to solve the problems of the world every couple of mornings at the Wagon Wheel over coffee and breakfast.

"Well Jerry, I have to admit that things haven't been looking too good from down here since they moved the capitol out of that liberal cesspool in Austin, but Atkins seems to be a good man. I find it hard to believe that the president would have him locked up for sedition. Along with everything else that comes out of his mouth, that talk is just hot air," Luke replied, although he was well aware of the growing concerns among the old timers that gathered at the Wagon Wheel almost every morning. Heck, he was one of those old timers now. Since getting shot and almost dying, Luke had not ventured far from Odessa except to attend Michael Tucker and Hanna's funeral. The two plus years since had done little to dampen the sense of loss that he felt when he recalled the young family that he had befriended.

"Luke, Luke, look!" Luke Moffett was jarred back to reality as Jerry shouted to him and pointed to the television that was showing the Vanguard News Channel.

"We interrupt our normally scheduled broadcast to bring this breaking news! These pictures that you are seeing are of hundreds of troops from the United Nations parading through Fort Worth, Texas just now. We expected some United Nations participation in the enforcement of the President's declaration of martial law that has most of Texas on edge, but no one has spoken about the exact number of these troops or what their role will be over the next few weeks," Vanguard News Anchor Maggie O'Brien continued on excitedly, while all over the restaurant, men were hurriedly gulping their coffee and paying their bills.

"I expect that guns sales just went through the roof!" Luke exclaimed as he stood and made his way to the checkout line, "If you men meant what I've heard you all talking about for the last couple of years, now is the time to pull those drag bags out of the closet and head for your mustering sites. If not, just park your weapons by the front porch and those blue hats will be along to pick them up from you."

Jerry slapped Luke on the back, "I'm too old for this crap Luke. Let me get your breakfast, and you go make sure Mary is safe before you do something foolish…like getting yourself shot up again."

"Thanks Jerry. I'll take you up on it today since I am in kind of a hurry," Luke shook his friend's hand before he made his way through the crowd and out of the door, taking a brief look back at the television just in time to see that the Texas Guard had assembled in force around the capitol building as the Texas Air National Guard helicopter carrying Governor Atkins rose swiftly behind the human barricade and flew off toward the south, away from the capitol.

The short drive to the house was made with a heavy heart as Luke thought of what he might have to do in the next few days, months, or years, depending on whether he survived or not. He had served in Vietnam during that war, and had seen the cost of a half-hearted effort by U. S. forces first hand. Now, just when he and his wife had a good retirement in sight, all hell was breaking loose in the country, and once again his service was needed to protect his homeland. This time that was Texas, and the way of life that he had always known.

Mary was waiting on the porch for Luke to pull into the drive and met him at the old Chevy truck.

"I've heard the news Luke. Is it time to go?" she asked quietly as he just set there for a second before answering.

"Yep, some of the 39th is mustering in Gardendale, but I don't think it will be as bad as all that, Mary. Still, I reckon it won't hurt for you to get over to Ruidoso for a spell. There will probably be a few folks that we know already there," Luke was having trouble speaking so he got out of the truck cab and gave his wife a hug, "Mary, if I don't..."

"Hush that talk Luke!" Mary quickly put her fingers on his lips, "This will be over with quickly. Besides, they won't hurt the cooks. Until then, I'll wait to hear from you."

Luke just nodded his head and choked back the tears that threatened to stream down his face. He knew that the "Old Guard" as they called themselves jokingly, probably wouldn't survive the first wave of conflict. However, they were determined to give a good measure to the enemy until the last man.

"Well, if you've got everything packed, get on out of here. Just remember to take the battery out of your phone until you get word that it is safe to turn it back on. I wouldn't want those idiots to sneak a drone up on you," Luke gave her one last squeeze before she walked to her car and drove off.

Now he had to hook up the one horse trailer that he hauled his old faithful quarter horse in. 'Lucky' would be turned out at John and Mary Louise Post's ranch until the coming conflict had been resolved. Finishing that chore, Luke went into the house to retrieve the custom Remington 700 that had been given to him by Otis Jamieson after Michael Tucker had died in the plane crash with his family. He had hidden the rifle and accompanying drag bag from Mary, not wanting her to think that he might have a more dangerous assignment than camp cook during his time with the Texas Militia, but they knew that he was an accomplished sniper from the Viet Nam campaign. Now, as he loaded the bag into the truck, he dreaded the idea of taking another man's life again, although Luke also knew that there would be no hesitation on his part when that time came.

As he headed to the small corral that held his old horse, Luke stopped by a barrel of oats and got a big handful to feed to Lucky. The horse saw his old friend and trotted briskly over to nuzzle Luke and get his reward. Luke scratched his ears while the horse took the oats from his open hand.

"Well old partner, I have all ideas that this might be our last time together. You need to behave yourself over at the Post's while I'm gone or Mary Louise will have you sent to the glue factory."

Lucky just snickered at that and followed behind Luke to the trailer.

CHAPTER 2

Jebediah Atkins, a tall, wiry, slow talking Texan that had served in the Gulf War conflict years before as an Army Lieutenant Colonel, was feeling the pressure of the Governor's mantle on this particular evening. His heroic service during a particularly brutal fire fight in Baghdad had gained him national recognition, and his friends urged him into politics after he retired from active duty. After several years of working his way up the political ranks, he found himself winning the seat of Lieutenant Governor, and then gaining the governor's office less than a year later with the sudden and suspicious demise of his processor, who had made a practice of poking his political finger in the eyes of the president on every occasion that he could. As Lieutenant Governor, Jebediah became well aware of the building tensions between Washington and Texas, and just how fine a line had to be walked between preventing the President from taking military action against the state and those that defied his authority, but still be the inspiration to the rest of the states to resist the tyranny that was being pressed on them. Now that martial law had been invoked and all elections suspended, it was time to make a decision about which side of that line Texas would step.

After an all night meeting with his Lieutenant Governor, Tom Hastings, and the new Texas Attorney General, Isaiah Ramirez, the decision was made to sign into law the articles of secession that had been passed with overwhelming bipartisan support of the legislature twenty four hours before. As soon as secession was declared, the Governor and his cabinet would flee to a safe area, deep in the Big Bend Park, that had been designated as the new headquarters of the Texas government until the hostilities were over.

"Tom, Isaiah, good luck and God speed to you both. You've probably got about thirty minutes from the time that I make this announcement before they try to take us, so get going. Transportation has been arranged. Make certain that your cell phones are on and in your desks before you leave. That should buy a few extra minutes if they ping the signal for location. I'll be right behind as soon as I put the Guard on alert," Jeb shook both men's hand in turn and watched them exit the room.

The Governor picked up the secure line that had been arranged for this one purpose, "General, we are go for Operation Separate Nation. I repeat we are go for Operation Separate Nation."

"Roger that sir, we are go for Operation Separate Nation," General Andrew Clarke responded and hung up the phone.

Jebediah hurriedly signed the document that was lying on his desk and summoned a trusted courier to run it to the House Speaker. He then made his way to the helipad and the waiting Texas Air Guard UH-1 that would take him to the safety of the new headquarters.

"Welcome aboard, Jeb…er… Governor," the voice came through his headset as soon as he settled into his seat.

From where he was sitting, Jeb couldn't see the pilot's face, but he recognized the voice, "Amos? What are you doing up there?"

"I volunteered for this trip Jeb. You didn't think that I was going to let a green pilot take you out of here, did you?" Captain Amos Whitehorse replied with a laugh, "Besides, it will be like old times when I saved your butt in Iraq!"

"I remember that a bit differently Amos," Jeb replied with a laugh, "Let's get this bird airborne."

"Yes sir, and not a minute too soon, either. Take a look out of your door," Amos responded as the old Huey climbed slowly into the air and started moving away from the capitol.

As they gained altitude, Jeb could see the militia troops that surrounded the capitol grounds waving to the chopper, and just beyond an advancing sea of blue helmets.

"Amos, get me a direct line to General Clarke, pronto," He ordered.

"Roger that, Governor, I'll have it in a second," Amos responded, then, "You're on sir."

"General Clarke here, Governor Atkins."

"General, are your men armed?" Jeb asked.

"Yes sir! We followed your orders to the letter," Clarke responded.

"General, we both feel the same way about firing on our own troops, but I want you to decimate that bunch of rapists and pedophiles in the blue helmets. As soon as that objective is reached, fall back and put my order 'Domino' in play," Jeb ordered, "And General Clarke, good luck."

"Yes sir! I understand the order sir," Clarke responded with what seemed to be a short laugh.

"Well, that will unleash a crap storm, Governor," His headphones crackled as Amos switched them back to internal comms.

"I suppose it will, Amos, but the first shot was fired when the President saw fit to send those United Nation's troops in to Texas. Keep me posted on any reports coming out of there," Jeb responded.

"Yes sir. I hope our boys kick those blue hats back across the Red River," Amos answered, "We've got an escort up high Jeb. Four of our Texas Guard air jockeys are flying cover for us."

"How long before we reach the rendezvous, Amos?" Jeb asked.

"I'm keeping her low to avoid radar, but maybe about two and a half hours. I'm bucking the wind a good bit here," Amos replied.

"Well, I'm not going to relax until we reach safety. All hell is going to break loose in a few minutes, and I know that our 'would be' king is going to come after me with all he can muster," Jeb replied with just a hint of nervousness in his voice. He was starting to wonder if sneaking out on this old bird was the wise thing to do.

The two guards that had accompanied him on this flight just exchanged looks and checked their weapons for the second or third time. Jeb gave them a smile and a 'thumbs up' as a gesture of reassurance. Both men nodded in the affirmative but it was obvious from the grim looks that covered their faces that they would rather be on the ground.

Two hours into the flight the headset came to life, "We've got company Jeb! It looks like five bogies coming in hot about fifty clicks to the east. Our little friends are going to intercept."

"Amos, I think that you had better get us on the ground. I like our chances better in the mesquite scrub than up here. Our boys are outgunned in this fight, and I don't want them to commit suicide for me," Jeb declared.

"They aren't doing it for you Jeb. They're doing it for Texas! This is our home, and by God, we won't give it up easily," Amos replied with anger in his voice, "I know a place a few clicks from here south of I-10 where you might find some cover, and just possibly a few friendlies. I'll drop you there, and then fly decoy straight south. There is another rifle, and a survival kit just behind you. It might come in handy."

"Amos, Texas needs you more on the ground than in it. They will destroy this chopper if you try to make a run in it," Jeb pleaded with his old friend.

"Relax Jeb, I'm not about to commit suicide. I have a plan," Amos reassured him, "Now you boys get the lead out, skids down in thirty seconds."

The Huey just barely touched the skids to the ground, and Jebediah and his escorts hastily disembarked. They watched the old war veteran nose down and pick up speed before lifting away for the southerly run that would draw off any pursuers from following Jeb into the small caves that lined the big bluff behind a natural camouflage of scrub pines.

The men knew that there was no time to waste in finding cover, and made their way through the thick mesquite brush and cactus up the steep slope at a run until they were well hidden from aerial view. They turned to face the direction that Amos had taken over the top of a distant bluff just in time to see a fireball followed a few seconds later by the shockwave of an explosion. Jebediah fought back the tears for his friend who most certainly had just given all that he had for the place and people that he loved.

"We'll make a cold camp here, men. I need to see what we have in our packs that might help us get out of here alive," Jeb said to the men as he started rummaging through the pack that Amos had on the chopper.

That search produced two full twenty round magazines of 5.56 mm ammo for the rifle, one compass, a map of the Trans-Pecos area, a heavy knife that Jeb recognized as Amos' prized K-Bar U.S. Marine Corp Fighting Knife that he had won during a card game in Kuwait, two MRE packs, one issue quart canteen of water, and a fire starter.

"Well things are looking up men. What did you bring to the party?" He asked of his escort.

"I've got six mags, my compass, map, and six MREs, sir. I've also got my canteen with me and about a quart of water," The slender one with 'Leonard' on his MultiCam nametag replied.

The bigger of the two was a rough looking ex-biker named Rodriguez that almost busted out of the sleeves on his MultiCam jacket. "I've got ten mags, six MREs, two grenades, map, compass, binoculars, my Marine Corps bivvie bag, and a length of parachute cord."

"Two grenades, how did you manage that?" Jeb asked in amazement.

"Well, Governor, I was helping unpack a few of our supplies yesterday and just thought they might come in handy," He replied with a big grin.

"They might at that. Men, we've got rough ground to cover if we are going to get to safety. I suggest that we bivouac here for the rest of today and tonight. We will have to leave early, and try to make some mileage during daylight while sticking to cover. If we move out at night, we run the risk of getting bitten by a late denning rattler or being seen by a drone with infrared. We are also going to need more water so Rodriguez, use the binoculars to look for a windmill. If we can find a tank along the route, we'll have plenty of water. Leonard, scout us a cave big enough to get all of our gear in before dark. It's going to be cold without a fire," Jeb gave the men orders to keep them busy and keep their minds off what might be happening to them very soon.

CHAPTER 3

The orders given to the Fourth Regiment Texas Guard ground commanders were simple, "Wait until the United Nation troops were within three hundred yards, kill as many as possible, and then withdraw. Execute 'Domino' as soon as the men are clear of the buildings."

There would be no political correctness controlling the leaders of the Guard. Every man was expected to make real time battle field assessments of the situation and act accordingly to maximize enemy casualties and minimize the casualties of their own men. In addition to the Texas National Guardsmen equipped with issue weaponry, many of the men that had been assembled to protect the Governor and the Capitol were Texas State Guard marksmen equipped with the best rifles that they could afford ranging from the AR-15s in 5.56mm, the new Savage 10/110 FCP HS Precision in .338 Lapua, a couple of Barrett .50 caliber sniper rifles, and a variety of others in the NATO Standard calibers. Those with longer-range capabilities were held in reserve until after the first opening volley to wreak havoc at ranges past one thousand yards as the enemy retreated.

The men that would do the initial killing were quietly hiding in the upper floors of the office buildings that surrounded the large common area leading to the new state offices on three sides, while the others stood in formation at parade rest outside as if to surrender on request. They all knew that many of those that wore the blue helmets and marched under the flag of the U.N. were seasoned fighters that would not be easily defeated, but they also had a reputation for treating the civilian populations of the areas that they occupied with a wanton disregard for personal rights. Stories of food being traded for sexual favors, pedophilia, rape and murder followed them from country to country. This was simply not going to be permitted on Texas soil.

Six heavily armored personnel carriers entered the upper end of the pavilion followed by what looked like a full battalion of troops marching by company. If the size of the force surprised or dismayed the Texians standing in formation, there was not a glimmer in their eyes to show it, just a ready resolve to carry out the orders as they were received, and, as many hoped, to take a blue helmet for a souvenir after the fight.

Closer and closer rolled the personnel carriers until they stopped about four hundred yards out, and the enemy drew up into a deep skirmish line.

General Andrew Clarke watched the procession of white vehicles and blue helmeted troops advance on the Texas Guard positions from his observation and command post sixteen floors above the ground. He smiled as he thought of the six M1A1 Abrams tanks that he had quietly requisitioned from the commander at Fort Bliss just two weeks ago. Just this morning with the news of secession breaking, that same commander had informed Washington that he was surrendering his base to the Texas Guard and General Clarke along with any personnel that wanted to side with Texas. Now the tanks were waiting for his orders from positions that were well hidden from the enemy air support, and located to the sides and slightly behind their columns in several large parking garages that had been built with this contingency in mind just a few weeks before.

The United Nations columns stood unmoving for several minutes before the phone rang in the command center. A young lieutenant answered the phone and then handed it to the general without explanation. They both had been anticipating this call for hours.

"General Andrew Clarke here," he answered.

"General Clarke, this is General Anthony Wayne, Vice Chairman of the Joint Chiefs. By order of the President of the United States, I am ordering you to stand your men down and surrender the capitol building immediately! Is that understood?" the voice on the other end of the call obviously was used to men cowering when he spoke.

"General Wayne, are you watching this treasonous act that has been perpetrated on the Republic of Texas by your president?" General Clarke answered in a calm voice.

"I am observing a lawful action by the United Nations in response to a request for assistance from the President," was the curt reply.

"Very well, you will witness our withdrawal and surrender of the capitol grounds in about thirty minutes," Clarke hung the phone up abruptly.

"Lieutenant, give the Air Guard commander the signal, 'Go for Willy Pete'!" Clarke barked the order as he reached for the comm link that connected him with the Tank commander, "Take out those personnel carriers, and then direct fire on the troops until they break!"

"Lieutenant, tell the field commanders to put the troops in battle formation and open fire as soon as the personnel carriers are hit, I want this trash swept off the field. Target any officers in view first."

"Yes sir!" the young officer replied as he relayed the order to attack.

The first explosions rattled the windows of the office building followed closely by six large explosions that caused several of the windows to shatter as the personnel carriers and several dozen troops disappeared in clouds of fire; raining hot metal and body parts on the troops that had been standing in formation.

Right on cue, four fifty caliber Browning M2HBs opened up followed by two mini guns in 7.62 NATO that had been mounted to provide a devastating crossfire to the field with a combined rate of six thousand rounds per minute! Four hundred men also opened fire while the shock of the attack gripped the U.N. troops, very few of whom were returning fire. Snipers effectively targeted the commanders that had stayed in the rear of the battalion while hundreds more fell to the devastating fire of the regulars.

The 'coup de grace' was delivered by three Texas Air Guard fighters that screamed in at tree top level to drop the deadly, and forbidden, white phosphorous canisters on the disoriented troops, killing most of them outright and delivering massive burns to those that survived.

"Give the order to cease fire, Lieutenant. Pull our forces back and execute 'Domino'," General Clarke said to his aide, "I hope the Governor was tuned in to this action. It would make him proud!"

As the last of the Texas Guard reached their fall back positions, a series of explosions went off in rapid succession bringing the entire capitol complex tumbling to the ground like a stack of dominos. Under cover of the billowing clouds of dust, General Clarke moved his command swiftly from the area.

CHAPTER 4

Luke unloaded Lucky at the ranch run by John and Mary Louise Post, and then waited for John to grab his kit and say his good-byes to his wife. They would ride together to their designated mustering point in Gardendale, where they would draw the gear necessary to fill out their kits, and also receive their orders for deployment.

John Post climbed into the cab of the truck after depositing his gear in the back, "Well Luke, it looks like it's going to be up to a few of us old cowboys to take this country back."

"Aren't you going to send Mary Louise away for a spell, John?" Luke voiced his concern for Louise's safety.

"She said she wouldn't go Luke. You know how women can get. I figured that the Lord will protect her while I'm gone," John answered, "What kind of odds you figuring for us coming back?"

"About the same that I get when I buy a lottery ticket," Luke said grimly.

"You could have lied and made me feel better," John declared, "Anyway, we've both had a good run, and planted a bunch of our friends. Maybe it's time to be heroes and get ourselves written into the history books."

"Only if our side wins John, otherwise there will be no mention of us except to call us traitors," Luke replied darkly and reached over to turn on the radio.

"…reports are coming in now of widespread casualties among the United Nation troops in the aftermath of the cowardly ambush by the Texas National Guard just an hour ago in Fort Worth. At least six hundred men are dead, and many are severely wounded. No reports of casualties on the Texas side as yet, and they appear to have withdrawn immediately after destroying the capitol buildings," An ABC network reporter was giving details of the attack in Fort Worth.

"Dang, it's started already!" Luke exclaimed excitedly.

"Sounds like our boys whipped them real good too!" John replied with a big grin, "We'll get the real news in a couple of minutes. If that communist broadcaster is reporting a victory for us, it must have been an impressive one!"

"Things are starting to look up John. We might just have a chance in this lottery after all!" Luke was definitely feeling better about his odds of coming back.

"Governor, you need to come take a look at this!" Rodriguez came running up the slope from the lower edge of the pines where he had been looking across the flatland for any sign of a windmill and water.

Jeb took the binoculars from him and trotted back down the slope. There below them at about eight hundred yards distance were two U.N troop carriers and about thirty troops. Two miles further across the valley, two military helicopters had landed on top of the butte where Amos had been shot down. Jeb looked both to the left and to the right of their position hoping for enough cover to ease out of their immediate area without being seen, but just a scant one hundred yards in either direction was bare ground.

He handed Rodriguez the binoculars, "Let me know immediately if they start in this direction. I'm going back up and see if we have any other avenues of escape."

Leonard was back at the gear when Jeb returned.

"Did you find us anything, Leonard?" Jeb asked expectantly.

"Well, no large cave to crawl in, but there is an interesting vertical chimney in the butte face down there about fifty yards that could be climbed. It would be real rough on your suit and those fancy boots," He replied pointing out the fact that Jeb was hardly dressed for a hard climb.

"Well, I wasn't exactly expecting to be walking this trip," Jeb laughed, "Can Rodriguez fit in that crack?"

"I think so sir. It's about three feet across in the front and narrower at the back. Looks like straight up about fifty feet with no cover though. If we go first, he can soften the fall if we slip," Leonard laughed.

"Ease down there and get him, but do it quietly. I'm going to have a look," Jeb said as he moved in the direction that Leonard had indicated.

Five minutes later he was joined at the base of the crack by Leonard and a very agitated Rodriguez.

"Governor, one of those personnel carriers has moved over here about two hundred yards from the base of this butte. It looks like maybe six men came with it," He reported.

"Damn! I was hoping for a little more time. We'll need to get up this rock and just hope they won't see us. You two men bring our gear over here, and I'll go check on the enemy. From here on, I want you to keep your rifles locked and loaded," Jeb gave them the orders, and headed back down the slope after picking up the AR that he had taken from the chopper.

The men from the troop carrier had not moved any closer to their position so it didn't seem as if they were part of a search effort. They had pulled the vehicle close to the edge of the fairly deep, cactus and mesquite filled wash that ran parallel to the butte where Jeb and his men were hiding. Jeb scanned the wash in both directions from his high ground vantage point and spotted a fairly large herd of hogs bedded down about two hundred yards down from the enemy. Sensing an opportunity, he ran several possible scenarios through his mind before going back to where Rodriguez and Leonard were waiting.

"I'm sorry sir, but that sounded an awful lot like you want us to go down there and take that personnel carrier!" Leonard protested weakly.

"It will be dark in two hours. We'll sneak in and dispatch the guards closest to the wash. Once they are in the wash, the hogs will come to the blood and raise a ruckus while they feed on our friends. While the others are engaging the hogs, we'll make off with the personnel carrier. What could possibly go wrong?" Jeb asked with a straight face.

"I'm in Governor. Why wait for them to kill us off up here?" Rodriguez spoke up.

"Okay, I'm in too," Leonard agreed, "Besides, if one of them is your size, you could get a decent outfit. Hey, we could even swap clothes with the ones that the hogs are going to eat. If they think that you are dead, they'll probably call off the hunt!"

"I hate to think of the hogs eating my kangaroo Luccheses, but other than that it is a tremendous idea," Jeb agreed, "Let's get ready. I want to be out of here in one hour after the sun sets."

Just before the last rays of the sun lit the sky, the sound of another helicopter coming in low and slow above the men made them dive for any cover that the pines offered. It was soon obvious that plan 'A' was not going to take place with another U.N. chopper sitting directly on top of their butte.

"Change of plans men," Jeb announced in a low whisper as he handed Leonard his knife, "Leonard, I need for you to climb that chimney quietly and scout the situation up there for us. If possible, we need to capture that chopper! We'll wait for a sign, drop a broken stick or something, and Rodriguez will climb up with the gear tied to his 'chute cord. When I get up there, we'll pull everything up and see about taking that chopper. Understood?"

"Yes sir, Governor," Leonard replied in a hushed tone while taking the seven inch bladed K-Bar out of its sheath and testing the edge with his thumb.

The men moved quietly to the chimney and prepared their gear while Leonard made his way slowly and quietly upward into the darkness of the shaft. Soon he was lost in the shadows. Now there was nothing to do but wait for either his signal to climb, or to be discovered and probably killed by whoever waited on the top of the butte.

The minutes passed by at a crawl, first ten and then fifteen. With their nerves on edge, both men held their M-16's at the ready, expecting an attack that became more eminent with the passing of each excruciatingly slow minute. Suddenly, the stillness of the dark night was broken by the sound of a heavy object crashing into the pine tops and landing on the ground with a thud.

"What the…?" Rodriguez spun to cover whatever had made the noise while Jeb covered the rim of the butte with his rifle.

A low laugh came from the darkness above their heads.

"Well, you told me to toss something down as a signal to climb," Leonard called down in a loud whisper.

"I said a stick Leonard, a stick!" Jeb whispered back up, "What did you throw?"

"That was the co-pilot sir. The pilot is up here," Leonard answered.

"Good job soldier! We are on our way up."

Twenty minutes later, the three men surveyed the United Nations chopper that stood in the darkness. It was a UH-1Y four bladed Huey that bore the markings of the U.S. Marine Corps, and was equipped with one 7.62mm GAU-17A machine gun in the door, and a 19-tube LAU-61 rocket launcher.

"I thought you said this was a U.N. ship Leonard!" Jeb exclaimed.

"Well, it may not be, but that co-pilot sure was. He was wearing the U.N. Insignias all over his flight suit," Leonard explained, "I couldn't kill one of ours, and that is why the Lieutenant is duct taped over there."

They looked in the direction that Leonard was pointing and saw a Marine Corps pilot bound hands and feet lying unconscious just behind the chopper.

"Throw him in and secure him so that he doesn't fall out. We'll turn the Lieutenant over to our people later," Jeb told the men.

"If we make it to the new headquarters, I'm putting you both in for commendations. Good job Leonard!" Jeb slapped him on the back, "Now load up and let's get our tails out of here."

What about those guys on the other butte, Governor?" Rodriguez asked nervously.

"We'll go pay our respects as soon as this bird is in the air. Saddle up!" Jeb replied and climbed into the pilot's seat, Rodriguez, man the mini. We don't want Leonard to have all of the fun do we?"

Jeb made short work of the pre flight check and started the engine. In just a few minutes, the Huey was airborne and headed for the other butte with its running lights off.

As they swooped down on the landing area of the two helicopters, Jeb loosed two MK-66 rockets into the parked aircraft, and the ripping sound filled the air as Rodriguez raked the butte with several bursts from the door gun as it fired at a rate of three thousand rounds a minute.

Primary and secondary explosions lit the top of the butte as the helicopters died violently along with their crews, and Jeb swung away from the carnage and on toward the southwest, and to their rendezvous point. Leonard was riding co-pilot and reached over to slap Jeb's shoulder while pointing excitedly to their left. A laser light was being directed at them in three short bursts repeatedly as they cleared the top of the bluff. Jeb nodded and swung the bird toward the light. When they reached the area where it had been seen, Rodriguez covered the darkness with the door gun while Jeb eased the chopper toward the ground and turned on the landing floods. Just as the skids touched, a familiar figure came running out of the mesquite with his arms raised, ran toward the chopper door, and dove inside. He motioned for Rodriguez's headphones and quickly put them on.

"Captain Amos Whitehorse, Texas Air Guard!" The familiar voice of Amos Whitehorse was music to Jeb's ears.

"Amos, how did you manage to escape that helicopter? We saw it explode!" Jeb asked in astonishment.

"Jebediah...how in the world...? Well Jeb, I guess this kind of makes us even, doesn't it? I put her in a climb and jumped out as she passed the butte. My chute just barely opened when they killed her, so they probably didn't know that any of us got out. ...told you I had a plan," Amos answered as he swapped places with Leonard, "now you had better kill the avionics and transponder on this bird or this will be a short flight!"

CHAPTER 5

About forty men were mustered at the pipe yard when Luke and John arrived, so Luke parked the truck in the spot where a young man in Texas National Guard MultiCams indicated. As they retrieved their gear from the back of the truck the young soldier approached them, "Are you men Moffet and Post?"

"I'm Moffet, that's Post," Luke replied.

"There is a General inside that wanted to see you both as soon as you arrived," The soldier informed him.

"Any idea why he wants to see us?" Luke asked as he and John exchanged puzzled looks.

"It wasn't my business to ask," the young man replied as he turned to continue directing traffic.

"Dang John, I sure hope he isn't going to send us home because we are too old. That will make it hard to live down at the Wagon Wheel," Luke seemed dejected at the thought that they might not make the cut.

"Relax Luke, I've got a few years on you, and I'm not worried about missing this fight. We'll just start our own army if that happens," John replied with a laugh and slapped Luke on the back. "Let's go see who this General is."

The warehouse, which had been emptied of equipment and then hastily converted with lanes of clothesline tied to the backs of chairs into a mustering center, was bustling with activity as the men were assigned to companies, and then drew their gear that was being dispensed from the trailers of two semi-trucks that had parked in the back.

"Luke, John, over here!" the men turned in the direction that the familiar voice called from.

"Pastor Jenkins?" John blurted out in surprise at the sight of a big man in the MultiCams of the Texas Guard with full bird Colonel insignias on the uniform.

Colonel Nathan Jenkins had a big grin on his face as he welcomed the men, "I probably should have told the congregation where I was going during the last few weeks when I disappeared, John, but everything has been played very close to the vest. Come back to the office so we can talk in private."

"Here it comes," Luke thought grimly, "Pastor Jenkins isn't going to let us get into the fight."

"The 39th is being reformed as a tactical unit of the Guard, and I have been appointed Commander for the duration of the hostilities. I need for you two to form me a mounted cavalry that will operate in the areas Southwest of Iraan and Sheffield. I've got twenty older men that will serve as your company, but none of them have the knowledge of that area like you do," Colonel Jenkins explained.

"What is our objective, Colonel?" Luke asked.

"The border is going to be a real hot spot for us, and the Guard just doesn't have enough men to watch all of it, much less fight an invading force that might come across. Since some of the enemy will most likely get through our lines and make it the sixty miles to I-10, we need a patrol down there that can spot any enemy forces that could hide in that rough terrain. When you find evidence of a hostile force, you will communicate that information back to our command post. If the force is small enough, you and your men will likely be ordered to engage," Jenkins answered, "From here on you both will have the rank of Captain in the Texas National Guard. Each one of you will direct a ten man unit and coordinate your activities with each other."

"I think that we would like to use our own mounts, Pastor...that is, Colonel. Is that going to be possible?" John asked the question that both he and Luke had been thinking.

"Of course, Captain Post, you can if you like, but we've got some good looking horse flesh in the corral along with six mules for packing supplies that I would like for you to look at first," Colonel Jenkins replied, and then, "Captain Moffet, your prowess with a rifle is in your service record. Do you feel like you can still work as a sniper if the situation calls for it?"

"Yes sir, although I really wasn't very proud of killing all of those men back then. It was just something that needed to be done at the time," Luke answered quietly.

"I understand Captain, but sometimes it is necessary to take a life, especially in the defense of your homeland. Speaking as a pastor, all life is precious to God, but I'm certain that the evil that has come upon this country warrants actions as extreme as those we are about to undertake," The Colonel replied.

"Yes sir, I understand that this is necessary, and I won't let any of it bother me until it is over, but I also won't let my mind be numbed to the value of a human life," Luke replied quietly.

"Good, let's have a word of prayer for our cause, and for Texas before we head to the corral," Colonel Jenkins removed his hat and bowed his head.

It didn't take Luke long to decide that the big buckskin gelding in the corral would be a better horse for this mission than old Lucky. Besides, Lucky might get shot out from under him if things got tough, and that would be hard to take. John, on the other hand, decided to make the run back to the ranch for his horse, Ahab.

"Take my truck, John. I'll wait here with the stock and meet the fellows that we are going to ride with," Luke offered.

"Thanks, Luke. I'm going to tell Lucky that you are stepping out on him while I'm there," John replied with a grin.

"He'll thank me when this is over. Besides, that buckskin looks like he wasn't gelded until about five years or so. Look at the neck and chest on that animal. I'm thinking that he will be the big pony in this show before it's all over," Luke said with a smile.

"I'll be back in an hour. Don't let them start this war without me!" John exclaimed as he walked away.

He had been gone less than thirty minutes when Colonel Jenkins stepped out of the warehouse building with a bullhorn, "We have word of imminent enemy attack men. Grab what gear you can and prepare for immediate deployment."

Luke grabbed the bag that the Remington was in and walked quickly to the warehouse for the briefing. He was passed by six young men at a dead run. "Those days are long past for me" he thought wistfully as he watched them disappear into the building ahead of him. He had never heard of anybody outrunning a bullet anyway.

Colonel Jenkins was standing on the stage when the men assembled in front of him. Behind them, the others were being hastily processed and taken out to be loaded into one of the personnel carriers staged in the parking area of the warehouse.

"Men, we've just received intel that suggests that the enemy is going to try and seize the Midland Airport and the oil depots, which means that the 39th Texas Guard will be in combat almost immediately. Our air force boys are harassing the column as we speak, but there is a large aerial force flying cover for the enemy. We have decided to blow the overpasses along I-20 and 191 to slow their advance into Odessa if we can't stop them in Midland, and there is already heavy fighting in Big Spring. The Guard there along with any civilians that are fighting will harass the enemy and slow them down until we can get set up in Midland. I need for all company commanders to assemble your men and depart for your duty stations immediately. Captains Moffet and Post assemble your troops and get those horses and gear loaded. You will split forces here and regroup in McCamey. Dismissed!" The colonel finished speaking, and everyone went hurriedly about the business of getting out of Gardendale, and away from the pipe yard before any possible attack could occur.

Luke was in the process of directing the twenty men that had been assigned to this small cavalry when John Post came roaring in through a cloud of Texas dust with Luke's Chevy and his double horse trailer. Inside was his chestnut quarter horse Ahab, Luke's horse Lucky, and the tack for both horses.

"John, what in the world is Lucky doing in there?" Luke asked partially in anger, "I told you that I was going to take the buckskin and leave old Lucky at the ranch."

"No time for that, Luke. We got hit by something high up just after you and I left, and the house is gone. Mary Louise was in the main barn when it happened and just got the crap scared out of her. She had Lucky and Ahab in there with her, so I brought them both with me."

"Where is she now?" Luke asked.

"She is in Goldsmith right about now, but I'm thinking that she will be in Ruidoso tomorrow with Mary," John answered. The old house had been on the ranch through several generations of owners and managers, and to think of a president that would order his own people bombed just added to his rage.

"We are supposed to get these horses and men to McCamey. The enemy is in Big Spring and headed for Midland, so we need to hurry the boys along. I guess you and I can run the back roads with this rig and lead them in safely enough," Luke told him.

"We'll be cutting across some oil field access roads, but nobody I know will object. It sure won't be safe to run down 385!" John exclaimed.

Luke set about helping get the horses loaded into the two trailers, and the men were given orders to make their best way down and meet up in McCamey where they would saddle their mounts. John requisitioned some provisions including ammunition and MREs for twenty men which were loaded into the back of

Luke's truck. When the order was given to disperse, the pipe yard emptied as if the men were a covey of quail flying in different directions.

Luke led the procession of horse trailers out of the yard and through the back streets of Gardendale, hoping to get to the other side of Odessa without being seen.

"He wasn't kidding about 'old men' was he Luke? Most of those men are almost as old as we are," John said.

"I'm thinking that they just want to make sure that we don't get ourselves killed. It wouldn't look too good for the Guard on CNN if a bunch of old men get gunned down early on," Luke replied.

"I suppose so, but we are probably going to miss most of the action," John sounded disappointed.

The rest of the trip to the rendezvous in McCamey was made in silence.

CHAPTER 6

The red blinking light and the blaring of the fuel warning alarm caught the attention of both men in the cockpit of the Huey.

"Jeb, this bird is out of fuel. I think we'd better sit down pronto 'cause they glide like a brick!" Amos sounded worried.

"We had plenty of fuel for this trip when we picked you up, Amos. I don't understand where it went unless somebody got lucky back there and hit the fuel tanks," Jeb replied, "I'm going to see if we can sit down right here without hitting anything.

"Hold on back there men, we're going in!" Amos called to Leonard and Rodriguez.

Jeb was flying below the butte tops to avoid being spotted by radar so the trip down only took a few seconds. The problem was where they landed. When the rotors quit turning, Rodriguez stuck his head out of the chopper.

"SNAKES!" he shouted as he hurriedly moved to the center of the chopper, visibly shaken.

Jeb slowly opened his door and looked at the ground under him. The sound of dozens of Western Diamond Back rattlers buzzing sounded like a gathering of Cicadas in the late summer back east.

"Well, talk about out of the frying pan and into the fire! What does it look like on your side, Amos?" He asked.

"I don't think that I've ever seen this many snakes in one spot, Jeb, and I'm only looking down at the skid. What in the world did you put us in?" He replied.

"I think they must be denning up right here, and we just happened to land on the den. All of the fuel running down there must have brought them out of the holes," Jeb said, "Leonard, what does it look like out of your door?"

Leonard shined his flashlight out of the door and looked at the ground under him.

"Snakes sir, but they are mostly under the bird. I can see a spot about five feet over where there doesn't appear to be any."

"I'm going to pick her up and move over a few feet. There won't be enough fuel to move far. Is the ground flat over there?" Jeb asked.

"Looks to be sir, but I can only see a few feet," Leonard responded.

The Governor brought the engine to life and the rotors started turning slowly as the turbine spun to life. The Huey lifted slowly a few feet off the ground and drifted twenty feet to their right side when the engine quit. She slammed heavily into the ground and bounced slightly before coming to a rest.

"Thank God that we weren't further up Amos. We really did run out of gas!" Jeb stated, "Can you get out over there?"

"No snakes here sir, none that I can see anyway. What do you want to do with our prisoner?" Leonard replied.

"Untie his feet and take the tape off his mouth. We'll take him with us."

"Uh, sir, we might have a problem with that," Rodriguez replied, still nervously watching his door as he rolled the captive over. "It looks like a round came up through the bottom of the ship and got him."

Jeb and Amos crawled back to the cargo bay of the Huey and examined the body of the young Marine Captain. He had definitely taken a small arms round in the chest and died with a minimal loss of blood.

"He probably didn't know that he was hit. Leonard clubbed him pretty hard back there," Jeb said quietly, "Well, there is nothing to do for him now. Let's get our gear and get out of here. I don't need to tell you to watch for snakes, but we have to move away from the ship. The residual heat from the exhaust can be seen with infrared."

The men exited carefully behind Leonard who led them out, and then they slowly moved away from the downed helicopter and, hopefully, away from the irritated snakes. The ground was flat and fairly clear of cactus, although there appeared to be an occasional Mesquite shrub within their limited visual range. The cold, dark night was illuminated slightly by the millions of stars that gleamed over head, but it was still difficult to see where they were placing their feet.

Suddenly, Jeb stopped and said, "Listen!"

In the dark to their right came the rattling, squeaking sound of an old windmill.

"Move slowly toward the sound men," Jeb ordered, and the troop eased their way to the windmill, and the water tank beside of it.

Leonard shined his light briefly in the direction of the overflow on the tank. Just past the tank was a water hole nestled in some cottonwoods and scrub that would make a good place to shelter until daylight.

"Let's stop here until daylight men. I think that we can figure out where we are at first light. There should be some kind of landmark visible," Jeb told the men.

"I've got the chart from the chopper, Jeb. By the way, you've got my bedroll," Amos told him.

"Well then, it looks like you will be taking the first watch Amos," Jeb responded with a slap on his friend's back, "Get some sleep men. Rodriguez will take the second watch, then Leonard. I'm going to get some sleep."

When daylight came at about five thirty in the morning, Jeb was sitting on the edge of the concrete tank listening to the others snoring. It was obvious that they were on a well maintained ranch, but which one was anybody's guess. He could make out a trail that ran around behind the tank and headed in the general direction that he thought might get them out of the area. His concern now was that they would be discovered by whoever might stumble across the downed helicopter, which couldn't be more than a mile from their current location.

The smell of smoke wafted in on the morning breeze, so Jeb decided to wake the men and investigate. After a hurried breakfast of MREs and water from the tank, the small troop followed the dirt road toward where they thought the smoke was coming from. After walking less than mile, they spotted the source.

"Governor, I see a column of smoke rising above that group of trees," Leonard spoke up while pointing in the direction of the sighting.

"Men, be careful from here on. We don't know who or what might be behind the smoke, but lock and load…just in case," Jeb directed them.

The sound of the three rifles being charged was somehow comforting to Jeb, although he had given Amos back his piece and was currently unarmed.

They made their way stealthily through the mesquite and cactus toward the fire until they were close enough to see the cause. A large ranch house was burning, and several men were standing over what appeared to be two bodies lying in the dirt close to a corral.

Rodriguez handed Jeb his binoculars, "You might want to see this sir."

As Jeb scanned the scene before him, the bile rose in his throat over the evidence of brutality that he was witnessing. The bodies on the ground were women, one older and one a young girl. From what he could make out, they had been savagely beaten, and worse.

"Leonard…Rodriguez, make your way around to those outlying buildings and wait for our signal. Amos and I will get close enough to kill these, but I'm certain that there are more that we can't see," Jeb gave the order and the men moved quietly to obey.

"Amos, I need your rifle," Jeb said quietly.

Amos handed him the piece, and they started their stalk toward the burning house. When they had closed the distance to less than two hundred yards without being seen, Jeb handed the binoculars to Amos.

"Let me know when the boys are in position," He said as he picked his targets.

They waited in the heat for what seemed like an hour with nervous sweat running down their backs, but only about ten minutes had elapsed.

"They are in position, Jeb. Give them hell!" Amos whispered. As soon as Leonard signaled.

Almost immediately the AR barked six times in rapid succession and three of the six men in the yard fell. As the others turned to face the threat of Jeb's debilitating fire, Leonard and Rodriguez shot them from a distance of less than fifty yards. The last man had barely hit the ground when five men rushed from inside the large shed that was giving their attackers cover. Jeb drew their fire by killing two, which gave Rodriguez time to slip around the far side of the building and come up behind them. He and Leonard killed the last three and waited for a signal from Jeb before moving into the clear.

Jeb and Amos came at a run to the first bodies, trying not to look at the battered bodies of the two women on their left.

"Grab one of those rifles, Amos," Jeb ordered, indicating the AR 15-M4s that were next to the men.

"Government issue, Jeb!" he exclaimed as he checked the magazine, and then pulled two more from the vest of the nearest corpse.

They moved slowly toward the building where Leonard and Rodriguez were covering their advance. Jeb motioned for them to look inside and the men eased their rifles into a high ready position and peered quickly around the door. They took a second look before motioning for Jeb and Amos to approach.

"What is it?" Jeb asked as he and Amos trotted up.

"A Hummer sir, it has our markings," Leonard replied.

"Keep watch out here men, Amos and I are going in," Jeb said as he stepped into the building.

Sure enough, backed into the large barn was a new Hum-Vee with United States Army markings. They looked around the inside of the building and found the packs of the troop, and Army uniforms with identifying patches indicating that these men were Rangers.

"What do you think Jeb?" Amos asked.

"I'm not sure that I want to voice what I think, but it looks like either we have been infiltrated or these men went rogue," Jeb replied while shaking his head in disbelief at what he had just said, "Check that Hummer for a radio, and see how much fuel it has. We'll get out of here after we bury those women."

"Yes sir," Amos replied and headed for the vehicle.

He walked back outside into the bright West Texas morning and just looked around for a minute before calling his two men. He had known that there would be repercussions for his defiance of the Federal Government, but somehow it had eluded him just how brutal those repercussions would be. The knowledge that the barbarism that they had come upon might be only the tip of the iceberg, made Jeb's blood run cold. He knew now that this war for Texas independence must be won.

"Men, there is a backhoe under that far shed. See if you can get it fired up. We'll give these women a decent burial before we pull out," Jeb ordered.

"What about the others, sir?" Rodriguez asked.

"Check them for identification and stack them in the barn. They don't deserve a burial with these folks," Jeb's voice made it clear how little regard he held for rapists.

Just over an hour later, the graves had been filled in, and Jeb had prayed over the women, asking God to grant mercy for anything they might have carried to the grave with them. All of the bodies of the women's killers had been stacked in the barn, out of sight of a casual glance. The military IDs had been collected and thrown into the back of the Hummer along with the uniforms. After trading their civilian ARs for new issue armament, the extra arms and ammo had been cached in the back with the uniforms except for a pair of boots that Jeb requisitioned to replace his Luccheses. They had just finished loading, and were getting ready to pull out of the barn when the sound of another vehicle pulling into the yard made them grab their weapons and ease to the partially opened door.

There was a second HumVee with two officers aboard sitting close to where the newly dug graves were.

"I want to take at least one of these alive, men," Jeb whispered, "Wait until they get out of the Hummer."

The officers looked in their direction, but the bright morning sun was directly over the barn and shining in their eyes. Not seeing any movement, they started walking in that direction, laughing as the approached.

Jeb let them close the gap to less than twenty yards before stepping out and ordering the two to drop their weapons.

The young Lieutenant complied immediately, but the older one, an apparently battle hardened Captain, held on to his rifle just a moment too long. Jeb shot him between the eyes, and before the lifeless body hit the ground, he had swung the rifle on the frightened Lieutenant.

"You need to tell me what you men are doing here!" He ordered.

"My name is Johnson, Willard T. Lieutenant, Service number 431-06-5555," The Lieutenant replied with fear in his voice.

"Amos, let me hold that Ka-Bar," Jeb held his hand out to Amos without taking his eyes off the Lieutenant.

"Leonard and Rodriguez, restrain the Lieutenant please," Jeb's voice had murder in it.

"We don't take kindly to our women being raped or civilians being targeted here in Texas, boy. Now I asked you a question, and I expect an answer immediately."

"My name is Johnson, Willard T. Lieutenant, Service number 431-06-5555," The Lieutenant stammered.

Jeb cut the Lieutenant's web belt in two with the razor sharp knife that he held in his hand, and then pulled the britches down to his knees. The point of the knife hovered close to the man's private area, and the look in Jeb's eyes was almost maniacal.

"Oh God, Please don't do this. I didn't hurt those women. I told them not to do it. Please don't do this," The Lieutenant was sobbing like a baby.

"One more time, tell me what your orders are and where you came from," Jeb's tone was menacing.

"We are supposed to make people think that we are the 8th Ranger Battalion from Topeka, but these were mostly Muslim mercenaries from several countries. We were to harass the enemy and destroy supplies behind enemy lines. I swear sir," The Lieutenant sobbed.

"So Texas is your enemy, eh? What about that oath that you took to protect and defend the Constitution?" Jeb asked.

"I followed my orders, sir. I would have been court-martialed if I didn't," He responded.

"How many more are in here with you?" Jeb asked.

"Two more units came with us. We are operating about fifty miles apart and working our way to the east. We are the middle unit," He replied.

Jeb motioned to Amos and walked away from the young man and his hearing.

"Amos, I'm about to do something that might leave a bad taste in our mouths, but justice needs to be swift in these cases. Will you support me?" He asked.

"If you are about to hang this fellow, I'm behind you one hundred percent," Amos answered.

"Thanks friend, we'll need to document the proceedings just in case some of my enemies bring it up at a later time. Find us some rope, and we'll hang him in plain sight right there in that cottonwood tree," Jeb indicated a large old tree next to a small pond.

The order was given to tie the Lieutenant's hands behind him, and they took him to the old tree limb where Amos had thrown a rope that he had found on a saddle in the barn.

"Lieutenant, for the crimes of rape and treason, the people of Texas, by the order of Governor Jebediah Atkins, sentences you to hang by the neck until dead. Do you have any last words before this sentence is carried out" Jeb read the hastily written proclamation bearing his signature.

"Please don't kill me! I swear that I didn't hurt those women!" he sobbed as the rope was placed around his neck.

"You did nothing to stop it either. Pull him up men!" Jeb gave the order and the Lieutenant was lifted by his neck with his eyes bulging and his feet kicking.

Rodriguez made a wrap around the tree trunk and tied the rope off, while Leonard averted his eyes from the gruesome dance that was going on in front of him.

As soon as the lifeless body was swinging gently, the men turned away and walked back to the vehicles. It would probably be days before anyone would find the young man with the word "RAPIST" written on his forehead with a black marker that had been found in the Hummer, but the message would resonate loud and clear to friend or foe; "Don't mess with Texas!"

Rodriguez and Amos pulled the first vehicle out of the shed while Jeb and Leonard looked through the contents of the second HumVee. Inside they found what appeared to be looted provisions, and a small amount of money and jewelry that must have been taken from the women that had been killed. There was also a Barrett .50 caliber sniper rifle with one hundred rounds of ammo.

"Take the money and jewelry over to the cottonwood and bury it. See if you can find a can or something in the shed," Jeb said to Leonard, handing him the money and jewelry, "Amos, you and Rodriguez take the Hummer with the gear and follow Leonard and me. This other one has a radio that I can use to get us some help finding those other two patrols."

"Are we going after them, Jeb? What about getting you to safety?" Amos asked.

"We have good men running the government of this state Amos. Right now it is imperative that we find these murderous bastards and send a clear message to the President that this type of savagery will not be permitted on Texas soil!" Jeb replied angrily, "We are going to back track this Hummer and see if they attacked anyone else before coming over here,"

"Yes sir," Amos responded before turning to get in the other vehicle.

CHAPTER 7

"Yes sir, I understand. I will have a mounted patrol in that area within two hours, sir," Colonel Nathan Jenkins received the radio call from General Clarke informing him of the disappearance of the Governor as his HumVee left the makeshift compound in Gardendale in route to the new command center in Midland.

"Are we still holding the airport, sir?" Jenkins asked since that was his destination.

"As of a few minutes ago we were, Colonel. It looks like these U.N. troops don't have the heart for a real fight. We've got them stalled, and the Air Guard is keeping the skies clear for now. I've been told that the Air Force is reluctant to send up their fighters because so many of them have defected to our side down in Louisiana already. Get us a ready room setup, and I'll brief all of the officers this afternoon when I arrive," The General gave him as much news as he could.

"Yes sir, I'll have it ready, and we'll get the ground search underway for Governor Atkins immediately," Jenkins replied, then to his aide, "Ralph, see if you can raise Captains Moffet and Post. Tell them about the Governor, and have them look for anything unusual as soon as they get South of I-10."

"Yes sir," Corporal Ralph Hastings replied.

The convoy ran up 1788 until it got to the 191 bridge, which had been pulverized by a well-aimed JDAM from a Texas Guard F-16.

"Take us around the rubble driver, and then let's cut cross country to get off this road. Make a straight line for the airport," Jenkins told the private that was driving his HumVee.

Running across the expansive flat land and through the various housing projects would not be as dangerous as staying on the highway past this point and taking a chance on an IED, especially since the Texas Air Guard controlled the sky.

The two big M932A2 Guard semis towing the horse trailers with the mounts for the makeshift cavalry unit followed Luke and John down FM1601 and then cross country on oilfield access roads after the road dead ended on Highway 329 close to Crane. Three hours later, they made the rendezvous just South of McCamey.

Sergeant Luis Gonzales ran to meet the truck as they pulled into the parking area of a long closed business.

"Captain Post, we have an urgent message for you and Captain Moffet from Colonel Jenkins," He said to the first one of the two that he came to.

"What is it Sergeant?" Jon asked.

"The Governor has been shot down somewhere to the Southwest of here, and Colonel Jenkins wants us to look for the wreckage," Luis sounded out of breath.

"If that doesn't take the cake!" Luke exclaimed, "Something doesn't sound right about this John. I'm thinking that there is a reason that the air guard isn't down there with helicopters conducting a search and recovery. Do you think the area is hot?"

"Must be or Colonel Jenkins wouldn't be asking us to conduct the search. Do you know how long this could take with horses?" John asked.

"Sergeant, get the Colonel on the radio and see if he can provide us a grid to start the search from," John gave the order to Luis.

"Minutes later, a young private trotted over with a message for the two Captains.

"The Colonel wants to talk to you both, sirs," He told them.

Luke just shot a glance at John who shrugged his shoulders and started for the HumVee with the radio on board.

"Captains Moffet and Post here, Colonel," Luke spoke into the mike.

"Men, we think that the chopper may be down just south of the Canon Ranch airport. That terrain is pretty rough, and we don't have any reliable intel other than there was a call to a 911 operator to report an explosion in the area about two hours after the governor left Fort Worth, which would put him in that general area," Jenkins told them, "Be extra careful though. We think that area may be hot. Call for air support if needed."

"Yes sir, we understand," Luke replied as he glanced at John Post before handing the mike back to the private.

"Well, we can't ride that far today. What do you think?" John asked Luke.

"We can trailer the horses down below I-10 on the oil field roads. If there are enemy troops in the area, they are probably going to be on I-10, wouldn't you think?" Luke answered, "If we can get across unnoticed, we'll camp on the other side, close to the Canon airport and start our search at first light,"

"Sounds like a sound plan to me. If we drop your troop off there, I'll take mine another few miles south and set up camp below you. Between us, we stand a good chance of finding that wreckage in the morning," John replied.

"Let's leave my truck here and get our horses and gear in the HumVees and the trailers. Make sure that we have two radios, and make sure that none of your men are carrying a cell phone. I'll do the same with mine," Luke told him.

"Roger that. Let's get this show on the road," John replied and walked slowly back to the trailer to retrieve his horse and gear.

Luke decided to run the convoy down little used FM 1901 until they came to I-10. At that point they would have to cross the interstate quickly and get the group into the hills beyond. As they approached I-10, Luke ordered the convoy to stop about one half of a mile away from a small gas station that sat on the interstate feeder to the north of the interstate. Taking his binoculars he glassed the area between them and the station for any indication that it might be unsafe to cross here. What he saw made him cringe for a moment. There was a small convoy of U.N. Vehicles parked at the station, and a road block set up with three crude oil haulers being inspected. Luke gave the order to take a right turn slowly into a producing oil field in the hope that they would not be seen. The trucks crawled along to keep the dust to a minimum, and the constant wind kept a swarm of dust devils active between them and the enemy forces, which numbered around fifty men.

After hiding the trucks behind a couple of tank batteries, Luke joined John Post to try and figure a way out of this situation.

"Well, Luke, It looks like that lottery ticket might just get cashed down here in a bit," John told him dryly.

"It appears so, I imagine. They've got us outnumber two to one, and it looks like they are a lot younger too," Luke answered.

"Younger can be stupider also partner. They've got a very large bomb sitting right there with those three trucks full of crude, plus the station tanks, if we can find a way to set them off," John told him, "I saw several road flares burning next to the tankers where they staged the road block; any ideas coming to you?"

"Well, it is about eight hundred yards from here to that lead truck. I can make the shot from the top of this battery, but we would have to scoot out of here before they can blow us up," Luke replied.

"That .308 isn't going to do what we need at this range. There is something in the gear that I think Pastor Jenkins put in just for you," John told him.

They eased back to the last HumVee where the men we're huddled, waiting for orders. There, packed with care with the rest of the gear was a McMillan A-1 fifty caliber sniper rifle with the R-2 recoil reduction system topped with a Schmidt and Bender 3x12x50 PM scope, and a box of armor piercing rounds.

"Dang, look at this beauty!" Luke exclaimed, "I think we have a plan going now. Get the men ready and tell them to lock and load. As soon as I make this shot, all hell is going to break loose."

Luke made his way back to the battery where they had been spying on the U.N. forces, and set up the McMillan with Sergeant Gonzales acting as his spotter.

Luke quickly checked his zero by pulling the bolt and bore sighting the big rifle, and then waited for a sign from John Post that the men were ready. With the trucks sitting at a slight angle away from them, the best target was the lower back of the tanker, close to the valve handle. Luke took two breathes and set the cross hairs of the scope just above the valve. The boom of the Browning .50 cartridge echoed off a dozen tanks, and several of the U.N Troops threw themselves to the ground.

"Six inches right and three high, Captain," Luis declared without lifting his eyes from the binoculars.

Instead of making adjustments to the scope, Luke moved his point of aim accordingly and cut another round loose. This time the U.N. troops started firing small arms in the general direction of the tank battery. Luke's first round had pierced a half inch hole in the tank which was leaking crude oil like a garden hose directly on the ground next to one of the road flares. The second round broke the valve on the tank bottom, and the entire back of the tanker went up in a massive fireball as the oil ignited in a cloud of black smoke.

Luis slapped Luke on the shoulder, "Not bad shooting for an old Roughneck, Captain."

Luke smiled and made two more shots into the back of the second and third trucks in the line with the same devastating precision just as the first truck erupted in a huge fireball with heat so intense that they could feel it at one-half of a mile distance.

With small arms fire from the surviving enemy pinging off the tank battery, Luke and Luis hastily retreated to a more secure location just as John Post led a charge with two HumVees loaded with old cowboys straight into the teeth of enemy fire. Taking advantage of the thick black smoke from the burning trucks, John had his men scurry for the slight cover of the mesquite scrub and deliver a devastating volley into the enemy as they tried to run past the burning tanker.

Just as twenty of the U.N. Troops made it into the clear about fifty yards from the last tank truck following an armored personnel carrier, both it and the middle tanker blew in a massive explosion that hurled men and vehicles many feet into the air. John and his men ducked their heads as the shockwave rolled over them, and then the air was quiet except for the roaring of the flames. The station tanks followed shortly thereafter, leaving a scene of apocalyptic devastation that left the U.N. troops in baffled disarray, and the Calvary troops staring in awe.

The next thing John saw were the survivors of their assault marching towards them with a white flag waving, and their arms up above their heads, followed closely by the drivers of the trucks that had seized weapons from the enemy during the confusion following the explosions.

"Round them up and search them, men," He ordered in a loud voice.

Luke joined them with Luis, and the transport trucks.

"What in the heck was that, John?" He asked, "I thought you all were dead."

"A cavalry charges from what I remember, Luke. It seemed like a good idea at the time," John answered with a grin, "I haven't felt this good in about thirty years!"

"What about these prisoners? We sure can't take them with us," Luke asked.

"I say that we burn the personnel carriers, take whatever we can use, and send them back in one of the horse trailers with those truckers as a guard," John said.

"Let's call the Colonel, and let him make that decision," Luke countered.

They walked to the lead HumVee and had Luis make the call. John looked across the road and noticed that two of the men had not moved since the firefight had ended.

"We need a medic over here!" he shouted and began to jog across to the men that were on the ground.

As soon as he got there, he knew that it was too late to help them. Both had received head and upper torso wounds that had proven fatal.

"Those are our first casualties Luke. Remember that we thought just a short time ago this was a mission to keep us safe?" John said quietly.

"They died heroes, John. What better way to go out. None of us here are far off from a nursing home. Would you rather pass away there on a bedpan?" Luke asked.

"Of course not, but it just seems kind of peculiar that all of us old farts are taking the fight to the enemy. What happened to all of the keyboard patriots that we've been hearing from the last few years?" John replied bitterly.

"We are the only ones that remember what America was like, John. Those men died for a belief that most people don't share anymore. I'm proud of them!" Luke told him.

"I've got the Colonel on," Luis shouted from the HumVee.

Luke got back first and keyed the mike, "This is Captain Moffet, sir," He said, "We've got prisoners down here, Colonel. What are we supposed to do with them?"

"Prisoners…how in the world? How many have you got, Captain?" Colonel Jenkins answered.

"Eighteen in all, sir. We killed thirty two men and destroyed their equipment," Luke told him, "Captain Post suggested that we put them in one of the horse trailers and send them back up to you."

"I think that might be too dangerous, Captain. Can you get them back to McCamey? There is a battalion of TXSG just staging there," The Colonel asked.

"We can sir. They probably will be there in about an hour," Luke waited until John had nodded his head in agreement before answering.

"Very well Captain. Are there any casualties?" He asked.

"Two men sir, Fitzgerald and Causey were killed when we took the enemy position," Luke answered.

"Send them back with the prisoners. They will be given full military honors. Good work men," The Colonel ended the transmission.

"Well John, I'm going to unload my horses here to free up that transport. We'll ride to a suitable campsite. Once you have the prisoners taken care of, take the other transport as far down as you can. Give me a call when you get settled," Luke told him.

"Okay Luke. We had four extra men with the drivers. I'm sending two back with the prisoners and taking the other two with me. I just hope they can ride," John replied.

"Those are just kids, John. They might not appreciate all of the old fart humor around the campfire tonight," Luke said with a laugh.

"I'm thinking that maybe we should cold camp after this, Luke. We don't know how many more of these buzzards are working the area. I'm betting that they're hunting the Governor too," John told him.

"I think you're right, John. There is a good possibility that Governor Atkins might be alive if the enemy has men all over this area looking for him. Maybe we'll beat them to him. I'm going to get those horses unloaded and the mules packed," Luke responded.

CHAPTER 8

Two hours later, Luke had put two ridges between his troop and the Interstate. Just ahead was a brush filled canyon that promised a secure campsite with a two hundred foot barrier to guard their backs from any ground attack, and a water tank with the windmill still pumping.

"Sergeant Gonzales, we'll set up camp here tonight. Make a picket line for the animals. Tell the men that we will cold camp here, and not to light a cigarette after dark," Luke ordered.

It was going to be a cold night without a fire, but the necessity to keep off the radar outweighed the need for heat. Luke was the oldest of the men in his troop by a couple of years, but he knew that many of them shared the same joint pain that he experienced, especially when it turned cold like it was doing this fall.

Lucky didn't share the picket line with the other horses; instead he followed Luke as he made his way among the men. A strong bond had formed between them, much like a faithful dog and his master.

"Hey, Jorge, Herman, Mark," Luke stopped to talk to some of the old men that were regulars at the Wagon Wheel restaurant most mornings, "did you bring enough warm duds? It's going to be a cold one tonight when the sun goes down,"

"Howdy, Captain Luke… boy that sure sounds funny don't it?" Jorge Ramirez answered, "Just a couple of days ago, we were all wondering if this day was coming, and look at us now,"

Mark Wheeler spoke up, "I guess none of us expected to be fighting another war, Jorge, but who else would do it if we didn't. Besides, we got the best duty of anybody that I know. This is what I've done most of my life, and if I've got to go, I'd rather go out on horseback than in a burned out HumVee,"

"Well, I was hoping that none of us were going to get killed on this assignment, Mark, but that got proven wrong real quick. We need to be careful from here on not to rush into a situation where that can happen again. Our job is to work as a recon unit, not to engage without orders," Luke told them and moved on to the next group of men not knowing that they would be battle tested again in just a very few hours.

"Captain Moffet, Captain Post is on the radio," Luis came to give the message.

Luke made his way to the radio and answered, "Go ahead John."

"We are about twenty miles in from the interstate, Luke. I've got the men setting up camp for the night," John reported.

"If nothing happens tonight, we'll move out at first light toward the West and start looking for the…" Luke started to say Governor but thought better of it, "treasure."

"Roger that. I'll call when we move out tomorrow," John ended the call.

It was late afternoon when one of the men reported hearing the sound of a helicopter to the East of their position. Luke grabbed his binoculars and scanned the sky in that direction. About two miles away he saw two helicopters circle the top of a butte, and then land on it out of his line of sight.

"Dang! Sergeant, pass the word that we have enemy birds close by and probably some ground forces. Everyone needs to check their weapons and stay low and out of sight," Luke ordered.

The afternoon wore on, and just as the sun was settling on the western horizon, the sound of another chopper was heard. Luke scanned the sky in the direction of the sound, but couldn't see the bird from where they lay in the scrub filled canyon.

"It's going to be a long night," He thought to himself.

"Luis, get me Captain Post on the radio," He said quietly.

Sergeant Gonzales, and old army veteran of several campaigns including the Gulf War, was feeling the surge of excitement coming back that he didn't think he would ever experience again after returning to civilian life. He hurried to get the radio and move it to where Luke was watching the bluffs to the east of their position.

"Captain Post, sir," Luis handed Luke the mike.

"John, we have at least three choppers that have set down to the east of our position. Have you heard anything?" Luke asked.

"Nothing here, Luke, do we need to work our way closer just in case you need help?" he asked.

"Not just yet, but keep an eye peeled in that direction. I'll call if we need help," Luke handed the mike back to Luis.

"Captain Moffet, what do you think those choppers are doing over there?" Luis asked.

"I'd say that they think the Governor is somewhere close, or what is left of him if he got shot down," Luke answered, "There will probably be an all out search tomorrow so we need to keep on our toes. You'd probably better call this in to Colonel Jenkins also."

"Yes sir, I'll do that immediately," Luis answered with a smile on his face.

Luke thought that Luis might be the only man in the small troop that relished the thought of more action. Well, he probably would get it pretty shortly. Mary was sure going to be upset that he wasn't cooking in a tent someplace. He hoped she would understand why he had not told her the truth about his assignment.

Darkness settled in and the cold air rushed in with it. Luke wished for a mesquite fired to warm his old bones as he drew the coat tighter around his neck. He had taken care of Lucky, and was just thinking about retiring to his sleeping bag when the whining sound of a helicopter revving up interrupted the stillness of the night. He reached for the binoculars and was straining to see any activity in that direction, when the night sky over the bluffs lit up like a fourth of July celebration. The sound of heavy explosions followed closely behind the fireballs, and then the ripping sound of a mini-gun in close succession.

The sound of a single chopper started moving nearer so Luke gave the order for every man to get ready. He saw the landing lights flash on well below the top of the butte that looked to be on fire, and then the bird went dark as it regained altitude and moved off in a westerly direction, passing to their south.

Sergeant Gonzales came over with the help of a small light and handed Luke the radio mike.

"Luke what the hell just happened up there?" John asked nervously, "Are you all right?"

"John, there is a chopper headed in your general direction with its lights off. I think it may have destroyed the other two, but we won't know until morning. I have a feeling that there are friendlies on that bird!" Luke answered.

"Roger that, we'll try and track the direction by sound when we pick it up, but it's too dark to ride tonight," John replied.

"Ten-four, call me in the morning, and we can try to triangulate a rendezvous point," Luke ended the call.

"Sergeant, call the Colonel and give him the report. Tell him that we will investigate at first light," Luke ordered.

"Yes sir," was the excited reply.

At four thirty in the morning, Luke had his fill of a fitful night trying to sleep on the hard ground with an issue bivvie bag. The joint pain from his arthritis that had developed over the years seemed to have multiplied in intensity from the cold night air, and he knew that most of his men were suffering the same discomfort in silence. Well, there was only one way to deal with it, and that was to build a good mesquite fire and make enough hot coffee to wake the old bones up. He got slowly up from the bedroll, and limped off to find some wood to make his fire while Sergeant Gonzales walked from man to man, waking them.

Soon the fire was crackling in the makeshift fire pit, and Luke had a large pot of coffee boiling on the irons that someone had the presence of mind to load on one of the mules with the rest of the provisions.

"Luis, just sitting here close to the fire sure brings back memories, doesn't it?" Luke asked Sergeant Gonzales.

"Yes sir", he replied, "I remember working this ranch when I was just a kid. My brother and I used to help with the branding in the spring. We used to hunt this place also, before it got too expensive when the new owners turned it into a hunting ranch."

"I remember working down here years ago before Viet Nam. I drifted into other things oil related after I got back, but those memories of working cattle have always been good ones," Luke told him.

The rest of the men started drifting towards the fire and the smell of the campfire coffee bubbling in the pot. Soon the early morning sun was peeking over the horizon and it was time to saddle up. Luke was concerned that there might be an enemy presence to the east of them so he made the decision to move in the direction that the other helicopter was heading; down to the southwest.

"Get Captain Post on the radio, Sergeant. I think we need to see if we can meet up and look for the bird that caused all of that commotion last night," Luke spoke to Luis after the men had eaten a cold breakfast and started saddling their mounts.

"Yes sir, Captain," Luis replied with his customary smile. He was enjoying the excitement of the moment more than anyone Luke had ever seen.

Shortly he handed Luke the radio mike, "Go ahead John."

"Luke, I couldn't stand it any longer. We built a fire here this morning and had hot coffee with our rations. I felt like it would be a relief to get shot after sleeping on the ground last night. I don't remember it being so danged hard!" John Post exclaimed with a laugh.

"Same here, John, I built a fire and got the coffee going real early. Listen, we are going to head in a southwesterly direction and look for that bird. Have you got a fix on where it might have gone?" Luke asked.

"I don't think that it went too far after it passed us to the north. It kind of sounded like they might have set down a couple of miles from here over near the Hubbard ranch. We're going to ride over there, and wait for you to rendezvous with us," John told him.

"Ten-four, John. Keep your eyes peeled for trouble. If you run into anything, wait for us to get there. We'll keep the radio hot just in case," Luke ended the call and mounted Lucky.

The men had the mules packed and their horses saddled when he had finished talking to John, so Luke gathered them together and told them the plan.

"We're going to ride over to the Hubbard ranch and meet up with Captain Post and his men," He told them. "Keep your rifles at the ready, and your eyes peeled. We don't want to walk into an ambush if we can help it."

With that, Luke mounted Lucky and led the way at a brisk walk, figuring it would take a couple of hours in that terrain before they would rendezvous.

CHAPTER 9

While Leonard navigated the rough terrain as they back tracked the trail recently taken by the now dead Lieutenant and his Captain, Jeb tried without success to raise another Texas Guard unit and give them the news about the insurgent force that he had encountered.

"Any Texas Guard unit, come in. Any Texas Guard unit, please respond, over," Jeb keyed the mike one more time, and then quit in frustration.

"Go ahead for the Texas Guard," The radio suddenly crackled almost incoherently.

"This is…" Jeb hesitated knowing that giving his identity might put them in grave danger, especially since he couldn't be certain that this was a Texas Guard member that he was talking to, "…Guard patrol Golf Oscar Victor, over."

There was a brief silence and then, "I copy that Golf Oscar Victor. This is Captain John Post with the 39th mounted patrol under Colonel Jenkins."

"Captain Post, if you can relay word to Colonel Jenkins for us, there are two bands of insurgents, one to the north of Interstate 10, and one roughly eighty miles to the south of the interstate, working their way to the east. They are dressed as Army Rangers, but they are mercenaries that have orders to terrorize the locals into submission, over," Jeb replied.

"Roger that sir, we will relay the news to Colonel Jenkins. I am about one mile from the Hubbard Ranch and see a column of smoke. Are you in the area?" John asked.

Jeb knew that it could be a trick to get him to reveal his position, but they had enough firepower to make an ambush work the other way.

"We are about one mile west of that ranch. I'll hold our position until you men catch up," He responded.

"Roger that, we are on the way," John ended the call.

"Leonard, pull into that gully and get us hidden as best we can. I've got a surprise for those fellows if they aren't ours," Jeb ordered.

Amos pulled in behind them and Jeb explained what might be going on, "I need that Barrett out here, and you take the men down the gully about one hundred yards. If they aren't ours, we'll make certain that they don't do any more damage on Texas soil."

"I understand, Jeb. Rodriguez, break out the Barrett for the Governor, and then you and Leonard arm up and follow me," He ordered.

Jeb found a place where he could view the trail for several hundred yards and still be hidden by a small mesquite. Amos gave him a signal when his men were in position to catch whoever was coming in a cross fire. They waited as the sun climbed higher into the sky, and the temperature climbed along with it. Although it was late in the year, the daytime temperatures would be in the eighties well before noon. With the constant west Texas breeze, the wait was about as comfortable as they could hope for.

The minutes turned into half of an hour, and then one hour had passed with no sign of the supposed Captain Post and his troop. Jeb was getting anxious and worried about waiting for so long in this one spot after sending out their approximate position.

Just as he was ready to call off the ambush and move away, a throat cleared behind him!

"Ahem…it might be best if you take your booger hook off that trigger sir. I've got you covered," John Post said quietly.

Jeb eased his hands away from the Barrett and turned his head slowly for a look at who had gotten behind him. There, squatted down on his heels and pointing an AR-15 M4 directly at his face was an old weathered cowboy that looked about as tough as a strip of jerked beef.

"I take it you are Captain Post?" Jeb asked without moving a muscle except to speak.

"I am, and you would be who?" John asked.

"Governor Jebediah Atkins. How about lowering your weapon?" Jeb asked.

John looked at him for just a second longer and then grinned as he lowered his rifle, "I knew who you were when I got up on you, Governor, but I always wanted to tell someone that I had them covered."

He stood up and waved in the direction that Amos and his men had been waiting. Seconds later they stepped out into the clear with their hands raised above their heads followed by several old men with rifles.

"How in the world did you men get up on us like that?" Jeb demanded with more than a little anger in is voice.

"When you have lived as long as we have, you learn a few things about people. I had you and your men in sight the whole time that we were on the radio, and Captain Moffett had you bore sighted when you stepped out with that big rifle," John responded as he turned and waved toward the high ground several hundred yards to the north of their position.

Jeb looked to the north and was amazed that where there had been nothing but landscape a few minutes earlier, a troop of mounted men were now riding toward him at a gallop!

"Well, Captain John Post," he chuckled, all of his anger gone, "If I had another hundred men like you, I believe we could take this war all of the way to Washington."

"We need to win this one first, sir," John said as he stuck out his hand to shake the one offered by Governor Atkins, "I called Colonel Jenkins and relayed your report. The Air Guard has secured this area and will be conducting a search for those insurgents."

"Captain Post, I was backtracking the men that had the vehicles that we are using. They killed the women at that ranch before we got there, and I am afraid of what we might find at the other end of this track," Jeb explained.

"That would have been Molly Hubbard and her daughter Melissa, Governor. Max Hubbard died last year about this time, and Molly chose to stay on the ranch. If they came from the direction that you are heading, they would have been over on Otis Jamison's place. He and his wife take off this time of year so they should be safe. I don't know about the hands though," John told him.

"Have you heard any word about the conflict since yesterday?" Jeb asked.

"General Clarke tore up a large United Nations troop in Fort Worth, something like six hundred killed, Colonel Jenkins has secured the Midland Airport and area oil fields, and we took out a group of U.N troops over on I-10 yesterday plus sent eighteen prisoners back to McCamey. I don't know how the rest of Texas is holding up or if there is any heavier fighting," John answered as the rest of his unit arrived with Amos, Rodriguez, and Leonard on tow.

"I'm never going to live this down," Amos looked embarrassed, "getting surprised by a bunch of geezers that we were supposed to be ambushing."

Beaming with pride, John's entire troop just grinned at the thought that they had caught these youngsters by surprise.

Luke's men arrived in time to watch Amos' humiliation, and the men riding with John Post grinning from ear to ear in celebration. He dismounted and walked over to where the Governor and John Post were standing.

"Governor Atkins, Captain Luke Moffett, 39th Regimental Cavalry," Luke saluted and then shook the hand that Jeb offered.

"You men are something! In this day of high tech weaponry, the Texas Guard has fielded a cavalry unit that certainly knows how to get the job done, age notwithstanding," Jeb said as he shook Luke's hand.

"Thank You sir, but we need to get you to safety, and this isn't it. There are U.N. troops, and probably a few of ours, back there about twenty miles looking for you. We have limited control of the airspace from what Colonel Jenkins told us, and I think we need to get a ride in here for you ASAP!" Luke told him.

"I want to find these insurgents that are conducting a reign of terror before I leave the field, Captain. We can't allow this to continue on our soil," Jeb was adamant.

"Well, Governor, I know that is important, but you are our leader, and the man that most consider to be the President of our new republic. You are needed elsewhere more urgently than here. Besides, Captain Post and I can certainly handle a few terrorists. That's what Colonel Jenkins sent us down here for," Luke insisted.

Jeb was silent for a full two minutes as he walked a little way from where Luke and John were standing. When he came back he shook his head in the affirmative.

"Get me a ride Captain," He said to Luke, "I'll take Captain Whitehorse as my aide and leave Rodriguez and Leonard with you. Tell Colonel Jenkins to give them a field promotion to sergeant for their role in my rescue. They can drive the vehicles, which might come in handy, but I don't think either of them knows anything about a horse."

"Sergeant Gonzales, give the Colonel a call and arrange for transportation for the Governor and his aide," Luke gave the order, "Give him co-ordinates to the Thunder Ranch Airport. That will keep anyone from sneaking up on us. Tell him that we can have the governor there in about two hours, and then tell him that Luke says 'shake a leg'. That will get him in here in about an hour, so we will have to hustle."

"Good thinking Luke," John spoke up, "Anybody listening will be looking for us further back, and they will be late getting to the party."

"Exactly, but we are going to have to take the HumVees, and as many men as we can get in them. The rest of the troop can meet us there with the horses," Luke replied, "What do you think, Governor?"

"I think that we need to 'shake a leg' Captain," Jeb replied with a grin and turned to walk toward the HumVees that Leonard and Rodriguez had retrieved from the gully.

Forty five minutes later, after a bruising ride at high speed across the rough terrain, the two vehicles raced up the access road that led to the dirt runway. At one time, the runway had been used for business jets coming in from Mexico with a clear five thousand foot length. Today, much of that had grown over and a scant two thousand feet was available. After parking the HumVees as close to some of the taller mesquite as possible, the men took up defensive positions on both sides of the vehicles.

Soon after their arrival, the air was filled with the roar of two USMC Harrier TAV-8A two seat trainers with Texas Air Guard emblems that had been hastily applied as they used their nozzles to achieve a near vertical landing about fifty yards from where Governor Atkins was hunkered down. Shielding his eye from the dust that had been kicked up by the Rolls-Royce Pegasus 103 turbofans during landing, Jeb shook hands with Luke and John, gave a wave to Leonard and Rodriguez, and then ran to the lead Harrier as Amos ran to the second. The canopies opened simultaneously, and both men had scarcely gotten seated before the dust rose in two billowing clouds as the Harriers performed a vertical takeoff before disappearing at near supersonic speed over the buttes to the south west of their position.

"Well, I reckon we did our good deed for today," John Post said to Luke as they watched the aircraft disappear in the distance.

"Yep, now we need to check on Otis' place before we look for those other two marauder units," Luke replied before giving the order for the men to return to the HumVees.

"From what I remember about this place, there is a gully just north of the house and sheds that leads to a ridge with enough cover that we can get all of the men up there without being seen," John said.

"I only remember the front and what it looked like while I was prone," Luke said, referring to where he had gotten shot two years previously.

"Well, I think we should get the Hummers into a hide up there, and then take the men through the gully and up on that ridge. Whatever we do, we need to be quick about it because the rest of the troops will be here in less than an hour," John replied.

"The ridge it is then. Let's get moving," Luke told Leonard to move out and John got in the second vehicle.

The spot that John had told him about was perfect for a stealth approach to the ridge. They left the Hummers in a group of trees several hundred yards from the ranch house, and made as quick a stalk to the ridge top as old men can. This was not lost on Rodriguez and Leonard who exchanged rolling eye looks with each other when they thought Luke and John were not looking. Even loaded with the two heavy rifles and ammunition, they had to wait frequently for the 'geezers', as they were now known, to catch up.

Luke positioned Rodriguez at the far end of the ridge with the Barrett rifle while he took the McMillan to the near end. With the other four 'geezers' besides John, they had a good position, and a real tactical advantage from the ridge with an elevation of about one hundred feet over the ranch house.

Luis was spotting for Luke when he tapped him on the shoulder and pointed to the viewing stand of the old bull ring that was south of the house and about three hundred yards distance from them.

"I see a man in the stand, Captain, but I can't make him out with the binoculars," He said.

Luke turned slightly and got John's attention and pointed to the stand and then to his eyes. John took his binoculars and looked in that direction before shaking his head in the negative.

Luke settled down against the rifle and turned the Schmidt and Bender to the twelve power magnification. He was having a hard time looking through the back of the stand because the roof slope towards them, but there was a man with a rifle standing guard and looking over the arena. Whose man he was or what side he was on Luke couldn't tell from this vantage point. Suddenly Luis tapped him on the shoulder and pointed to the front door of the house. Standing in the doorway was a swarthy looking man with a black cloth tied around his head.

Luke motioned for John, and told him in a loud whisper to have Rodriguez take the shot on the man in the arena when he fired on the man in the doorway of the home. John nodded in the affirmative and passed the word to Rodriguez.

Luke dialed the scope back to six-power magnification, and chambered one of the big fifty caliber rounds with a six hundred and sixty one grain projectile and almost ten thousand foot pounds of energy at the short range that they had to the door.

With his mind clear about what he must do, but in his heart not wanting to do it, Luke waited until Luis gave him the signal that Rodriguez was ready, and then shot the man in the chest. Both rifles roared almost together, and the man in the observation stand at the bull ring flew out and away from them when the bullet impacted him between the shoulders.

Almost as if they had struck a wasp's nest, ten men poured from the bull ring and into the roadway in the front of it, firing indiscriminately in every direction except the ridge. Luke kept his eyes on the ranch house while the troop returned a deadly barrage that dropped all ten of the enemy in seconds. Luis tapped him on the shoulder again.

"Right window, left side," He said.

Luke moved the rifle to the new position and looked in the window that Luis had indicated. He instantly recognized that there was a shooter training a rifle on their position and hurried another shot from the McMillan through the window. When the bullet impacted whatever was in the room beyond the window, two men ran in terror from the front of the building with their arms raised. Before either Luke or John could tell their men not to fire, another figure with a black bandana on his head ran out behind them with what looked to be an AR 15 M-4 raised and ready to fire on their backs. He was suddenly flung backwards several feet from the shock of Rodriguez's Barrett, and the multiple 5.56 mm rounds that impacted his body.

"Here comes the cavalry Luke!" John exclaimed loudly, pointing toward the east of the house where their men were making their way slowly towards the bullring and house with their rifles at the ready.

"Rodriguez and I will give them cover fire, if they need it. How about taking the men down and helping sweep the place up?" Luke asked.

"Sounds like a plan. I'll signal when we're ready for you to come down," John had already started moving back down the ridge toward the vehicles.

"Yes sir, that is correct. We have attacked another enemy position down on the Thunder Ranch. No casualties Colonel, but there are eight confirmed enemy dead and three civilians that they tortured before we arrived. There are also two civilian survivors," Luke gave his report by radio to Colonel Jenkins while John and the men piled the enemy bodies in the bull ring after removing the bodies of the ranch hands that had been executed there, "I am going to say that these men were all Muslim sir. I think that we need some help down here."

"Good job Captain Moffett. We are having a difficult time keeping the air space around you clear, so I would suggest that you men move out as soon as possible. I'll send a detachment of troops down to further secure the area and take care of those folks that survived the attack. I'm also keeping two Apache gunships on standby, just in case you uncover another nest of snakes," Jenkins told him.

"Sir, how bad are things going?" Luke asked.

"Well, I would say not bad at all. Fort Hood is under our control, along with Fort Bliss, and just within the last hour, Dyess Air force Base was taken without a shot being fired by our people. Navy flyers from a carrier group in the Gulf are deserting right and left, and six F-16s have come into Midland in the past hour," Jenkins told him.

"I'll pass the word on to Captain Post, Colonel. He will be happy that the outlook isn't as bleak as we thought it was," Luke replied.

"We haven't won yet, Luke, but there are thousands of militia men from the neighboring states that are helping defend our borders. It's just a waiting game now for the next move from Washington. By the way, Governor Atkins is safely in the new secure command bunker. I thought that you would like to know," Jenkins said.

"Thank you sir, I'll call in as soon as we are mobile," Luke hung up the mike and walked over to where John had gathered the men for a makeshift funeral for the three victims.

"Almighty God, we are gathered here to pay our last respect to these men that were killed by the evil that came upon them, and I would ask in the name of Jesus that you would remember their suffering on that day of judgment when they stand before you. Amen" John prayed a simple prayer, more for his men than for the ones already dead.

Several of the men didn't move at the end of the prayer. Instead, they stood with their heads bowed, just looking at the grave.

"Anything wrong Jim?" Luke asked the one standing close to him.

"I was just thinking, and maybe the others were too. What if it was me in that hole? I'm not sure that I'm ready for that 'Judgment' Captain Post spoke of," Jim Wheeler, a sixty plus heavy set rancher from West Odessa told him.

"Does anybody else feel the way Jim here does?" Luke asked softly.

Six men moved closer around Luke as John came quietly back behind them and started praying silently.

"I reckon all of us do," Jim answered for them.

"Do all of you want to make certain that you're ready?" Luke asked.

All of the men nodded in the affirmative.

"Bow your heads and repeat after me…" Luke led them in prayer, and for the first time in their long lives the men were at peace within themselves.

A search of the outlying buildings turned up two more new HumVees and military uniforms like the ones that the Governor had found earlier, although these men were wearing civilian clothes and Islamic headgear.

"Take all of the ammo and leave the vehicles and the weapons for the sweepers, men," John ordered his men.

Luke mounted Lucky and took his men towards the west with Leonard driving the HumVee and running drag. John broke off to the south to get some space between them, and the Geezer Patrol, as they had started calling themselves, rejoined the war.

CHAPTER 10

"Durrah, what are our options in Texas now?" President Onbekend whined after learning of the debacle and rout suffered by the United Nations troops.

His senior advisor came over behind him and rubbed his temples, "Relax Mister President. We will have the Texas terrorists at our mercy soon enough. I've been assured that it will only be a few short hours before their governor is our prisoner, and when that is announced, the Texas Guard will surrender!"

Durrah's cell phone rang and she took the call, "Yes, what is so urgent? I will tell him."

"Tell me what Durrah?" the President asked.

"Governor Atkins…" she started.

"Good, they've got him!" he exclaimed with glee like a small boy.

"No Sir, he has eluded us with the help of the Texas Air Guard who have taken over Fort Dyess," She told him.

He slammed both fists on is desktop in a rage, and the look in his eyes revealed pure evil. His senior advisor waited until he had calmed down.

"Mr. President, we have to take some action, or you will be perceived to be weak," Durrah whispered to him all the while thinking that he couldn't be perceived to be weaker than the people already thought him to be.

"What do you propose?" was his only response.

"Fort Hood is in the hands of the Texas Guard along with the armor that they will need to continue their campaign. We have the carrier strike force sitting off the ship canal. Why not loose a barrage of Tomahawk missiles into Fort Hood and Fort Dyess? With one stroke, we can end this rebellion once and for all," She told him.

"Get the Joint Chiefs in the Oval Office immediately. Let's see what they think of your plan," He answered.

She nodded as an evil smile spread across her face, "Immediately, sir!"

Governor Jebediah Atkins smiled as he ran his hands over the polished top of his mesquite desk. How they managed to get it out of the capitol building without him knowing was probably going to be a state secret for some time, but finding it in this bunker located three hundred feet below the Big Bend Lodge in the heart of the Chisos Mountains was a pleasant surprise. He looked around the well-lit room as his cabinet and advisors gathered for his first meeting in the new command center.

"Bring me up to speed, Tom," He addressed the Lieutenant Governor, "Please tell me that we still have the element of surprise that we hoped for."

"Jeb, except for our initial 'shock and awe' attack, General Clarke has kept to the defensive strategy as we planned. So far, that seems to be working, although we haven't heard from our sources in Washington since yesterday morning. As you are now aware, we have Fort Dyess and the 317th Airlift Group, along with six B1-B bombers that came in from Barksdale AFB in Louisiana yesterday morning. Fort Hood is in our possession along with Fort Bliss. The Carrier Strike Group is still blockading us, but they have had so many desertions that they are not launching any aircraft. I think that if those boys could swim to shore, most of the sailors would have already joined us by now," Tom Hastings replied.

"Did you get those advisors that I asked for before we left?" Jeb asked while looking over his outline.

"I did, Brigadier General Isaac Hand will be joining us by Skype conference in about three minutes, and Rear Admiral Paul Johns has agreed to assess our situation regarding the blockade. We should hear from him later today," Tom replied.

"Very good Tom, let's get the General on screen," Jeb walked around his desk and into the area of the oval conference table and the large screen monitor that was displaying an elderly gentleman with short silver hair and disturbingly gray eyes. He was wearing a dark charcoal suit with a black tie over a white shirt, and appeared to be very much the man that Jeb studied during his career.

"Hello Governor Atkins, Tom," General Hand greeted them as soon as they stepped into view.

"General Hand, I want you to know that both Texas and I thank you for your help. Has Tom brought you up to speed yet?" Jeb asked.

"I'm happy to oblige my home state, Governor, and yes, I've already looked at what has transpired since yesterday morning. That was a brilliant move, by the way. If we had acted in our numerous skirmishes abroad as you did in Fort Worth, our country would be held in a bit more esteem than it is now. I see a real problem with Fort Hood and Fort Dyess since they are within range of the USS George H.W. Bush and her escorts. My council would be to get as many of the planes in Dyess airborne immediately, and get as much armor as possible moved out of Hood," General Hand told him.

"Tom, call General Clarke and have him issue the necessary orders immediately. Load those B1-Bs with as much ordinance as they will carry, and get a couple of tankers up over Oklahoma. General Hand, are you in a secure location? We have adequate room here if you want us to make the necessary arrangements for your travel," Jeb said.

"My location is presently secure for the moment, but make the arrangements, Governor. It will be easier for us to communicate face to face if something disrupts the internet," Hand replied.

"Will do General, one of our team will contact you with instructions shortly. I'm looking forward to your arrival," Jeb cut the Skype connection to end the call.

"Excuse me Governor," a young man stepped over with a note that had been hastily scrawled on a piece of paper, "Lieutenant Governor Hastings said this was urgent."

Jeb took the paper with a nod of his head and read the note, "Clarke says six hours before bombers can fly."

Jeb motioned to Amos who was standing on the other side of the large room.

"Amos, I need for you to arrange for General Hand to be delivered here quietly. Can you make this happen?" Jeb asked.

"I can try sir. Where is he located?" Amos asked.

"He is on the Goodfellow Air Force Base in San Angelo, and we don't know how secure it is," Jeb answered.

"Well, I know the Colonel in charge of the base, Jeb. Jack Hawkins is a patriot for sure. I met him in Iraq a few years back, but I don't know which way the wind is blowing him now," Amos told him.

"Get in touch with Colonel Hawkins and see if you can get a read on him. If he is leaning in our direction, I can get a couple of men to pick the General up and deliver him here," Jeb said.

"Right away Governor, but I would be happy to go up there myself and pick him up," Amos answered hopefully.

"We just got here Amos. Are you getting jittery all of a sudden?" Jeb laughed.

"Jeb, you know that I have to have some action going on or I get a little stir crazy," Amos returned the laugh.

"Have Tom come back in here when you go out, if you don't mind," Jeb smiled as he dismissed his aide.

Tom Hastings came back in shaking his head, "Jeb they are doing something electronic to those birds that is going to take a few hours to complete, something about the transponders. I don't understand all of that jargon."

"What did Clarke say besides the bad news?" Jeb asked.

"Well, there is heavy fighting above Amarillo between the volunteers and the Feds. They don't appear to have a military presence, mostly uniformed Federal police and such. Our losses have been fairly light so far, but General Clarke says that we can't expect to win a prolonged assault without more casualties. He suggested that we adapt a more guerilla style campaign. He also thinks that Washington will try to take out Dyess and Hood just like General Hand predicted," Tom gave the report, "He is on line two and wants to speak to you."

Jeb picked up the phone, "Hello General."

"Hello Governor Atkins. I tried to relay the urgency of our situation with these bombers that kind of dropped in our laps over at Dyess. The techs down there are trying to change the transponder codes so they can't be identified or tracked by the enemy. Unfortunately, that is delaying getting the birds up. We may lose them," Clarke gave him the bad news.

"General Clarke, I want at least two of those planes in the air in thirty minutes, with or without the electronics configured. In the air, we have a bargaining chip. On the ground we have nothing. Can you make it happen?" Jeb asked.

"Governor, hold the phone for a minute. I've got them on the other line," Jeb's line went to an instrumental version of 'Moon River'."

Thirty seconds later, General Clarke was back on the line, "They are rolling two out right now, sir. Technicians are going to fly with them and work on them in the air."

"Very good General, as soon as they are up, I want them patched in to this command center for orders, understood?" Jeb ordered.

"Yes sir! I'll have our people make the arrangements," Clarke responded and hung up.

"Governor, Admiral Johns on line one, sir!" the shout came from the other end of the room.

Jeb mashed the button for line one, "Hello Admiral, thank you for calling. I've got you on the speaker; Lieutenant Governor Hastings and my aide Captain Amos Whitehorse are present. Have you got any news for us, sir?"

"Hello Governor…Gentlemen. Well, I do have some news, but it is all bad. My sources in Washington are reporting that an assault on Fort Dyess and Fort Hood is imminent. It looks like they may try an airborne assault on Hood to retake the fort immediately after the Tomahawks are used," Admiral Johns reported.

"What is your suggestion sir?" Jeb asked.

"If you had something with enough payload capability, you could attack that carrier group. The only other option is to try and shoot down as many of those missiles as possible," Johns replied.

"Well, we don't want to look like the aggressors here, Admiral, and if we sink that carrier, we could kill or wound over three thousand men," Jeb told him.

"There is no such thing as a war with zero casualties, Governor. Warn Washington not to fire on your state beyond what they already have. They won't listen of course, because you drew first blood," Admiral Johns told him, "When they fire the first Tomahawk, you need to have an instant retaliation planned."

"Thank you Admiral. You have been very helpful, and I hope that I can count on your continued support. We've made provisions for you to be patched in to me directly," Jeb told him.

"If I have anything else, I'll call immediately Governor. Good Luck," Admiral Johns ended the call.

"Well?" Jeb looked at the two men sitting at the table with him, "What do you think?"

"It doesn't make sense to stage an airborne attack on Fort Hood, sir. That would give the enemy a physiological victory, but probably not a strategic one. Most of the armor is rolling, and an air strike will damage what is left. I'm betting that the Admiral is planting false information to throw us off, and Fort Bliss is the real target!" Tom Hastings exclaimed, "I also don't think that it is our best interest to fire on that carrier, especially since it is named after one of our own! That would just give them an opportunity to show the people that we're the real terrorists in this conflict."

"That makes sense to me also, Tom. Something about the way the Admiral sounded made me think that he is compromised. Get word to General Clarke to reinforce our people in Fort Bliss and put the base on REDCON 1. Have him send a fighter squadron to patrol inshore of that carrier group and intercept any Tomahawks that are inbound," Jeb issued the order, "Amos, I need a link to the B1-B group leader ASAP. I think that I've got a plan."

CHAPTER 11

"I don't know about you, John, but my men and I are worn out. We need to find a safe place to set up a decent camp and get these men fed and rested. That goes for the mounts also," Luke said to John Post.

"You're not alone, Luke. I feel like I've been dragged through a knot hole backwards. What do you suggest?" John replied.

"I remember that there is a high ground water tank a couple of miles from here that could afford us a good vantage point, plus cover for a couple of days. It has enough tree cover that we could picket the horses out of sight and hide our tents in with them," Luke answered. He was thinking of where he and Michael Tucker had faced the black jaguar two years before, but it seemed like only yesterday.

"Well, I reckon that Otis won't mind us camping out for a spell. I wonder what he'd think about us taking one of his steers for camp meat. The Colonel would pay him for it," John planted the idea firmly into the head of a man with an empty stomach.

"I saw a three hundred pounder on the other side of that bull ring a few minutes ago. I think that Mark would like to help me get a rope on him. We'll lead him up there and do the butchering close to the tank. Why don't you send Rodriguez and Leonard on ahead to set up the cook stove and gather enough mesquite for a good fire. I'm thinking medium rare steaks for the troops tonight!" Luke replied as he drew a map in the dry ground at their feet.

"Some of us will like that, but most of the men don't have their own teeth anymore. You're going to have to cut their meat real small, Cookie," John slapped him on the back with a laugh as he limped away to retrieve Ahab.

"Well, I'll be danged! I'm going to be a cook after all!" Luke exclaimed to his friend's back and a big smile came on his face.

Three hours later, the steer was quartered and Mark had started boning out the loin and tender loin at Luke's order. He figured that the tender loin would be easy enough for the men to gum if they had too. It would be cold enough for the next few days that they could hang the meat that they didn't cook immediately and cut it up as needed. One of the other men found a camping saw in the HumVees, and he was working one of the hindquarters into steaks as fast as he could saw. Rodriguez and Leonard had built a fire pit next to the cook stove that was almost three feet long. After finding enough large stones to encircle the pit, they laid some pieces of pipe over it to hold up a section of woven wire fencing that Leonard had spotted at the ranch house. It was obvious to Luke that these men had some barbequing experience, which they were planning to put to good use.

The men had pitched their tents among the pines just above the picket line that was strung for the animals. They shared one fire pit for each two tents, and Luke had them build log reflectors on the down slope side of the fire so that they could not be seen from the road way, just in case the enemy drove up that way. The vehicles were hidden in the brush and covered with scrub to make them invisible from the air.

"Luke, I do believe that this is the best steak that I've ever had!" John exclaimed around a mouthful of the tender meat.

"That's because we rustled it, kinda like stealing watermelons when we were kids," Luke laughed.

"Just keep that fact quiet. Old Jasper Coggins over there used to be a Texas Ranger. He might just want to string us up for that," John took on a serious tone.

Luke turned around and watched Jasper biting into his second thick cut of loin.

Jasper waved to them and said loudly, "Great piece of meat, Captain, even if you did rustle it!" To which all of the men roared with laughter.

"You'd better eat up John. There is a lot of evidence left," Luke said with a smile.

"Captain Luke, Captain John, Colonel Jenkins is on the radio for you," They were interrupted by Sergeant Gonzales.

"Thanks Luis. We'll get it while you eat another steak," Luke handed him his plate.

"What do you reckon he wants?" John asked as they walked to the tent with the equipment.

"I guess we'll find out in a second, but I'll bet it's not good news," Luke replied.

"Captains Moffett and Post here sir," John picked up the mike and spoke.

"Men, There is a ridge line about three miles to the west of where you are camped. I need for you to set up an observation post on the top of it tonight, if possible," Jenkins declared.

John looked at Luke who just shook his head in disbelief.

"Colonel, it is just about an hour until dark. I don't think that we can move men over there tonight," John told him.

"We interrogated those prisoners that you sent back to McCamey, and a couple of them mentioned that there was a sizable group of infiltrators staging over there. We've had two flyovers, but it is almost impossible to see men that don't want to be seen. I just need for you to locate the force and report the position. Our boys will do the rest, but it is imperative that you move quickly," Jenkins replied.

"We understand sir. By the way, the Guard owes Otis Jamison for a three hundred pound steer, and could you send us in some potatoes with the next supply drop?" John asked with a laugh.

"I might have to deliver that myself John. Ya'll be careful, and keep those eyes peeled," Jenkins ended the transmission.

"Well, that ruined a perfectly good cookout!" Luke declared, "I think we should send Rodriguez with those two infantry drivers that you picked up. One of us needs to go along to keep them out of trouble.”

“I’ll go with them, and you bring the relief crew in the morning. Let’s leave this place set up as a base camp. Jasper would make a good cook, and he makes a mean biscuit. Maybe we can leave Leonard with him tomorrow to kind of keep an eye out for trouble,” John replied.

“Let’s get it going then. Pick a spot on the map, and I’ll round up the men for the trip,” Luke said as he turned back to the tent opening, “Listen John, Mary Louise won’t take it too kindly if you get yourself killed over there, so don’t do anything foolish.”

“You worry too much, Luke. There’s not a foolish bone in my body,” He replied with a laugh.

Luke just shook his head and went back to the cook fire to give the necessary orders. Something didn’t feel right about this mission, although it seemed safe enough, but Luke chose to ignore the churning in his stomach and passed it off as a case of nerves. They decided to send the HumVee by itself since it would be too dangerous to cross the rough terrain on horseback in the dark, so John told Luke to keep an eye on Ahab for him. Luke watched the vehicle roll out across the brown fall desert through the mesquite, cactus, and scrub that had lost their foliage. He tried to tell himself that the extra chill in the air was because winter was just around the corner, but the nagging in his spirit wouldn’t quiet down.

CHAPTER 12

The operations center was alive with activity as Governor Jebediah Atkins waited for the connection to be made to the White House. Across the oval shaped table sat his Lieutenant Governor, Tom Hastings, retired General Isaac Hand, retired Colonels Anthony Schaeffer, USAF, and Thomas Bridges USMC. They had been discussing a plan to strike a truce with the President by using the small leverage that they had gained with the B1-B bombers that had defected.

"I'll admit that it is a risky proposition, Governor Atkins, but it could get those jackals off our backs," Colonel Schaeffer spoke up.

"I also agree, sir," Colonel Bridges added, "either he will agree to a truce or we will have stirred up a hornet's nest, but it is certainly worth a try,"

"Tom, what do you think?" Jeb asked.

"Well, I agree with General Hand's assessment earlier. If we come out of the corner and bloody his nose, we at least will gain some respect and an advantage," Tom replied.

"That's the plan then. Let's get this show on the road. Amos, I want a video feed with Vanguard News and Margaret O'Brien set up. She gets an exclusive. No other news media talks to us. We'll break the news to the world as soon as we finish with Washington," Jeb finished and walked to the camera area for the Skype feed to the White house.

"Governor, you are on in three…two…one," Amos gave him a hand signal as General Anthony Wayne's face came on the screen.

"General Wayne, I thought that we were going to be talking to the President," Jeb showed a little surprise.

"The President has delegated all of his authority to the Joint Chiefs to deal with your insurrection Governor. Do you want to discuss your surrender?" Wayne replied coldly.

Jeb looked at General Hand who was standing outside of the camera view and got a neck chopping motion from him.

"General Wayne, I believe that the President is listening to this conversation. If he will not make himself available then we have nothing to discuss," Jeb signaled Amos to kill the link.

"What now, gentlemen?" Jeb asked of the men in the room.

"I would go ahead with the strike on the first target, sir. That would certainly get some kind of response," Colonel Schaeffer offered.

The others signified their agreement by a nod of the head.

"Have the B1s strike the first target in stealth mode. I don't want them to know what hit them," Jeb ordered, "How long before they are in position, Colonel?"

"They've been ready for about thirty minutes, Governor. We will know the outcome in about five minutes," Schaeffer responded, "I wish that I was flying this mission myself!"

Jeb just smiled at his response, "Don't we all Colonel...don't we all."

"Amos, can you get us the visual on those Tomahawks? I'd like to watch the fireworks if we can," Jeb asked his aide.

Amos gave the order to one of the technicians and a sixty inch screen came to life, giving them a multiple image view through the cameras that were mounted in the missiles' noses. The action was over quickly as first one target and then another came into view and the screens went white, starting with the clubhouse of the golf course at Fort Belvoir, and ending with the clubhouse of the golf course at Andrews Air Force Base, the two favorite courses of the President.

"Let's see if he wants to talk now," Jeb ordered and sat back in the chair in front of the camera.

The Skype line rang twice and was picked up by Durrah Jowles, the President's senior advisor who answered curtly, "Governor

Atkins, President Onbekend wants me to talk to you. He is having a migraine and needs to lie down for a while. What do you want?"

Jeb looked across at the men again and General Hand just shrugged, "Why Not?"

"Durrah, we all know that you are the power behind the throne, so I will make my proposal to you. We want a cessation of hostilities between the United States of America and the Republic of Texas. In return I can guarantee you that there will be no more aerial attacks, and I will give you adequate time to pull your troops out of Texas safely," Jeb threw the proposal out on the table.

Durrah's look and tone changed to that of a venom dripping snake, "You launched four missiles at us in a hostile action that is unparalleled in the history of this country, and you expect us to just throw up our hands and quit?" Jeb raised his right hand ever so slightly in a pre-arranged signal as she continued speaking. "You are a filthy infidel that has no rights. I am going to personally see to your defeat!"

The room that she was broadcasting from suddenly took on a life of its own with the generals and cabinet members all talking at once. News of the second strike that took out both Air Force Ones simultaneously while they were on the ground at Andrews Field had just reached them.

"Consider that a love tap from this infidel, bitch," And he gave the signal disconnect the call.

"Is Maggie O'Brien on yet?" Jeb asked.

"She is ready sir," Amos motioned him to get ready.

"Governor Atkins, this is an unexpected pleasure," Maggie started in graciously, "The World is hearing about a series of explosions in Maryland this evening. Would you care to comment?"

"Are we broadcasting live, Miss O'Brien?" Jeb asked.

"We are running a few seconds delay for censoring purposes, Governor," Maggie responded.

"Here's the deal, no delay or no interview," Jeb said sternly.

Maggie looked off camera for a brief moment and then responded with her characteristic smile, "We can do that sir, now about that comment."

"A few minutes ago, I had a brief and unsatisfactory discussion with Durrah Jowles at the White House via Skype. My aide has sent an unedited video recording of that conversation to you, please run it now," Jeb sat back and waited.

The short video played in its entirety while Maggie O'Brien was visible in a split screen shot. The look on her face was priceless when Durrah lashed out at the Governor of Texas as being an 'infidel' since some in the news media had been vehemently denying for years that the President and his advisors were Muslims.

"Governor Atkins, is there anything that you would like the American people to know about the conflict between Texas and their country?" Maggie asked as if unsure just what questions she should be asking.

"Maggie, Texas is now a sovereign nation, and we want recognition of that fact. As you have heard, I am willing to sign a truce with the government of America and put a stop to the killing that is going on inside our borders. We are not threatening anybody or any target if the President does not agree to a truce, but, as you have seen, I will not be threatened. The time for political correctness in Texas is over. As we speak now, I am told that in the few days that we have been at war, our forces have killed or captured many Muslim insurgents that have been terrorizing and killing innocent civilians, and we know that there are many more to be captured. After hearing the rhetoric of the President's Chief Advisor, I can only believe that they are acting on direct orders from the White House. From this point forward, any Muslim that refuses to accept Texas Constitutional law and refuses to assimilate into Texas society will not be allowed residence in Texas. All of their mosques are going to be destroyed, and those that are here, and desire to leave peaceably, will be given safe passage across our borders to any state that will have them. Those that choose otherwise, well…" Jeb finished by raising his hands slightly and shrugging his shoulders.

"Governor Atkins, we have some film that shows the devastation to the clubhouses at Andrews Air Force Base and Fort Belvoir a few minutes ago when several massive explosions occurred there. Did you order this strike and also the strike that destroyed both Air Force Ones?" Maggie asked.

"We needed to underscore a point, Maggie. The clubhouses were on the courses that are the President's favorites, and we struck them at night when they were less likely to be occupied. I had credible intel that none of the planes were occupied, and that President and his advisors were with the Joint Chiefs in the underground command bunker. As I've already said, Texas will not be toyed with," Jeb answered.

"I have one more question, Governor, and this is not being recorded, since you have honored me with this exclusive interview, would you give me permission to bring a film crew to document the things that you've told me?" Maggie asked.

Jeb thought for a minute with his brow wrinkled and his fingers tapping the table top, "I'll tell you what, Maggie, We are generally not allowing any imbedded news services in the Guard, but there is a group that we can probably fit you right in. You can ride can't you?"

Back in Midland, Colonel Jenkins looked over the reports that had been coming in all evening to General Clarke, who was now the Commandant of the Texas Guard per Governor Atkins orders. The personnel casualty reports were the hardest to sift through. Texas Guard forces had suffered substantial losses in the first two days of fighting, but they had lost only three aircraft, F-16s, and had gained several more than that number due to the desertions of the Navy pilots and the Air Force bombers. The drone attacks against both civilian and military targets had started on the first day of the conflict right after the ambush of the United Nations forces in Fort Worth, and there had been two attacks thwarted by alert Texas Guard fighter pilots in the past three hours at the Midland airport complex.

He was interrupted by a loud cheering from the men that were assembled in the hanger area just outside of his office, and the door being flung open suddenly.

"Sorry Colonel, but there is some news on Vanguard that you really should see!" a young corporal burst in excitedly.

"That door is on the office for a reason, son! Don't enter without knocking again, understood?" He answered in irritation.

"Yes, sir, but you really need to see this!" the young man insisted.

Nathan followed him outside to the break area where fifty men were gathered around a sixty-inch TV screen just in time to see the Governor's interview with Maggie O'Brien.

"He bombed the golf courses and blew up the Air Force One planes!" they all shouted to him.

Laughter began filling the air at the thought of the Governor ordering a strike on the two golf courses that the President frequented most often.

"Corporal, get me a smaller TV installed in my office immediately," Jenkins ordered with a smile.

"Yes sir!" the young man shouted and ran off to find someone to fill that order.

Jenkins continued to stand in the front of the big screen television with his men as they watched pictures streaming in showing tens of thousands flooding the streets of almost every major city in celebration of the Texas attacks. Other footage showed fighting breaking out along the Oklahoma and Texas

Border as militia men clashed with U.S. Army regulars that were trying to stop them from crossing into Texas. These men were armed with heavy weapons and seemed to be gaining ground when a brilliant flash of light illuminated the battlefield, followed by the shockwave of a massive explosion and the camera going dark. The report was suddenly returned to the newsroom where Maggie O'Brien and her fellow reporters sat in shock and disbelief that the government would use a weapon of this magnitude to quell an uprising against its own people.

Colonel Jenkins rushed back into his office and put in a call General Clarke.

"General, are you aware of what just happened in Oklahoma a few minutes ago?" He asked when the General answered the phone.

"I'm just seeing it now, Colonel. My advisors are telling me that the blast has triggered earthquake alerts over one hundred miles away! They only have two weapons that would do this; either a Daisy Cutter or a tactical nuke. I can't imagine what idiot sanctioned this kind of strike that would kill the fighters on both sides. Hell, we hesitated to use them in Iraq or Afghanistan. We'll know more tomorrow; in the meantime, you are going to need to build some bomb shelters immediately. Utilize whatever you need in the complex, but try to get everyone below ground if we get an alert," General Clarke ordered.

"I'll give the necessary orders immediately sir," Jenkins ended the call and went outside to find some of the oil field construction hands that were under his command.

Deep under the West Wing of the White House, the President listened intently to the discussions between Governor Atkins and his people. When all of the news had come in regarding the air strike on the two golf courses and his aircraft, he finally broke his pouting silence.

"General Wayne, I want the order given to respond in kind with an attack from the carrier group off Galveston. I especially want one missile programmed to strike the Governor's personal residence. Who knows, we might just get lucky!" He ordered.

"Yes sir, Mister President. Do you want to include a bombardment of the Midland Space Port with that order?" Wayne asked.

"Yes, I believe that an attack on Fort Hood and a prolonged attack on the airport will serve as a sufficient diversion for the assault on Fort Bliss, don't you?" the President responded.

"I'll give the order immediately sir!" Wayne exclaimed as he signaled to one of the aides for attention, "Sir, you should know that there has been some fallout from our use of the twenty thousand pound bomb on those militia troops in Oklahoma. We lost one hundred Army regulars in the blast."

"I'm aware of the casualties General. It is an unfortunate, but a necessary evil if we are going to conclude this business in a timely fashion," He answered, "If we don't get a surrender of the Midland Space Port after the next attack, we'll drop one in there also."

Durrah Jowles had the last word as she and the President stood up from the table, "Gentlemen, you have your orders, now we want to see some results."

The members of the Joint Chiefs stood as the President exited the room, and then turned to look at General Wayne.

"Drinks are on me, gentlemen. Let's adjourn to Mickey's," He said quietly, knowing full well that their every move was being monitored, "The first round is on me."

CHAPTER 13

Maggie O'Brien, one time cheerleader, local news anchor in Myrtle Beach, SC, and now the lead anchor at Vanguard Nightly News in the Washington, D.C. studio, jumped at the opportunity to embed her news crew with a group of Texas Guards while they patrolled the sprawling expanse of the West Texas Desert. Her main problem was that the President's advisor had forbidden any commercial air travel to the embattled nation of Texas unless she embedded with the United Nations forces that had paused to lick their substantial wounds in Fort Worth. With all of the commercial flights into and out of Oklahoma, Louisiana, Arkansas, and New Mexico coming under the close scrutiny of the U.S. Military and their local law enforcement counter parts, her options were extremely limited as far as travel was concerned.

"Maggie, this news agency will not underwrite a trip to Texas while the country is at war with them! Now I hope that I've made myself clear on the matter. As news worthy as this might seem, we will not risk sticking our corporate finger that far into this administration's eye, especially since they are getting more dangerous every day," Blake Greer, News Director for the network was adamant.

Maggie thought in silence for a minute and then replied, "Blake, I'm taking a leave of absence for an unspecified period starting tomorrow. I trust that you will have all of the necessary buttons pushed by broadcast time."

"You're what? Maggie, you can't do this to me…to us. What am I going to tell Robert about your leaving?" Blake asked in a pleading tone.

Maggie looked across the desk at her former boyfriend and now boss. She had found him attractive until the last time she had gone to Texas. Since then his perfectly styled hair and expensive clothes, his taste for flashy cars and equally flashy restaurants, plus the need to always be seen, seemed foreign to her. They had broken up shortly after her father's death, and her return from the funeral of Michael and Hanna Tucker and their baby girl, Emily. The type of relationship that those two had was what she wanted also, and her emotional reserves had been depleted with their passing.

Maggie stood up before she answered, "Blake, number one, there is no 'us', and number two, tell Robert that I have had a nervous breakdown. Tell him anything, but you had better cover my butt on this or you won't have a job after I get back. Am I making myself clear enough?"

He hesitated for a minute, face flushed with anger, "You'll be sorry for this, I promise."

"You'll be sorrier if I bring my story back to CNN!" She snapped as she walked out of the office, letting the door slam behind her.

"Well, what did he say? Do we get the gold card for expenses or what?" Her best friend and camera woman Julie Meyers had been waiting around the corner while she had talked to Blake.

"No gold card, no support. I'm going to have to do this on my own…somehow" Maggie replied without slowing her walk to the elevators.

By network standards, Julie Meyers was not a head turner, although she was attractive in a small stature, cute sort of way. She wore her hair in various styles, mostly short, and various colors which seemed to change with her often shifting moods, but she was one of the best videographers in the business.

"I've got a news flash, Honey, where you go, I go! Are we clear on that?" Julie took Maggie's arm and matched the hurried pace.

"Jules, I don't know how in the world I am going to get out there, much less how we could get out there, especially with all of your equipment," Maggie said.

"Take me by my place, and I'll pick up my GoPro. If nothing else, we can make You Tube videos!" Julie quipped with a laugh.

"I need to stop by Wal-Mart first and pick up a burner. There is a person that might be able to help," Maggie said in a conspiratorial whisper as she gave her best friend a slight sideways hug.

Amos Whitehorse looked up from a session with two of the military advisors that had been brought on board in the past few hours to see Governor Atkins motion to him from his office.

"Excuse me gentlemen, I'll be right back," He excused himself from the meeting.

"Amos, you are just the man that I need to volunteer for a mission," Jeb said with a laugh.

"Is this going to be like the mission that you 'volunteered' me for in Kuwait?" Amos asked anxiously.

"Relax, this is a cake walk compared to that one. We need to get Maggie O'Brien out here without being seen…if you know what I mean, and you are the best smuggler that I know. Well, make that the only smuggler that I know. What do you think?" Jeb asked.

"Maggie O'Brien, you mean beautiful, red haired Maggie, the reporter? Heck yeah I'm game! When do I leave?" Amos asked.

"She is leaving tonight for Cozumel, so you will need to get down there and pick her up along with her camera woman. We have an ops team coming in from the company airport at Mina Hercules tomorrow. Have them up there to make the flight in and bring the whole team back here," Jeb told him.

"Cozumel is one place that I've always wanted to visit, Jeb. Can't we afford just one night R and R for me?" Amos almost pleaded.

"Not this trip partner, you will catch a ride with Sergeant Emmanuel Hernandez, our front desk man in the lodge, across the border and down to the Mina Hercules. Catch a ride over to

Monterrey and pick up your plane there. When you pick up Miss O'Brien, fly back to Mina Hercules and load the team. Any questions?" Jeb asked.

"Well, I probably wouldn't be too far off if I guessed that this was a hazardous undertaking, would I?" Amos asked with a smile.

"Is there another kind, old friend?" The Governor replied, "Amos be careful and use whatever resources that we can muster to pull this off safely. We need Maggie out here reporting the facts, and we need this team that is coming in."

"You know that you are going to owe me on this one, Jeb," Amos said with a laugh as he shook the Governor's hand and then walked out to get his gear.

Jeb gave Amos a brief wave and turned back to his desk. Signaling to his military advisors, he gave them a brief command.

"Let's get first strike underway, gentlemen. I've all ideas that we're within minutes of being hit, and I would like to bloody their noses," He said.

A young Lieutenant issued the order, "Black Swan one, you are go for 'first strike', over."

The comm line was silent for a second and then came to life, "This is Black Swan confirming 'First Strike' is a go."

"Well gentlemen, see if someone can patch us into the Admiral onboard the George H.W. Bush," Jeb ordered.

They all waited while the comms room attempted to establish communications with the carrier. After several attempts, one of the young men gave Jeb the high sign that the line was hot.

The speaker in the room came to life, "This is Captain Horatio Spires speaking."

"Captain Spires, this is Governor Jebediah Atkins of the Republic of Texas speaking. I need to cut to the chase here sir. Please direct your attention to your aft flight deck area," Jeb greeted him while the room looked at the video from the camera on the two thousand pound guided bomb.

"Three…two…one…I'll hold for your response Captain Spires since it appears that you are busy," Jeb chided him.

The two thousand pound relic of the Viet Nam era had been equipped with the latest strap on guidance system from Raytheon, and had penetrated the flight deck before coming to rest among the aircraft in the hanger deck below, destroying two and damaging several others.

"That was a warning, Captain. We took the charge out of this bomb, but if you fire one Tomahawk at any target in Texas, I will send a half dozen of these puppies down with full charges. One other thing, when I call again the Admiral had better pick up the damned phone!" Jeb signaled for the transmission to be cut, "Get those bombers to Roswell immediately. Once they are inside the old hangers there, it will be difficult for them to be found. I've talked to the New Mexico Governor to make the arrangements."

"Governor, General Clarke is on line two," An aide called in to him.

"Yes General, what's going on?" Jeb asked as he picked up the phone.

"Sir, the enemy detonated something very large up on the Oklahoma border near Shamrock about thirty minutes ago. From what the news footage shows, and the reports from the ground, I'm guessing that they dropped something similar to a BLU-82, only larger. We don't have a casualty report yet, but there was a company of about one hundred Army regulars fighting to keep a militia group out of Texas, and both have gone dark, along with a complete news crew that was up there reporting live!" the general reported.

"My God, they've killed their own troops! What kind of soulless animals could do such a thing intentionally?" Jeb replied to the news.

"A man that could destroy his own country…but it might be worse, Sir. I've got people headed to the area to check for radiation, and I've given an order for all of our troops to dig shelters in any location that they can find. If they have resorted to a nuclear strike, this could be a short conflict," Clarke finished.

Very well, general. Please keep me on speed dial," Jeb ended the call.

General Hand came to the open door of the office area and knocked politely, "Excuse me sir, but there is some news coming in from Texarkana that you should see."

Jeb got up and headed for the conference room where they were playing a cell phone video that had been shot a few minutes after the explosion in Oklahoma by an apparent survivor. The carnage that it showed was unbelievably harsh even by battlefield standards with the charred remains of at least one hundred militia and one hundred U.S. Army soldiers and their support equipment lying scattered among the debris.

"Where did we get this video, General?" Jeb asked.

"It came in from an Army battalion commander in Texarkana just a few minutes ago. Governor, they want to defect to our side and bring two other battalions with them!" General Hand exclaimed.

"How did he get the video, General? Shamrock is a long way from Texarkana," Jeb asked him.

"The video was loaded up to You Tube, sir, and the whole world is watching it now. The commander had it sent to him by the person that took it," Hand replied.

"If the story is true, then it is a stroke of luck for us!' Jeb exclaimed, "But I think we need to move carefully with this. Arrange a meeting with the battalion commander and feel him out. Do you have anyone in that area trustworthy?"

"Yes sir, Major John Deese has his guns bore sighted on that Battalion as we speak. He assures me that they have stood down," Hand declared.

"Very well, have the Major open talks with the commander and keep it quiet, but let's make this happen quickly! Also, make certain that any Muslim troops are excluded before we bring them in," Jeb answered with a feeling of elation rising in his chest.

CHAPTER 14

"Come in Luke. Have you got a copy on me?" the radio crackled with John Post's voice.

"Luke here John. What's going on?" Luke replied.

"It's real quiet here, Luke…too quiet I think. What am I supposed to be looking for?" John asked in a low tone.

"Colonel Jenkins didn't say specifically, just that when they questioned those prisoners, that area was mentioned as a location for hostiles," Luke replied.

"Well, it is darker than four foot up a well diggers hind quarters out here. How in the world are we going to see anything if it's there?" John sounded a bit cranky.

"Bundle up until morning, and I'll get some replacements over there. The Colonel is sending out some reinforcements to set up a real cook tent and latrines, so I guess we'll be staying in the area for a while. Now remember, John, don't engage the enemy without help…if there is any enemy," Luke cautioned him again.

"Just make sure to get us off this danged hill in the morning!" John grumbled back.

"Will do, Luke out," Luke ended the call and walked back to the warmth of the fire.

"Coffee, Captain Luke?" Luis asked as he approached.

"Thanks Luis," He said as he took the cup and moved to where Lucky stood with the other horses.

"Hey boy, I just wanted to see how you were doing before I hit the sack," Luke talked to his friend as he scratched behind the horse's ear, "We'll get us a good ride tomorrow, I promise."

Luke headed for the tent that he shared with John. It was going to be good to have the latrine set up and a shower, he thought. The men were all getting a bit ripe, although a couple of them always seemed to be that way before. He drifted off to sleep on the hard cot with his head buried in the sleeping bag to ward off the cold night air.

Four thirty came early, and the Geezer Patrol, as they had taken to calling themselves, moved slowly to the cook fire for a hot cup of campfire coffee and fried beef strips. Jasper and Leonard had taken to cooking for the men like ducks to water, and could hardly wait for the mess tent to arrive with the reinforcements that would dig the latrine and build the shower. Luke tried walking off the stiffness in his joints, but the morning cold exacerbated the pain from the many places in his body that had been bent or broken over the years. What he wouldn't give for about an hour in a hot tub this morning or a handful of Aleve!

"Sergeant Gonzales, pick two men to relieve Captain Post and his men. Get them over to that ridge on horseback, and have Captain Post bring the Hummer back to camp," Luke said to Luis as he passed by the fire and got his coffee.

"Right away Captain," Luis saluted, "I think that I should stay over there with these men sir. Not many of them have any military training."

"That's a good point, Sergeant. We'll send replacements out this afternoon when the new men get here," Luke agreed with him.

The sun was just rising in the east and lighting up the few wispy clouds that floated high up with no promise of rain. Luke moved to the radio to get word to John, when it squawked.

"Come in Luke, do you read me?" A gravelly whisper came from the speaker that Luke knew belonged to John Post.

"Go ahead, John. What's wrong?" Luke replied.

"You know those Apache gunships that the Colonel promised us? You need to get them out here, pronto!" John whispered into the radio, "We've got about two companies of rag-heads down below us, and I don't think they are going to stay there."

"Standby John, I'm going to call Colonel Jenkins," Luke responded.

"Luis...Sergeant Gonzales, muster the men immediately and get them mounted. We've got a bunch of Moslems over that far ridge!" Luke gave the order to Luis as he made the call to Colonel Jenkins.

"What do you mean 'the Colonel isn't there'? I need those Apaches that he promised, and I need them yesterday! Is that clear?" Luke let his frustration show.

"Sir, I'll keep trying to raise him, but they are on the move and communication is spotty," The voice on the other end replied.

"Just make sure that he gets the message, son, or his favorite 'Geezer Patrol' might cease to exist," Luke told him, and then ended the call in frustration.

"Come in John, do you copy?" Luke tried to raise John, but the radio was silent.

He walked over to the remuda where Lucky was waiting for him to saddle up, "Not this morning old boy, I'm going to ride the buckskin because I don't want you to get shot."

Lucky blew at him as he passed like he understood, which he probably did, and stomped the ground as Luke saddled the big gelding.

"Everybody in the saddle men; weapons at the ready!" Luke commanded as soon as he was mounted.

His rear had no sooner hit the seat good when the buckskin balled up and shot straight up in the air, putting all of that muscle into a jump, three hard crow hops, and a series of jumps and twists that had his belly almost pointing straight upward. Luke had broken plenty of horses in the day, but he wasn't expecting a keg of dynamite with this horse, and especially when he was turned halfway in the saddle. He lost his hat on the first jump, and managed to get his left hand on the saddle horn before the horse went crazy. His last thought just before he hit the hard ground was, "This is going to hurt a whole lot!"

When he got enough of his wind back and opened his eyes, Lucky was standing over him looking into his face as if to say, "Serves you right!"

Two of the fellows checked him for broken bones, and then asked as they lifted him to his feet, "Can ya ride Luke?"

"You wouldn't think so after that spill, but I guess I'll make it," He replied.

With every bone in his body feeling like it was out of joint, Luke retrieved his saddle and bridle from the buckskin that was standing quietly with the remuda, and saddled Lucky. He eased into the saddle again, but his old horse had no intention of doing anything that would hurt him.

The men then circled up around him while he explained what was waiting for them over the ridge where John was, hopefully, still keeping a lookout.

"Luke," Jasper called out, "How about leading us in a word of prayer before we go over there. I know that I'd feel better, and I sure these fellers would also."

Luke removed his hat and bowed his head, "Dear Lord, please protect these brave men as we go into battle, and put the enemy to flight before we get there. Amen."

A big "AMEN" rose from the men as they fell into formation behind Luke and Lucky, with Leonard bringing up the rear in the second Hummer. Fifteen minutes at a gallop put the men within sight of the area that John Post was supposed to be in, so they drew up in the deep cover of the mesquite growth which had not lost its leaves. Luke checked the terrain with his Leupold binoculars for any sign of life, but there was no movement on the ridge in front of them. After waiting for ten minutes in the cover of the big butte to their left and the mesquite scrub, Luke decided to split the men and advance from two points. At least this way, they probably would not all get caught in an ambush, although there was absolutely no sign that there would be one.

"Keep those peepers peeled men! Lock and load your rifles," He ordered before taking the lead.

The men had spread out until they were in a line about three hundred yards across and approached the three hundred foot ridge slowly. About fifty feet from the top, they dismounted and continued working their way to the top as quietly as if they were hunting deer.

Suddenly the air was filled with the sound of high speed turbines screaming up behind them, and they froze in position, expecting the worst. What happened next was nothing short of a miracle. Two Apache helicopters roared in overhead like angels of death, and disappeared over the ridge top above them. Almost instantly it sounded as if all hell had broken loose on the other side with small arms fire being audible first, then the sound of Hellfire missiles finding targets.

"Let's get up there men, those boys might need some help!" Luke shouted down the line, and the old timers charged the hill at a pace much slower than they would have twenty years before, but charge they did!

Leonard reached the top first and immediately began laying down fire in three shot bursts, quickly followed by Jasper and then the rest as they ran smack dab into twenty ISIS terrorists running up to meet them. Down below, the dust from the Hellfire impact was still settling and Luke could make out the Hummer that John had taken sitting out in the open while six other vehicles were burning in the brush at the base of the rise.

Luke's men made short work of the Islamists except for the ones that escaped the two Apache pilots who were still dogging their trail as they ran through the mesquite, and the Geezer Patrol suffered no casualties except for sixteen old men gasping for air like wind broke horses.

Luke signaled Luis to come over with the radio, "Get me Colonel Jenkins, Sergeant."

Luis made the call, and then handed the handset back to Luke.

"Captain Moffet here sir," Luke was still gasping for air.

"Luke, are you men all right? Those pilots said that they encountered a large contingent of Islamists," Jenkins asked.

"We have no casualties sir, but I've lost track of Captain Post and his men," Luke answered.

"Start the search, but be very careful. Tell the men not to touch any of the dead enemy, I'm right behind you with more troops and some of our intelligence gatherers. I'll see you in about ten minutes. Jenkins out," The Colonel ended the transmission.

Luke walked back down to where Lucky waited and mounted up. He didn't intend to do anything on foot the rest of the day if possible, except find John Post.

Ten minutes later they had all gathered behind the Hummer that John had driven over. The Barrett was gone, and the radio was smashed, but there was no sign of the men that had been driving it.

Leonard was with two other men searching the area around the burning vehicles for any sign of their friends, with no success, when the Apaches came back and did a slow turn just outside of the battlefield perimeter before coming back and landing close to the patrol. One of the pilots got out and walked over to where Luke was sitting.

"Sir, there is a body on the ground about three hundred yards to the north of this position. It is definitely not one of the enemy," He told Luke.

Luke thanked the pilot and immediately headed Lucky at a dead run toward the area that the pilot indicated, flanked by six of his riders. He came to a sliding stop in the front of a mesquite bush where the body lay face down with its hands tied behind its back, knowing immediately that it was John Post. The men gathered around the still form of their friend and cut his bonds before slowly turned him over. It appeared that his captor had been interrupted in an attempt to remove John's head, and had only accomplished cutting his throat.

Luke's eyes were full of water as he put his hand on his friend's chest, and then loudly exclaimed,

"He's alive! Thank God Almighty, John is alive! Get him some help!"

"Captain Moffet!" a voice behind him exclaimed.

Luke turned to see Colonel Jenkins standing there with a medic and a Texas Guard ambulance.

"Colonel, he's alive!" Luke couldn't find anything else to say.

"Let the medics do their jobs, we'll get John flown out of here if they can stabilize him. I'll make certain that Mary Louise is with him," Jenkins put his arm around Luke's shoulder and led him away from where they were working on his friend.

The unsuccessful search for Rodriguez and the two infantrymen continued for several hours after John Post was flown to Odessa for treatment of his severe neck wounds, and the loss of oxygen to his brain, so Colonel Jenkins ordered all of the men to regroup at their base camp.

"Think of it as home for the next few weeks anyway, Luke. You men have done an outstanding job out here, better than we could have hoped for, all things considered. We got word from Otis Jamieson to use what you need here, and we'll settle up after Texas wins its statehood," Jenkins told him in private.

"Well, sir, to be truthful, John and I didn't expect to last the first firefight, so everything from here on is gravy. I know the men appreciate the mess tent and the latrine that you boys fixed us. That will help us out a good bit now that the weather is taking a turn," Luke answered but his mind was on John's injuries.

"There is something else, Luke. We are embedding a news crew in here with your troop to get public opinion working for us worldwide," Jenkins said.

"A news crew? You've got to be kidding me, sir! We don't have time to bird dog a couple of tenderfeet out here. What about if we get run over in another attack like John and his men?" Luke protested sharply.

"It's Maggie O'Brien, Luke, and her camera woman," Jenkins said with a smile.

Luke just looked at him for a second in dumbfounded amazement, "Maggie O'Brien? Red haired Maggie O'Brien? Well…that puts a whole 'nother light on it! Dang, wait until the fellas hear about this."

"Listen Luke, if this is going to be a problem, I can always have her work out of headquarters," Jenkins was having fun now.

"Now don't you worry about a thing, Colonel. It will be like that little girl has twenty daddies out here. We'll take good care of her!" Luke said with a grin that looked like it would split his face.

"All right then, it's settled. I want her to have a tent set up in the center of your compound, and remember, 'The eyes of Texas are upon you'!" Jenkins ended with a laugh.

"Yes, sir, Colonel, Well make you proud! Before you go, would it be too much to ask if you would lead the men in prayer?" Luke answered.

"Not at all. In all of the activity today, we must not forget who delivered us from the enemy," Pastor Jenkins said quietly.

Later that night, Luke sat by the fire drinking a cup of coffee with Luis and laughing at how the men acted like schoolboys when the news of Maggie O'Brien's visit circulated through the camp.

CHAPTER 15

Sergeant Emmanuel (Manny) Hernandez met Amos at the Big Bend lodge dressed in old blue jeans, and driving a 1972 Chevy pickup that was so rusted that it left an outline of the body on the ground when the doors were slammed. Amos was dressed to match with a well worn park employee jacket on and a fake passport in his pocket in case they were questioned. Manny's grandmother still lived in Las Garzas, Mexico just across the border. They arranged to have other transportation waiting for them there through a special relationship that Manny had worked out with family on the other side. From there, it would be a rough, noisy run of almost seventy miles to Mina Hercules where their ride to Monterrey waited in a dusty hanger.

Amos worked to quell an anxiety attack as the old truck vibrated its way closer to the border. Finally, when he could stand it no longer, he raised his voice to shout over the roar of the broken exhaust on the V-8 engine that labored under the hood.

"Manny, what are we going to do at the border? You know that there will be U.S. and Mexican Army guards posted that will know that I am not a Mexican," Amos asked.

"Senor Amos, you worry too much. Of course you are not good enough looking to be a Mexican, but I know a shortcut that will put us across the river before they can find us," Manny laughed at his joke, "Seriously Captain, the Rio Grande is very low this time of year, and I have a spot where we can drive over. I used it many times when I was a young man and my future wife, Maria, lived in my Grandmother's village."

Amos just nodded his head and smiled in a half hearted attempt to let Manny know that he was okay. In less than ten minutes, Manny turned off the road onto a dirt path and killed the engine as soon as they were out of sight of the main road.

"Let's listen for any sounds that might not be friendly," he said as he got out of the truck.

They listened intently for anything out of the ordinary, and then Manny open the hood to make an adjustment. When he fired the engine up it was as quiet as a Cadillac.

"What did you do?" Amos asked in amazement.

"Well, we had this old crate fixed to look and sound like a dirt poor Mexican's truck, but it has a good suspension and a three hundred and fifty horse motor under the hood. You know, in case we want to run down a jack rabbit or something," Manny replied with a laugh.

They drove slowly and silently down to the edge of the river bed with the lights off. Manny waited for two minutes and then flashed his lights once, and then twice. Directly across the river, there was an answering flash.

"Well, Captain Whitehorse, its pucker time!" Manny laughed and slowly forded the river toward the vehicle that waited on the other side.

Amos could feel his jaw drop when they pulled up next to a bright red, brand new Toyota Tundra driven by a boy that could not have been more than fourteen years old.

The two men got out and Manny introduced Amos to the youngster.

"Captain Amos Whitehorse, meet my nephew, Isaac Gonzales," Manny said as he exchanged keys with the boy.

Amos shook the boy's hand and followed Manny to the Toyota, "What in the world…?"

"Just keeping the family business going, if you know what I mean. The kid needed the motor in the Chevy for a project that he has, so I traded him for a ride. Pretty nice too!" He answered as he patted the hood, "Let's get going!"

Two hours later after running the circuitous route that took them through Chihuahua, the two men arrived at the secluded airstrip of the Hercules Mining Company. Manny pulled the Toyota up to the side of a small hanger and grabbed his kit bag from the back seat.

"Time to go, Captain," He said with a grin.

"What about the keys?" Amos asked when he saw them in the ignition.

"We're trading this for an airplane!" Manny laughed, "I hope you can fly it."

In the deserted hanger sat an old Piper Super Cub that had been painted a desert camouflage pattern.

"Does this relic fly?" were the first words out of Amos' mouth.

"Si, this one used to belong to my brother-in-law who also used it in the family business. I think it is about a 1960 model, but he took good care of it until the Federales came for him," Manny volunteered.

"That explains the bullet holes in the fuselage, I suppose. Well, let's check it out and get out of here. This place gives me the willies!" Amos exclaimed as he shined his flashlight down the fuselage of the small airplane, illuminating three holes about the size of a dime that exited the other side of the fabric and tube fuselage. Manny rolled the hanger door open, and then he and Amos pushed the Piper outside into the starlight. Amos got in to the pilot's seat and switched on the cockpit lighting. At first glance the cockpit instrumentation looked like what he expected to find in an airplane that was controlled by Visual Flight Rules, but on closer inspection, Amos found a radio direction finder, radar scope, and a new VHF radio with a twenty watt booster. It was becoming very apparent what the 'family business' must have been.

Manny finished the quick preflight on the retrofitted one hundred and eighty horse power Lycoming O-360 engine and signaled Amos to turn it over. The motor spun twice and then coughed to life, and Manny ran to get in the passenger compartment.

Amos knew when he heard the engine cough that this was not an ordinary Piper, regardless of appearance, but a real thoroughbred that was waiting to jump off the runway. He taxied past the hanger a short way before turning his landing lights on, and seeing more than two hundred feet of open space in the front of him, he opened the throttle and released the brakes. Inside of one hundred feet they were airborne and on the way to Monterrey.

"I told you that she was a good airplane Captain," Manny's voice crackled in his headphones.

"She certainly is, sergeant. What are we trading this one for?" Amos laughed.

"This actually is my personal plane senor. It is the only thing that I have left of my brother's. Governor Jeb arranged for an airplane for us to fly to Cozumel. We'll pick that one up when we land. I also think that you should probably fly a little bit lower and turn off the running lights. I don't think Governor Jeb is on such good terms with President Fuentes," Manny said nervously.

"Now you tell me!' Amos replied, "Any more surprises?"

"Well, there is one other thing, just a small thing really, but the ladies have to be blindfolded on the trip back," Manny replied.

"What in the world are you talking about, Manny? Why would we have to bring those women back with blindfolds on?" Amos demanded.

"Because, my friend, they aren't the only ones coming back with us!" Manny exclaimed, "You were told that we were going to pick up an ops team on the way back, correct?"

"Yes, at Minas Hercules," Amos answered.

"Well, that was a false trail that we threw up because someone is listening to those conversations in the Governor's office so the Governor made all of that up. However, we are going to bring a team back across the border."

"But what about the spy in the office? How are we going to catch him?" Amos asked.

"Well, my brother Carlos will fly this plane back to the mine, and those guys that are waiting for us will come out of hiding. The rest of my family will take care of them, and use some old family secrets to extract the information that we need. I expect that Governor Jeb will have heard from them before we land," Manny told him.

"Well, where is that going to be, exactly?" Amos sounded put out.

"You'd better turn on your running lights Captain, that's Monterrey up ahead. Let me handle the tower," Manny evaded the question as he called the tower for landing instructions.

Amos brought the little airplane in expertly and taxied to the hanger that Manny indicated. In stark contrast to the dirt at the strip mine of Minas Hercules, this hanger was well lit and bustling with activity as the ground personnel rolled out a new Beechcraft King Air 350i.

"Wow, I'd sure like to fly that baby!" Amos exclaimed.

"Isn't that a coincidence, that's the one we'll be flying!" Manny laughed at him, "There's Carlos. I'll give him the instructions and then meet you at the plane," Manny told him as he stepped out of the Piper.

Amos grabbed his kit bag with his street clothes and headed for a small lounge to change. He was still puzzled by the change in plans that he had not been made privy to, but he was sure that Jeb had his reasons for not telling him. Manny came in to change, and they laughed at the upgrade that this new airplane represented.

"Well, Captain Amos, I suppose that I can now tell you that this airplane belongs to the United States Government, and we need to be very careful not to scratch it up when we cross the border again," Manny told him.

"A government plane? Why are we flying one of their airplanes on this mission?" Amos asked.

"Because, these are some seriously high level ex-spook dudes that we are bringing in, and these news women can't know or even suspect that Governor Jeb is recruiting outside of Texas for an intelligence team," Manny informed him.

"Sergeant Gonzales, if that is who you really are, how do you know so much about the inner workings of our new government?" Amos asked.

"I am just a simple man, Captain Amos. I've never wanted to do more than run my business and take care of my family. However, there are things in my background that made me suited to work on the Governor's intelligence gathering detail. That, coupled with the fact that I love Texas enough to give my life for her, is why Governor Jeb entrusted me with this information," Manny answered, "How about you? Are you willing to die for an ideal as big as the Nation of Texas?"

"Of course I am, Jeb and I go a long way back!" Amos sounded displeased with Manny asking.

"We'll see…we'll see," Manny answered.

Thirty minutes later the Beechcraft was wheels up and on the way to Cozumel. This was certainly not turning out the way that Amos imagined this trip going, and it looked like he might not even get to talk to the famous red head that they were picking up. Oh well, he knew when Manny had told him that they were going to fly back across the border, that it was his skills as a fighter jock that made Jeb pick him for this mission. Amos just hoped that they wouldn't get shot down before he got to meet Maggie O'Brien!

"The Flamingo Hotel, really Maggie? I've never been to Cozumel, and I'm thinking like we'll be staying in a luxurious place like the Cozumel Palace, but noooo…we have to stay off the beaten path. Do we even know if this place is clean or not? Do any single men stay there?" Julie was on a rant as the taxi took them on the short ride from the airport in San Miguel to their lodgings.

"Listen Jules, we have a meeting with some people a little later in the evening, so we probably won't be staying very long…depending on how that works out, and you know that a brief vacation here is just a cover story to get us out of the country. Besides, this is out of the way, it has great reviews, and there is less of a chance that we will be noticed than if we stay at one of the bigger hotels. Remember, I'm not on an expense account for this one either, so no shopping!" Maggie laughed, "Cheer up, we still have about four hours of daylight left, we can act like tourists until this evening anyway."

"Maggie O'Brien! Look everybody, it's Maggie O'Brien!" a loud, and obviously drunk voice began shouting as soon as they entered the lobby of the Hotel Flamingo.

The two women tried to walk around the heavy set man in a green flowered silk shirt that barely covered the stomach hanging over his belt, but without much success. It was fortunate that there were not many people in the lobby at this hour of the day, but the situation that he was creating had already drawn unwanted attention to Maggie's arrival in Cozumel. As the big man moved to intercept the women, he appeared to stumble, and Maggie found herself entangled in an embrace with the big sweating drunk. What happened next astounded her.

"Play along," He whispered as he struggled to regain his footing, then in a loud voice, "I'm sorry Mish O'Brien, let me buy you a drink."

"No thank you. Just leave us alone!" Julie spoke up just as two men with close cropped hair and muscular builds came up on either side of the man.

"Sir, you need to leave these women alone!" One of the men spoke in a lowered voice directly into his ear.

The drunk began mumbling apologies as they led him away, and another man walked up behind them. Taking both women by the arm, he escorted them past the small crowd to the desk area. Seeing the puzzled look on their faces, he laughed.

"Now that we've made certain that everyone in America knows that you are vacationing in Cozumel, I'll leave you ladies to check in. You will be getting a phone call on this around seven this evening," He said as he discreetly handed Maggie a cell phone.

"Who are you?" She asked, but the question was met with a smile, and the man left the hotel.

"That was weird," Julie said just before the front desk attendant, who had been standing patiently off to the side, approached the pair.

"Weird indeed!" Maggie exclaimed as she realized that Julie had not heard the drunk when he had fallen into her.

"Greetings ladies," The man behind the counter said in a contrite and sincere voice, "I would like to apologize for the rude behavior of that gentleman. Please accept a free room upgrade as a token of that apology while you are with us."

"Yes, of course, and thank you," Maggie told him as he finished his paperwork and handed them the key cards for the room.

What they didn't see was that the room the man entered into the desk computer was not the room that they had been assigned. As soon as they walked away with the scant luggage they had brought with them, the desk clerk left the counter and made his way to the exit in the rear of the hotel, just as a young woman came from a small room to the side and took his place.

When Julie arrived at the room ahead of Maggie, she opened the door and saw the piece of paper on the floor just inside of the threshold.

"Maggie, look!" She said excitedly as she picked up the hand scrawled note that had been written on the hotel letterhead.

Maggie took the note and read it, "Don't unpack. Stay in the room until you are contacted. Stay off social media; others will be looking for you."

Maggie turned the note over to see if there was anything written on the back, but the cryptic message on the front was all that they had.

"What's going on, Maggie?" Julie asked. The tone of her voice told Maggie that she was worried.

"The drunk in the lobby was a ruse, Jules. We may be in danger if we leave the room, especially if someone in the State Department found out that I was sneaking into Texas. I think we might have some new friends that are looking out for us," Maggie responded as she locked and bolted the door.

"Well, those two that helped with the big drunk guy were sure cute! If I had to pick my body guards, those would be them," Julie told her with a laugh.

"Be careful what you wish for," Maggie laughed.

The rest of the afternoon and evening, Maggie worked on her laptop, being careful not to visit any of her social media sites. Julie alternated between wistful glances out of the room which overlooked the pool area, and talking to Maggie about what kind of trouble they might have gotten themselves into. At exactly seven o'clock, the cell phone that Maggie had been handed rang.

"Yes?" she answered carefully.

"Grab your clothes and leave your electronics in the room. Use the back stairway and I'll meet you on the ground floor," The voice said.

Maggie started to reply, but the call ended abruptly.

"Come on Jules, we've got to go. Leave your phone in the room along with the camera. We are only taking our clothes," Maggie told her.

"What? Leave my camera? No way!" Julie was angry.

"We have to do it, Julie. They've got cameras in Texas, I'm sure," Maggie reassured her friend.

"Well, all right, but this is turning out to be a real drag of a trip!" Julie pouted as they tossed their electronics on the bed and left the room.

The stairwell was about six rooms from the room that they had just left, and the elevators were about the same distance in the opposite direction. Just as they entered the door to the stairs, Maggie heard the chime of the elevator ring down the hall.

"Hurry up Jules!" She exclaimed as they ran down the three flights of stairs, "I'm thinking that whoever was on the elevator might have been coming to pay us a visit."

Julie made the bottom landing first and had just reached for the door, when it swung open to reveal a stocky Mexican gentleman in boots blue jeans holding the door for them.

"Hurry up ladies, I think that you might have some company out here in a very few minutes," He admonished in perfect English.

They quickly ran from the back of the hotel to an older car that was waiting at the curb and piled in. As he sped away from the hotel in a cloud of blue smoke, the man introduced himself with a big smile. "I am Stefan Hernandez, ladies. My twin brother, Manny, is waiting for you at the airport. There are two black hoods in the seat back there. I'm afraid that you will have to wear them until you get to Texas."

"Why do we have to wear the hoods, Stefan?" Maggie asked.

"There are people traveling with you that don't want to be known, especially by the famous 'Maggie O'Brien'," Stefan told them.

"The next time that I want to tag along with you Maggie, just shoot me in the head!" Julie said as she grudgingly pulled the dark hood over her head.

"It will be okay, I promise," Maggie tried to reassure her friend, but she was starting to have her own doubts.

CHAPTER 16

The private, smoke filled back room at Mickey's, the upscale D.C. bar known for its seedy atmosphere, was empty except for General Wayne and the members of the Joint Chiefs, now in civilian attire, that had decided to convene an emergency meeting outside of the prying ears and eyes of Durrah Jowles' growing network of Muslim sympathetic spies and informers. What better place than Mickey's, where local politicians had gone to great lengths and considerable expense to sterilize the establishment from any type of eavesdropping, spying, or lip reading technology. It was not unusual for long time members to arrive at the dimly lit bar and hangout to find that their favorite bartender had left town the evening before under mysterious circumstances, but no one ever asked the obvious questions that begged an answer.

Wayne waited until all of the men were seated and the drinks served before he proposed a toast by lifting his double Wild Turkey and orange juice and saying in a loud voice for the benefit of anyone in hearing range, "Here's to victory over our enemies!"

The men all took long pulls on the drinks and responded, "Here, here!"

"Gentlemen, we have a serious problem," Wayne started, "I don't know how many besides myself watched the President this evening, but I am beginning to believe that Durrah is the power at the helm of this nation."

One of the men across the table, Navy Admiral Lucas Smith, turned his head in both directions as if looking for an eavesdropper in the empty room. "Anthony, if we are caught so much as whispering what I think that you are getting ready to whisper, our heads will be adorning the White House fence by morning!"

The others hurriedly drained their glasses and reordered.

"Gentlemen, if we destroy the infrastructure of Texas the way that he is talking about, with a nuke for Pete's sake, Russia and China will be cruising up the San Jacinto River within days!" General Wayne continued, "Up until now, Governor Atkins has not attacked us with deadly force except for the United Nations troops in Fort Worth, which in my opinion was justified. He damaged the carrier to get our attention, and made certain that his strikes on the golf courses and Air Force One were non-lethal. The world is watching, gentlemen, and right now they are cheering for that bugger in Texas!"

"What do you propose to do with the order that was given to bomb the daylights out of Midland then?" Admiral Smith asked before the others could get into the discussion.

"We need to bomb Midland into submission, but stop short of using another daisy cutter or tactical nuke. The attack on the George H.W. Bush will keep us from using their Cruise missile option on Fort Hood, but we have other delivery methods that will work. What we need to consider is the mental condition of the President, and whether or not we are going to follow the orders of Durrah Jowles," Wayne replied.

"You are talking a coup then?" General Tom Doggett asked quietly while twirling his drink.

There was an uncomfortable silence around the table after that question was raised, broken only by the sound of ice cubes clinking in their respective glasses. Each man at the table was well aware that their individual character flaws had brought them to this place, and they were now bound to play the cards as they were dealt.

"We'll work our strategy to bomb Midland while the U.N. ground forces quell any opposition in the cities. Let's take Fort Bliss back, and then we will decide on any other course of action that might be expedient," Wayne finished his speech, slugged the rest of his drink down, and stood to go.

Not another word was spoken as the men finished their drinks and left the bar one by one, not knowing that their every word was recorded by devices in the room belonging to Durrah Jowles and her Muslim Brotherhood compatriots.

The bombardment of the Midland Space Port began at 0200 hours with Predator drones leading the attack, but, thanks to the ingenuity of the oilmen that made up a large part of the Texas Guard and their makeshift bunker systems, the initial strike only broke a few coffee cups. Sitting under six plus feet of steel and concrete that had been hastily blown in to cover a few tons of steel from several oil rigs, the men waited for the bombing to end, and the ground assault to begin. Neither the Daisy Cutter nor the tactical nuke strike manifested, and the bombardment ceased at 0430. In the eerie silence that followed the bombing, Jenkins had his men quietly deploy to strategic positions around the Spaceport and wait for the next phase of the attack.

At 0530, after aerial reconnaissance showed no signs of life among the ruins of the terminal building and the outlying structures, Colonel Ahmed Farook ordered an assault on the Spaceport using two companies of Middle Eastern troops and heavy armor. The well hidden Texians, outnumbered two to one, waited as one man for the enemy to pass their perimeter defenses. On the pre-arranged signal of six A-10 Thunderbolts attacking the armored column, the deadly crossfire of the Texas Guard began cutting the United Nations troops to ribbons. Within five minutes, after the A-10s had devastated the tank column and armored personnel carriers, they turned their firepower on the ground troops, and thirty minutes later, the surviving fifty United Nations troops threw down their weapons and surrendered.

Daylight was breaking on the battlefield as the victorious Texians rounded up the prisoners and took a tally of their personal losses. The Texas Air Guard gave cover while heavy equipment cleared the debris from the fighting and opened the airstrip for incoming traffic.

At the same time as the attack on the Midland Space Port was underway, Fort Hood received numerous strikes from Cruise missiles that had apparently been fired from offshore. Since that area had been evacuated quietly and the armor moved, the damage was contained to the base structure. The main assault target was Fort Bliss, and that attack was carried out by airborne troops in what they had hoped would be a surprise. What wasn't figured in the equation was that the several brigades of troops defecting to Texas would be rushed to Fort Bliss to help turn the tide when the attack started. Coupled with the heavy armor at the fort, and the Texas Air Guard on alert, the attack was over within an hour after the last of the airborne assault team was on the ground.

At 0700 hours, the Joint Chiefs , a representative of the State Department, and twenty aides, reconvened in the War Room with the President and a furious Durrah Jowles. Conspicuously absent from the table was General Anthony Wayne. As the men looked from one to another for an answer to the question that they didn't want to ask about the General's absence, the silence in the room became like a thick fog.

"In case you are wondering where the General is this morning, I regret to inform you that he was killed by a hit and run driver last night as he left the bar where you were meeting," Jowles stated coldly, "As for the debacle of last night's attacks on the Texas positions, some explanations are in order, starting with why there was no tactical weapon used in Midland, and why there was not a heavier bombardment of Fort Hood from the carrier group? Who wants to start giving excuses?"

The President sat silently at the table, staring at his hands, which were folded in front of him.

"Mister President, Miss Jowles," General Doggett cleared his throat nervously before continuing, "unless we had resorted to a ballistic missile, the logistics of deploying that weapon in Midland was impossible given the control that the Texas Air Guard has of the sky in that region. Two of our cruisers fired their missiles on Fort Bliss, but the Admiral onboard the George H.W. Bush issued a cease firing order based on the fear that Governor Atkins would make good on his threat to sink the carrier. As for Fort Bliss, I can only say that we somehow lost the element of surprise, which was essential to taking the post with a limited loss of equipment and lives."

"Anyone else up to making excuses this morning?" the President said without looking up.

"Sir, if I might add," Admiral Smith replied, "Most of our Naval Fleet is now facing the threat of mutiny among the enlisted men as well as the officers. With the viral video of our attack on Shepard, Oklahoma and the loss of friendlies in that attack going up on the internet, the world is condemning our tactics. We've had desertions and defections running into the hundreds of troops with every decision that we've made to escalate the war in Texas, as well as enforcing martial law elsewhere. The situation is making it difficult to carry out the type of operations that will win the war for us."

The rest of the group remained silent as they thought of the events of the night before, and the death of the one man that had broached the subject of a coup at Mickey's. That they had been overheard was now topmost in their minds, and the fear of being next had acted to cement their tongues to the roof of their mouths.

"Admiral Smith, I want you to personally fly to the George H.W. Bush and relieve Admiral Stokes of command. From this moment, you will assume full control of the carrier group, and, I might add, you alone will be held responsible for any more failures of that group. Do I make myself clear?" The President raised his head to stare directly into the eyes of the Admiral from the short distance across the table.

"Absolutely Sir! Thank you for your confidence in me," Admiral Smith sucked up in the best way that he could think that would gain him a couple of more days of life as he looked into the eyes of a mad man.

"General Doggett, you will assume the responsibilities of the Head of Joint Chiefs. Bring in as many personnel as you need to make certain that we have no more screw ups…subject to Durrah's review of course," The President finished with an evil smile crossing his face as he stood up to leave the room with his entourage of Secret Service bodyguards.

Durrah took over the meeting, "First of all, I want an explanation from the State Department as to why Maggie O'Brien was allowed to go to Cozumel on vacation while this country is under Martial Law. I want her found and escorted back immediately! Secondly, it is imperative that we seize control of the oilfields in the Permian Basin, have a plan to do just that by this afternoon's briefing. I also want a plan to find the headquarters of Governor Atkins, and to eliminate it. Am I making myself clear? Two retired Generals, one from Pakistan and one from Afghanistan, are coming onboard as advisors to fill our leadership gaps on this team, and I expect you to cooperate with them on every matter. Is that also understood?"

A very nervous nodding of heads signified that all were in agreement.

"Gentlemen, we've got a war to win, And I expect immediate results. She finished and left the room.

Admiral Smith immediately rose from the table, "Gentlemen, I've got to get my 'A double' on a flight for the Gulf of Mexico. Good luck to you all."

General Doggett stood to shake hands with the Admiral, thinking to himself, "Lucky bastard! If I could get on a plane, I'd head for South America," What came out was, "We'll hold the fort here while you're gone, Lucas."

Admiral Lucas Smith had always thought of himself as a survivor, especially in situations that other men figuratively lost their heads in, but there seemed very little chance of coming out on the top of the dilemma in which he now found himself. When hundreds of officers had retired or been forced out of the service for not answering in the affirmative when the question was asked if they would fire on United States citizens, he had thrown his support behind the President, believing that action was what was best for his career, and also believing that those orders would never be given. Now he had to fire an old friend of his and take over a wartime command that would force him to kill hundreds, if not thousands of men and women that believed that their freedom from tyranny was more important than life.

What he needed was a plan, and he had precious little time to come up with one before his Navy Seahawk SH-60 touched down on the flight deck of the George H.W. Bush on station off Galveston, Texas. He was escorted by a Marine guard in full dress uniforms to the Admiral's quarters where he was met by both Admiral Stokes and Captain Horatio Spires.

"Lucas, this is a pleasant surprise," Admiral Stokes greeted his old friend after the formal salute.

"It probably isn't going to be for long, gentlemen. The President has authorized me to take command of the carrier group immediately which doesn't bode well for either of your careers," Lucas told them point blank.

"Admiral Smith, sir, if I might say in our defense that we are on very shaky ground here. Half of our crew is on the verge of mutiny, and the other half is thinking about it, including the officers! The first sortie that we sent just took off and didn't come back, and I'll bet that the first one you send will do the same. Begging your pardon, sir," Captain Spires weighed in.

Lucas was silent for a minute letting what he was hearing from these two senior officers sink in.

"Let me get this straight. You are telling me that this ship would rather support a mutiny against the United States Government than attack a rogue state? Does that include you two?" He asked.

"Well, Admiral, if you put it that way, then I would have to say that I do not support the actions of our Commander-in-Chief, although I won't speak for Captain Spires," Admiral Stokes told him.

Lucas turned to Spires, "…and you Captain?"

Nervous sweat stained his uniform at the armpits as he answered in a strong voice, "I concur with the Admiral, sir!"

"Gentlemen, you have made this transition too easy for me," Admiral Smith let his words sink in, "It's time that Texas had it's own Navy! Captain, find a way to contact Jeb Atkins, I want to negotiate our surrender, and keep all of this between us, please. We'll also need to know if there are any Marines that we can count on. There will probably be a few men that will need to be kept in the brig until they can be transferred off the ship."

"What about the rest of the carrier group, sir? How do we break the news to them?" Captain Spires asked.

"I would say that both of you men have had your hand on that pulse for some time. Give me a list of those that we think we can trust in the fleet," Lucas responded, "but first, get me the Governor on the horn so we can see if he will let us steam up the river."

"Aye, Aye, sir," Captain Spires replied and left the boardroom.

"Well, Benjamin, I guess we have stuck our feet firmly in it now, haven't we?" Lucas addressed Admiral Stokes.

"Why did you change sides, Lucas? This isn't quite like you," Stokes asked as he poured a small glass of bourbon for the both of them.

"Jowles had Anthony Wayne killed last night, and the rest of us have a target on our backs. I just figured that this was the lesser of two evils," He replied as he raised the glass, "A toast to mutiny!"

"To Mutiny!"

CHAPTER 17

"We should load the women in the back first so they don't have to get jostled by the team. The aisle is kind of narrow," Amos said to Manny as they waited for their passengers to show up.

"My brother Stefan is on the way with the ladies, but I think that our other passengers might be doing a little cleanup work before they come," Manny told him, "Let's get her warmed up and ready to leave just in case they don't get all of the dirt out."

"Another brother? Didn't your father ever sleep?" Amos cracked as he climbed into the cockpit and started his pre-flight check.

As they were getting ready to start the engines, the old Volvo Taxi rolled to a stop in a cloud of blue smoke, and Stefan gave a wave to Manny as he helped the women out of the car.

"I'm going to lead you to the airplane now senoritas. It has been a very big pleasure for me to meet you!" He said with a laugh.

From beneath the hood Julie replied sarcastically, "Likewise."

Manny helped them climb into the plane and ushered them carefully down the narrow aisle to the rear seats.

"Good evening ladies, this is your Captain speaking. No really, this is Captain Amos Whitehorse with the Texas Air Guard," Amos laughed, "We apologize for the precaution of the hoods, but our other passengers must remain anonymous. I hope you understand."

"Crank it up Captain, our guys have arrived," Manny said as he saw the SUV with the others pull into the hanger area in a hurry.

The powerful Pratt and Whitney Turbines spun to life as Amos finished his checks and fired them up. It was obvious that the six big men that had exited the SUV and were headed at a dead run for the airplane were in a hurry to leave, and he certainly wanted to oblige them!

"Tower, this is Beechcraft November Two Zero Whiskey Tango Tango, requesting takeoff clearance, over."

The men were in the cabin of the plane now and finding seats. Two of them looked at the back seats of the airplane at the women and exchanged glances. Amos was certain that he had seen them before, but the tower interrupted his thoughts.

"Beechcraft November Two Zero Whiskey Tango Tango, we have to ask you to hold your position; clearance is denied."

Manny slid into the seat opposite Amos and leaned over to whisper, "What are we going to do now? These guys have gotten us in big trouble!"

"I need at least three thousand feet to get this bird off the ground. Does that look like a straight shot through those parked planes?" Amos was already pushing the throttles up and starting to roll.

"Tower, this is Beechcraft November Two Zero Whiskey Tango Tango, I copy your last, and we are holding for clearance."

"What the…we aren't holding Amos. Those guys are going to go nuts in about a minute," Manny was excited.

"They can't see me for another thousand feet, and by that time we'll have enough jump on them that they won't be able to block us," Amos replied as he shoved the throttles up and felt the combined twenty one hundred horsepower of the big engines, "Let's see if this bird has a wartime emergency built in."

Manny crossed himself and closed his eyes so he couldn't see the wingtips and tails of the parked aircraft shooting by dangerously close as the big Beechcraft thundered between the rows and then out into the open, narrowly missing a jet liner that had just landed.

"Beechcraft November Two Zero Whiskey Tango Tango you are not authorized for departure. You will cut power and return to the paddock area for inspection!" The voice barked from the tower.

Amos kept his eyes on the instruments and watched his airspeed building to minimum takeoff velocity.

"It's now or never," he said under his breath as the end of the concrete rushed toward the plane. He pulled back gently on the controls and felt the plane grow lighter under him. As soon as there was no ground feel, Amos toggled the gear up and eased the controls further back, watching the airspeed climb even as the wheels locked into place.

"Ladies and gentlemen, we've just departed the beautiful and scenic Cozumel, but I would advise keeping your seat belts buckled for the duration of the flight," He spoke into the cabin speakers.

"Aren't we flying a little low, Captain?" a voice from behind his shoulder asked.

"I wouldn't have to normally, but you guys disturbed the locals, and they will be hunting us with radar, so I am flying under it," Amos replied without looking back.

"Nice flying by the way. Most men would have frozen back there and left us stranded on the tarmac," The voice said again.

"Thanks, I guess, although I think that the take off is probably going to be the least exciting thing about this flight," Amos answered.

Manny looked up from his praying and said, "I have the return path right here," as he took a piece of paper out of his pocket.

Amos punched in the coordinates for the various waypoints and watched his radar for any ground clutter. He reached up and switched off all of his navigation lights and just prayed that they were alone in this airspace as they flew at maximum airspeed along the return route. His special skills wouldn't be needed unless they picked up a tail, which could come at any time now that they were flying across the street flat Yucatan Peninsula low enough that they could be swatted by a tall man with a broom.

"You can turn off the radar now Amos. I had my brother fly this route so we could get through here without any surprises," Manny told him, "but we will have to be very careful until we get into the Sierra Madres. After that it is not likely that they will be looking for us that far North."

"I wouldn't put money on that, my friend. Somebody tried to stop Maggie O'Brien from leaving Cozumel, and I think our other passengers probably killed them. If I am just a little bit right, they know that we are headed for Texas," Amos told him.

"Stop being so pessimistic and look on the bright side. If we don't get killed between here and Texas, you will be a hero in the eyes of a very beautiful senorita. Besides, this is why you get paid the big bucks," Manny said with a nervous laugh.

"One small thing, did you make sure that the fuel was topped off before we left? I'm pushing her pretty hard right now at two hundred and ninety knots, and that is going to cut into our range. By the way, I haven't been told where we are going yet. That information is always useful to the pilot," Amos told him.

"The coordinates are on that sheet that I gave you. It is a dirt strip about seventy miles from the border," Manny told him, "Don't worry, we'll probably get shot down before we get there anyway."

Amos flew across the Gulf of Mexico right on the deck, hoping that the wave pattern would minimize the chances of the big plane showing up on somebody's radar. They would have to be careful as they came across land again because of several airports along the coast, but once past that…well it was anybody's guess.

"Excuse me, pilot," The voice behind Amos' shoulder spoke into his ear, "This aircraft is equipped with a radar avoidance system and some diversionary flares and chaff, if the need arises,"

He turned his head slightly to look at the man and found himself looking into the coldest blue eyes that he had ever seen. He just nodded his thanks as the man pointed to the instrument panel where the switches had been added skillfully to blend with the rest of the instrumentation.

Amos reached for the switch that controlled the radar-jamming device and flipped it on.

"I hope that this thing works," He whispered to Manny who was watching his every move.

Manny responded with an affirmative nod of his head as he watched the coastline approach at close to three hundred nautical miles an hour. As they flew across the coastline and proceeded inland, Amos waited for a hail from one of the control towers or a military jet that would indicate they had been spotted. When it didn't happen, he breathed a sigh of relief.

"Well, Manny, it looks like we might just make this run after all..." he started to say, when, "Unidentified aircraft heading two hundred and eighty five degrees. Identify yourself, over," Came through the headset.

"Crap boys, we're busted!" Amos exclaimed as he pulled back on the controls to gain some altitude.

"Wait a minute, Amos. Keep us low and let's see if we are the ones that they are after. This area is a drug runners hot spot, so there just might be someone else in the sky with us," Manny said.

Amos eased the nose back down and waited. Sure enough, the radio squawked again with an angry voice calling for an unidentified aircraft to identify itself. Suddenly, about three miles to their starboard side, there was a brilliant burst of light as an air-to-air missile found its target, and some burning wreckage fell to earth.

"I hope that wasn't family, Manny," Amos said quietly as he thought about how they had just avoided that bullet...or missile as the case might be.

"Probably not. My family pays off the right people most of the time. Besides, drugs are not what we deal in," Manny answered,

"We've got about two hours left. Do you think we are going to make it?"

"Piece of cake!" Amos said with a bravado that he did not feel, "Hey, can one of you fellows check on our other passengers? The ladies might not be used to all of this excitement."

The man sitting closest to the two women turned so he could speak to them, "Pardon me ladies, but the pilot wants to know if you are all right."

"Tell him that I have to pee, and I might puke, but other than that, I'm having a ball!' Julie answered sarcastically.

"How about you. Miss O'Brien?" he asked next.

There was something familiar about the voice, but Maggie couldn't put her finger on it.

"I'll be fine as long as we don't die," She responded.

That drew a laugh from the man and he called to the front, "They're fine!"

"Manny, when we get about fifty miles from the border, I'm going for maximum altitude. That should be around thirty thousand feet or so. I can then put her in a shallow dive and pick up about fifty knots as we come across. The Army will be looking for us to make a low run across to avoid radar, and we might just blow past them overhead. What do you think?" Amos asked.

"We are going to have some air cover if we can get across. That's a big if though. Are you catching the radio chatter?" Manny asked.

Amos had heard the alerts being broadcast by a half dozen ground stations, and he was sure that the Mexican military was up looking for them. He pushed the throttle full open and picked up another fifteen knots of airspeed. They flew over Minas Hercules, which was now lit up like a Christmas tree, and roared toward the border at full throttle.

Amos pulled back on the controls and the aircraft climbed at a rate of twenty seven hundred feet per minute. It was now or never to use every trick in his arsenal to evade the enemy, because they knew he was coming.

At thirty five thousand feet, Amos leveled off and started running scenarios in his head. If they were going to get jumped, it would be soon, and probably from behind. There would probably also be no warning, since the powers that tried to stop Maggie O'Brien in Cozumel would just as soon kill her rather than to have her go back on television with a gruesome report about their activities.

"Okay guys, everyone take a sector and keep an eye peeled for anything coming up behind. If it is military, the running lights will probably be on," Amos shouted into the cabin, "If not…well…"

"Hey Whitehorse, this is Texas Air Guard Red Angel flight, Angel One. If you read me, there are two bogeys five miles back and closing. We've got your back if you can make the border."

"Copy that Angel One. I've got maybe three hundred and fifty knots max when I start my descent. Keep your fingers crossed," Amos responded, and dropped the Beechcraft toward the deck.

He could hear the groans of the passengers as their stomachs reached their mouths, and all he could think of was, "Lord, let me get this crate across that little river up there."

Twenty miles from the border, the radio squawked again, "Whitehorse, they've fired two heat seekers! Make a move!"

Amos quickly released the flares that had been added by some forward thinker for such a time as this, and was rewarded with two explosions at a very close distance behind them.

"Okay Angel One, I could really use some help here. It's not like it will start a war or anything," Amos said in frustration.

"Copy that Captain, we've got the bogeys locked on. You should see our smoke any second now!" Angel One laughed.

Amos felt the hair on his neck prickle as he waited for the missile that was sure to come right up their exhaust any second.

All of a sudden, there were the tell tale streaks of four SAMS flashing by his windscreen.

"Holy Crap!" One of the men in the back shouted as first one explosion, and then two more were seen behind them.

"Angel One, that was some good shooting!" Amos told the unseen pilot.

"I had a good teacher, Amos. Angel One out."

"Something tells me that I know that man," Amos thought to himself.

The Beechcraft was over the border now, and Amos slowed her speed by pulling the nose up. Ten minutes the Beechcraft touched down on the brush lined dirt runway illuminated by several dozen Texas Guardsmen with flashlights.

CHAPTER 18

Sergeant Leonard had the HumVee at the airstrip to pick up the women when Amos landed, and held back from approaching the aircraft until the other passengers had left. As he walked around to the cabin door, Amos was helping Maggie O'Brien and Julie Meyers out of the plane.

"I'm terribly sorry for the hoods, ladies. Please let me make it up to you somehow," Amos was almost whining.

"It wasn't your fault, Captain Whitehorse, so there is nothing to make up," Maggie was direct in her response. There was going to be no 'make up' anything if she could help it.

"Maggie, I'm freezing," Julie said as the cold night air of the late Texas fall hit her.

"Ma'am," Leonard called as he heard Julie complaining, "I've got warm clothes in the HumVee. I'm suppose to take ya'll back to the camp with me."

The women left Amos abruptly and walked shivering to where Leonard was standing.

"You don't look like a cowboy," Maggie said as she gave him a once over.

"Who cares Maggie, he's got heat in that Hummer!" Julie said as she took Leonard's arm and propelled him toward the vehicle.

Maggie followed close behind without turning to say goodbye to Amos, who was left standing next to the plane with Manny.

"Man, she sure shot you down, Amigo," Manny laughed.

"I suppose so, and I don't blame her. Why in the world did they have to wear those hoods, anyway?" Amos asked.

"You'll have to talk to Jeb about that when we get back. Now we need to get this plane out of here and down to Redford where our ride is waiting," Manny replied.

Within minutes, the Beechcraft was winging toward their next rendezvous, and Leonard was taking the women back to the base camp.

Julie was sitting up front fiddling with the heater controls and talking to Leonard as he drove.

"Do you have a first name, Sergeant?" she asked.

"It is Jackson, ma'am, but my friends call me Jake," He replied.

Maggie was surprised at her friend's uncharacteristic forwardness, and attributed it to Julie being nervous about what might be happening over the next several days.

"So Jake, I thought that we were going to be traveling with a bunch of old soldiers out here, but you certainly aren't that old," Maggie said from the back seat.

"No ma'am, but my friend and I were with the Governor when we got shot down out here. He and I stayed with the patrol until last night. We had a dust up with some Muslims yesterday, and Rodriguez went missing with two Texas Guard soldiers," Leonard told them.

"I'm sorry about your friend, Jake. How far is it to the camp?" Maggie asked to change the subject, which she saw was painful for him.

"It's just up ahead. If you look close, you can see the glow from the fires," Leonard answered.

Leonard drove up the incline to the main camp where they were greeted by Luke and half-dozen older men that looked like they stepped out of a painting of the old west.

"Welcome to the 'Geezer Patrol' Miss O'Brien," Luke greeted them warmly as they got out of the vehicle and put on the field jackets that Leonard offered, "I'm Captain Luke Moffet, and these are some of your biggest fans. We've got a tent all fixed up in the middle of the camp, and we also managed to round up some clothes and the equipment that Governor Jeb said you would be needing. Jasper over there has got some dinner prepared if you are hungry, so just make yourselves at home."

"Luke…Captain Moffet, you were the friend of Michael Tucker that got shot out here by those cartel men, weren't you?" She asked.

"Yes ma'am. That's been couple of years ago, and I still hurt when I think about it, like tonight," Luke answered.

"I'm sorry, Luke. I thought the doctors had taken care of all that," She replied.

"It's not that kind of hurting, Ma'am. Tuck and Hanna were my friends," He said.

Maggie took Luke's hand for a second and squeezed it, "Mine too, Luke, mine too."

"I'm starving, Maggie!" Julie exclaimed to break the tense moment, "Let's get some dinner."

She took Leonard by the arm and dragged him to the cook fire with Leonard looking back helplessly at Luke.

"I think that young filly has got her brand hot for Sergeant Leonard," Luke chuckled to the others that were standing close by, "Well, let's all get over there and show these ladies some cowboy hospitality."

After two hours of eating, talking, and signing autographs, Maggie and Julie politely excused themselves and asked Leonard show them to their tent. They were met by two tough looking old hombres that stopped the young man six feet from the tent flap.

"Far enough, youngster," One of them laughed as the other escorted the women to the tent flap and showed them their quarters.

"Yours is the only tent with a stove," The old gent said politely to the women as he held the flap back, "You will probably want to throw a few pieces of kindling in it by morning. It's been getting pretty cold up here at night. Your gear is in the corner, and we put extra blankets on the cots for you."

"Thank you so much…ah…I didn't get your name," Maggie responded.

"Charlie, Ma'am. My partner's name is Elroy. We're your security detail while you are staying with us," He explained.

"Thank you Charlie. I think that we can figure it out from here. Good night," Maggie said as she walked into the tent with Julie and closed the flap.

"Maggie, look at the equipment, It's the camera and sound gear that we need!" Julie was busy digging through the pile of gear that Governor Atkins had sent in.

"We can sort it out in the morning Julie. I'm turning in," Maggie crawled into her cot and pulled the wool blankets over her ears.

A general uproar in the camp woke the women at about three in the morning after only a few hours of fitful sleep. Maggie stuck her head out of the tent flap and asked the one called Elroy what was wrong.

"I don't know Miss O'Brien. Charlie and I turned out to guard ya'll's tent just in case. The noise is coming from over by the water tank."

"Grab a camera and follow me Julie. We've got a story!" Maggie exclaimed as she dug for some warm clothes and pulled on a pair of boots.

"Why do stories always happen at zero-dark-thirty in the morning?" Julie grumbled, but worked quickly to get some gear and clothes together.

Maggie stopped short upon hearing her friend's words. She had heard her father use that saying many times when he talked about having to get up early. His voice was in her head for a brief moment before Julie pushed behind her to get out of the tent with the camera.

The women ran out of the tent toward the sound of several men talking at one time, followed closely by Charlie and Elroy.

"Captain Moffett, what is going on?" Maggie managed to get Luke's attention.

"One of our missing men has returned with a prisoner," He answered.

Julie had the camera rolling and turned to the man that they were talking about. There in the viewfinder was a big bear of a man, cut and bloody from his neck to his waist, looking for all of the world like a pirate demon from a kid's worst nightmares. He was holding a rope that was attached to the neck of a trussed up bearded man in a black uniform with the emblem of ISIS on the chest.

"This is the man that killed Captain Post!" he exclaimed loudly to the camp as more men gathered, "I followed this bastard after the attack and finally got the drop on him."

"Sergeant Rodriguez, where are the other two men?" Luke asked quietly.

"Dead, Sir," was the simple response.

"I need that rope you're holding, soldier," Luke said again in a quiet tone with his hand outstretched. He had seen this before in a man that had been driven beyond his ability for rational thought by the horrors of war.

"I can't do that until he pays for what he did to Captain Post, Sir," Rodriguez replied.

"Rodriguez, It's good to have you back!" Leonard walked right up to him and threw his arms around his neck, "What did you bring me?"

Leonard reached down and took the rope from his friend's hand as the big man started crying like a baby. He handed the rope and the prisoner to Luke and walked Rodriguez to the campfire where he could sit and get medical attention.

The prisoner had a defiant look in his eyes as Luke took the rope from his neck and had two of the men tie him to a fence corner post for safe keeping. It took every ounce of Luke's self-control to keep from pulling his 1911 and putting a forty-five caliber slug right between the man's eyes.

"You filthy American pigs," the man spit vehemently at them, "My men will cut your heads off tomorrow and rape these infidel whores until they are dead also. Allah be praised!"

Luke had just turned to walk away when the tirade started, so he turned back and walked to the prisoner, standing directly in front of him.

"Are you the leader of that bunch?" he asked quietly.

The man just glared at him in silence.

"Did you try to cut my friend's head off?" Luke's voice rose a notch as he asked the question.

"I will personally cut yours off the same way, you old, weak, infidel swine!" he spit out.

Luke turned to the men and said, "Get me a rope."

He turned back to the prisoner, "This here is the Republic of Texas, and we Texians do things a little different than what they do in the rest of America. Out here we hang rustlers, horse thieves, and lying, murderous, devil spawn like yourself. Your boys will find out that Texas justice doesn't take twenty years to met out, and, in your case, there is no appeal. String him up on the water tower men. I want his body visible tomorrow!"

Luke turned toward the men and found himself looking directly into the lens of Julie's camera, "Keep it rolling young lady, this will send a message to the rest of these animals not to mess with Texas or Texians!"

As the crowd of men surrounded the prisoner, who up to this point had been defiant, screams started coming from his throat. Luke pushed back in and saw that several of the men had placed slices of bacon on his clothes and rubbed them on his face.

"Leave him alone, men, that's an order. Get him some water to clean him up with, and then hang him. He will be in hell as soon as the dance stops, so let him have the last peace he will get on this side," Luke told them over their objections.

Fifteen minutes later, the man had cleaned himself and prayed. His last act on this earth was to spit in Luke's direction. Luke gave the signal and six men pulled the kicking body ten feet up the side of the windmill where it jerked and twisted in the dark with the shadows from the harsh white camera light lending a macabre touch to the scene.

As Luke turned to leave the area, he saw a visibly shaken Julie Meyers trying desperately not to vomit, and Maggie O'Brien watching silently as the camera ground on.

"Put the bacon back on men. It will give them something to talk about in the morning if they try to take the camp," He ordered over his shoulder, "Double the guard tonight, and get some of the younger fellows up on top of this butte."

CHAPTER 19

"Have they arrived yet?" Jeb Atkins sound impatient as he asked one of the men in the ready room the question.

"They touched down twenty minutes ago, sir. We are covering a lot of tracks to get her in here unnoticed, but I think probably another hour or less," The aide told him.

"Good news at last!" Jeb exclaimed, "Now bring me up to speed on how the war is going."

"Well, sir, we've had moderate losses so far, but we haven't lost any ground. Midland is still in our hands thanks to Colonel Jenkins' ingenuity, Fort Hood suffered heavy structural damage, but we managed to keep Fort Bliss from being overrun…brilliant plan by the way, Governor. Moving along, the Muslim immigrants are rioting in Houston. We don't have good data from there, but it seems like they are trashing the Montrose area and throwing all of the gay men they find off the highest buildings."

"That could keep them occupied for a long time," Governor chuckled, "Sorry, but it just struck me as funny that these barbarians are killing the very people that argued so strongly for them to be given quarter here. What is the mayor doing about the problem?"

"She is advocating for calm and won't let the police department stop the violence," The aide responded.

"Get me the Harris county sheriff on the line when we finish. I'll put a stop to this crap," Jeb told him.

"There has also been a Captain Spires trying to get in touch with you for about thirty minutes. You were out of the office so I told him to call back."

"Spires…Spires…Captain Horatio Spires of the U.S.S. George H. W. Bush, of course! What did he want?" Jeb asked; his curiosity peaked.

"He said it was important, and for you to call this number, sir," The aide handed Jeb a slip of paper.

"Well, don't just stand there, get the man on the horn!" Jeb barked.

"Right away, sir," The aide responded as he reached across the table for the phone.

"Captain Spires, sir," He handed the phone to Jeb and left the room.

"Captain Spires. I'm sorry that I missed your call, my aide said that you had some urgent news?" Jeb cut to the chase.

"Admiral Smith of the Joint Chiefs is here, and he wants to broach the subject of our defecting," Spires said hopefully.

"What? Am I hearing you correctly? For the love of God put the man on!" Jeb was in a scramble, throwing bits of chalk and pencils at various people on the large room to get their attention, and to get the call on the speakers.

"Governor Atkins, this is Admiral Lucas Smith of the United States Navy on board the George H. W. Bush. Are you open to discussing the terms for us to bring this ship into Texas, along with two cruisers and three destroyers? I'm sorry that there are no submarines available with this particular carrier group," Admiral Smith told him.

"Admiral, what is driving this mass defection? Aren't you playing a very dangerous game with those people in Washington?" Jeb asked.

"Last night, the Joint Chiefs held a clandestine meeting in a local pub, and the topic of the President's mental health was brought up by General Anthony Wayne. Durrah Jowles subsequently had him murdered shortly after the meeting broke up. This morning she announced that she was bringing in two Muslim Generals as advisers to the Joint Chiefs. I doubt any of us would have survived more than a week from today. I hate to say it, but we certainly backed the wrong horse in this race," Smith finished.

"Admiral, I will have to have some assurances of course, but right now my people will check with the harbor master to see if we can bring you in. How many hostiles among your crew will we have to contend with?" Jeb asked.

"Surprisingly, there are only about five hundred men and women that are against us. My Marines and shore patrol have them locked in various safe areas of the ship under heavy guard. I don't have a count on the ships though, but all of the line officers of the group are onboard with the plan," Smith told him, "Governor, why don't you fly out and meet with us under a flag of truce? You can bring as many body guards and dignitaries as you would like. If we can come to terms, my carrier group will patrol the Gulf for you and protect your shipping assets."

"Set up the meeting, Admiral, but you can launch no aircraft, and I want the senior line officers from all of your ships present," Jeb replied as his aides were all shaking their heads violently "NO!"

General Hand had come into the room as they finished talking, "I've got to hand it to you Governor, you are swinging some heavy brass, if you know what I mean."

"Do you think that I made a mistake, General?" Jeb asked after he had hung up the phone.

"If you can pull this off, it will be one of the biggest coups of this short war. If they kill you, we can always sink them," He responded dryly.

"With that in mind, how about arranging to have some heavy air cover over that fleet tomorrow…just in case," Jeb answered.

"Will do…by the way, I saw Amos coming in when I was on my way up here. There he is now!" General hand said pointing toward the back of the conference room.

"Talk about timing! Amos, get over here. We've got some serious planning to do!" Jeb waved and shouted excitedly to Amos Whitehorse.

"I'm glad to see you too, Governor…General," Amos said as he shook the men's hands.

"Well, how did the trip go? Did you get to meet Miss O'Brien?" Jeb laughed.

"Well, yes and no. She and her photographer had to be blindfolded for the entire trip which made them a bit airsick, so I wasn't exactly her favorite person when the cowboys picked them up," Amos replied, "Where did you find those other guys? I think they killed somebody in Cozumel, at least the Federales were after us like they did."

"I wouldn't be surprised, Amos. Those are some of the best special ops men in the business. I'm glad that they are working for Texas right now. Anyway, I've got to find an ex-Navy pilot that can set me down on a carrier deck tomorrow. Does anybody come to mind?" Jeb asked him.

"I should have jumped ship in Cozumel!" Amos replied, "Why in the world do you want me to fly you to an aircraft carrier anyway?" Amos asked.

"I knew you'd volunteer old buddy. Now go find us something fast that is befitting a man that just got his own navy," Jeb laughed.

General Hand broke in, "You don't have it yet, Governor. Please proceed very carefully with these men, and remember who they work for."

"Will do, General. Amos, let's plan for an 0530 start tomorrow. Can you get us set up by then? General, we'll need those bombers up there tonight, if you can coordinate it with General Clarke, and please brief him for me on this new wrinkle. I've got to handle the Houston situation," Jeb told them.

"I'll take care of everything, Governor," General Hand left the office.

"I'll see what we've got in a sporty two-seater with a tail hook," Amos laughed as he left.

"Amos, I'll see you in the morning for coffee," Jeb smiled at his friend.

"Certainly Jeb, and see if you can find a good donut to go with it," Amos replied.

Jeb made the call to the Harris County Sheriff's Department and got a young woman on the switchboard.

"This is Governor Jebediah Atkins, Miss, and I need to speak to Sheriff Tate please."

"I'm sorry sir, but the sheriff is busy. Can I have him call you back?" she responded in a sweet southern voice.

"Did you catch my name, Miss?" Jeb was annoyed.

"Yes, Governor Atkins, but Sheriff Tate said that he didn't want to be bothered," She replied.

"Tell the sheriff that if he isn't on the phone in thirty seconds, I will have a company of Texas Rangers remove him from office!" Jeb was extremely annoyed now.

"Yes sir, right away sir," She replied and put him on hold.

"Sheriff Tate here, Governor," The sheriff responded in less than five seconds, "I'm not used to being threatened, sir, and I want you to know that I take offense at you delivering that threat through my secretary."

"It wasn't a threat you pompous, liberal windbag! Now listen up because I am only going to tell you this one time. I am the authority in this state-nation, and I want the mayor removed from office tonight. Next, you have one day to work with the Houston Police Department and get those sand fleas over in Montrose controlled. There is no room for political correctness here, Tate, so if you are not up to the task, I'll appoint a provost marshal within the hour that can deliver results. Did I make myself understood?" Jeb was on the edge of his seat with anger as he delivered the ultimatum.

"Perfectly clear sir. I'll get right on it," Sheriff Tate said as he hung up.

"We had better find a Provost for Houston. I have a feeling that Sheriff Tate is whining on the mayor's lap right about now. It might be a good idea to get General Clarke involved in this decision since it will be some of his men going in," Jeb told the aide that was standing next to his desk.

"Right away, sir!" he answered sharply and left the room.

CHAPTER 20

"Good morning Jebediah!" Amos greeted the Governor in a loud voice as he strolled into the command center at 0430 hours the next morning, "Your chariot awaits!"

"Good morning Amos, where do we have to go to pick it up?" Jeb answered as he slid a box of plain cake donuts across the table.

"About five miles south of here. Colonel Schaeffer pulled some strings and got us one of those two seat Harriers back down here. We can leave when you are ready," Amos told him.

"We are on for 0530 hours just as soon as General Hand checks in. I suppose we can communicate from the air," Jeb replied and finished his coffee.

Manny Hernandez was waiting for them with a Hummer that he had camouflaged near the hidden command center entrance, and they made a quick run in the early morning light to the wash where the Harrier pilot had stashed the jet and was waiting with two flight suits.

As soon as the two men suited up, they climbed into the Harrier and headed for the Jefferson County airport at Port Arthur to wait for a confirmation on the meeting arrangements. Jeb made his call to General Hand as soon as they were airborne to confirm the bombers were flying cover for them.

"Governor Atkins, we are not going to be able to use the B1Bs on this mission," Hands told him, "Someone tipped off Washington that they were in Roswell, and they are locked down."

"What other resources do we have, General?" Jeb asked.

"We have a flight of those F-18s off the carrier up here at Dyess. They could sure give you a pretty powerful escort and air cover," Hand replied.

"That will have to do. Arm them up and let me know when they are in position. We will be at the Jefferson County airport near Port Arthur until time to go in," Jeb replied.

"Roger that, Governor. You boys be smart and get out of there if the situation looks hostile," General Hand finished.

"Did you get a copy on that, Amos?" Jeb asked.

"Well, I don't like the way the odds have shifted, but these guys might be on the up and up. We'll know soon enough," Amos replied, "Jeb there's another transmission coming through."

"This is Governor Atkins…go ahead," Jeb spoke into his mike.

"Governor, we are under heavy bombardment at the command center!" Manny's voice came over the radio, "It started right after you left, and they have destroyed the motel and several of the tunnels. What should we do?"

"Sergeant, get all non-combatants out through the emergency exits, post our best sharpshooters, and I'll try and get some support in there…Atkins out. Amos, we need to get back there. Our people are going to be trapped!" Jeb exclaimed.

"Governor, we can't go back and risk you getting killed. Let the military work through this one while we take that carrier," Amos told him.

He had just finished talking when they got a call from General Clarke, "Governor, I've got F-18s inbound to the Hive and Apaches on the way in the case of a ground assault. What is your location?" Clarke asked.

"General, were are headed to Jefferson County, ETA in about forty five minutes," Jeb told him.

"I'm sending reinforcements for your security, Governor. They'll meet you at the airport," Clarke ended the call.

Amos buzzed the Jefferson airport before landing to make certain that they wouldn't be surprised by hostile forces and saw two Chinook CH-47D heavy transport helicopters sitting on the tarmac with their rotors idling.

"Texas One, this is Major Rory Peterson, over," The radio crackled.

"Go ahead, Major," Amos responded.

"I've got sixty troops in these birds awaiting the Governor's orders," Jenkins said.

"Roger that, we'll be down in a second. Stand by," Amos told him.

"What do you think, Jeb?" Amos asked him on intercom.

"I think that I'm starting to feel safer already," Jeb replied with a smile, "Set her down close by."

As the Harrier landed just to the south of the helicopters so that its takeoff couldn't be blocked, they saw the tail door open on one of the Chinooks and a tall officer in full combat gear exit the craft and head in their direction. When the canopy opened on the Harrier, he gave Jeb a smart salute and held it until Jeb returned it in an equally military manner.

"Good to see you Governor!" he shouted to Jeb as he and Amos climbed out of the Harrier cockpit.

"Tex Peterson! I knew that there was something familiar about that voice. How long has it been…ten years?" Jeb asked as he shook the man's hand.

"Yes sir, I was a young lieutenant the last time that you saw me in Iraq," Peterson replied.

"Amos, this is Major Rory Peterson, better known as 'Tex'. Major, this is Captain Amos Whitehorse, formerly of the United States Navy," Jeb made the introductions.

"Well Governor, what's the plan?" Peterson asked after the introduction.

"We are going to board the U.S.S. George H.W. Bush and arrange for their surrender," Jeb told him without breaking a smile.

"Seriously sir? I might not have brought enough men," Peterson looked worried.

"Relax, Tex, we have an arranged meeting with Admiral Smith to accept a mass defection, and I don't expect too many problems," Jeb laughed, "If you will take your men and fly on out to the carrier, I'll inform the Admiral that my advance guard is en-route. Amos and I will set down as soon as you provide a secure perimeter."

"Roger that sir," Tex said with a salute before running back to his helicopter and giving the signal to get airborne.

"Let's give them a few minutes, Amos. I'll call the Admiral while we wait," Jeb said as they climbed back into the Harrier.

Minutes later, Amos was airborne and headed for probably the most historical rendezvous in the history of the United States and Texas. The Chinooks were flying in low, using the carrier to shield them from any offshore eyes, and Amos had to throttle back to keep them ahead of him.

"How does it look Admiral Smith?" Jeb asked into his radio.

"Everything is ready on this end…wait…we've got a perimeter alarms, and the Phalanxes are coming online. Pull back and wait…I repeat pull back and wait," The radio went silent.

Suddenly, a gigantic fireball erupted up the offshore side of the carrier!

"This is Guard One, Abort, Abort, Abort!" Jeb screamed into the microphone, "Tex, get those men away from the ship! Do you copy?"

"Roger, Guard One, we are turning back," Came the calm, battle proven voice of Major Peterson.

"Admiral Smith, do you copy?" Jeb made another attempt to contact the carrier.

"Governor, this is Captain Spires. Can you read me?" A voice came across the radio.

"Go ahead Captain," Jeb answered.

"Admiral Smith is dead and Admiral Stokes is severely wounded. We think we were hit by one of our subs since the attack did not originate from the surface. We are listing to port and the engine room is flooding. Sections of the hanger deck are on fire and some of our munitions will be going off momentarily," Spires concluded.

"Copy that Captain. What can we do to help?" Jeb asked.

"Our carrier group is back up and operational. They let down their defenses for this meeting, but their commanders are getting back to the business of protecting this craft. Unless we find and sink that sub, it would be very dangerous for you to stay in the area," Spires told him.

The radio crackled again, and a new voice called for attention, "Texas Guard One, Texas Guard One, this is Captain Vladimir Petrovich, Commander of the Russian submarine Tango Charlie. We have eliminated the threat to your aircraft carrier."

"Russian Submarine, Tango Charlie, what are you talking about?" Jeb responded.

"One of the United States attack class submarines fired on the Bush, but we sunk her," Came the voice back.

"Who am I talking to again?" Jeb demanded.

This is Captain Vladimir Petrovich, we wish to make diplomatic contact," He replied.

"Captain Petrovich, you might have just started World War Three. I need for you to withdraw quietly and let me see if we can salvage this operation," Jeb answered while shaking his head.

"We understand that you need allies and customers for your oil, Governor, but I will withdraw for now," Petrovich ended the call.

"Amos, set me down on the carrier. We just got it, and I'll be damned if that lunatic in Washington is going to take it away from me!" Jeb told him by intercom, "Get Major Peterson on the horn and let's get those Texians to help fight this fire, and also get hold of Bay-Houston Towing and authorize them to help fight the fire and bring the carrier inside."

"Jeb, that flight deck has got a nasty list to it. There is a platform about two miles back that I can probably sit this bird down on, and we can have Tex pick us up there," Amos told him.

"Let's make it happen quickly, Amos. I've got to get on that ship!" Jeb responded.

The war room briefing under the White House started with Durrah Jowles introducing her new military advisors on loan from the Pakistani and Iraqi Governments.

"Gentlemen and women, before we get into the briefing of last night's activities, I want to introduce Generals Mohammed Salimi, and Nadir Jahanbani who will be advising us on the conflict in the state of Texas. Now, General Doggett, the President would like a briefing on our campaign, specifically where we are with capturing Governor Atkins."

General Doggett nervously cleared his throat, "Mr. President, we started an aerial bombardment of the suspected location of Governor Atkins command center early this morning, but Texas Air Guard Fighters intervened, and drove our aircraft from the area. A ground assault was also repelled by the Texas Guard, and we experienced at least fifty casualties on the ground and the loss of two aircraft. Following the intelligence that we received from the George H.W. Bush that Admiral Smith was defecting the entire carrier group to Texas, one of our attack submarines launched a torpedo strike against the carrier. We subsequently lost all contact with the submarine which leads us to believe that it may have been lost. There has been no word from the carrier, although sources have reported it burning off the Texas coast,"

The President looked as if he was pouting at the news, so Durrah spoke for him, "Let me make this perfectly clear, we are not going to lose this war with Texas and they will not become a separate nation…ever! Now I want some battle plans drawn up and presented to these two gentlemen," indicating her Generals, "and I want them to include whatever measures must be taken to insure our victory. If we don't make an example of Texas, we will lose more than half of this country."

She got up from the table and left the room with the President on her arm.

General Mohammed Salimi addressed the table while looking directly at Tom Doggett, "The problem with you Americans is that you are weak when it comes to making the hard choices in battle. We have learned that for a nation to be victorious, it also needs a ruthless military presence. From this point forward, we will oversee the fighting forces at our disposal, and we will make them feared in every household in the country."

"I don't think that you understand the resolve of the American people, General," Doggett replied, "What you are going to do is wake a fearsome beast instead of making it cower."

"Weakness gentlemen, will not be tolerated in this room. We have the full authority of your President to direct the wartime policy of this country, and from this point forward, we will become as ruthless as necessary to win!" Salimi shouted as he slammed his fists on the table.

The next sound that was heard in the room was that of General Tom Doggett's smuggled in M92 barking three times in quick succession, and General Mohammed Salimi falling backward with a loud soggy thump to the floor, the result of two 9mm holes in his heart, and one tearing off the back of his head. Tom Doggett then immediately put the pistol under his chin and shouted, "GOD BLESS AMERICA!" before pulling the trigger. As his head snapped backwards, the recoil from the M-92 drove his right hand forward, and a spasm caused the pistol to discharge one more time before falling to the floor. That bullet struck Nadir Jahanbani just over the left eyebrow, and exited in a spray of blood and bone from the upper left hand side of his head. While not instantly fatal, it did reduce the Pakistani to a quivering heap on the floor. Several in the room that professed a type of very quiet Christianity suddenly recognized that the events they had just witnessed could not have been anything other than an intervention by the hand of the Almighty. That night they would gather a few belongings and quietly disappear.

CHAPTER 21

Maggie tossed restlessly on her bunk for the next three hours that they had until daybreak. Images of the gruesome dance that they had witnessed flooded her dreams, and she also heard her father speaking to her when she was a little girl, before her mother made him leave. There was something in that voice that haunted her, but it was not until the hustle and bustle of the camp woke her from a fitful sleep, that she realized her father had somehow been on the plane with them the night before!

"Come on Maggie, we're going to be late for breakfast!" Julie called out.

Maggie stuck her head out from under the covers to see Julie putting on some Texas Guard MultiCams over a pair of long johns.

"Why the hurry, Jules?" she asked.

"I don't want to miss Jake is all," She replied.

"What in the world has gotten into you, anyway?" Maggie asked.

"I've never been around anybody like him. Something just clicked last night, and I want to see if it is still there," Julie replied.

"Well, throw some wood in the stove, and I'll meet you out there in a few minutes," Maggie pulled the blankets back up around her ears.

Thirty minutes later there was a voice at her tent flap.

"Miss O'Brien, Captain Moffett here ma'am. You need to get ready to travel with us," Luke called into the tent.

"I'm almost ready Luke," Maggie replied as she hurried to pull on her britches and boots.

"I'll meet you in the mess tent and brief you while you get a bite to eat," Luke told her.

Ten minutes later, Maggie and Julie were chewing on a thick country bacon biscuit and drinking a cup of Jasper's coffee that they both thought would make a better drain cleaner but didn't voice the opinion.

"We aren't going to be riding hard today ladies, so you have the option of riding with us or riding in the Hummer with Sergeant Leonard," Luke told them, "We might see some action though, and it is likely that we won't be back here until tomorrow, depending on how far we scout today."

"Captain Moffett, I think that it would be best if I rode in the Hummer with the camera equipment," Julie spoke up, "I can put a remote mike on Maggie and record her as she rides with you guys."

"Well, Maggie, if you are going to ride with us, you'd better go with Sergeant Gonzales and pick something gentle out of the remuda. He'll get you saddled up and ready to ride. A word of warning though, if we come under fire, you are to ride quickly to the back of the troop and dismount. Is that understood?" Luke asked as he finished his briefing.

"I'll be fine, Luke, but could I talk to you in private for a minute outside?" She asked.

They walked out of the tent and Maggie told him about the man on the plane.

"I know that was my father's voice," Maggie told him, "Now I am wondering who else was on the plane with us."

"All that I was told was that the men that came in with you are working for Texas in a special operation. I didn't know your dad, Maggie, and I didn't see those men, but Leonard might have. I hope it was him because it might mean that Tuck made it also," Luke told her, "Let's keep this between us for now, anyway. I don't want to jeopardize their mission."

"I understand, Luke. Thanks for listening. Maybe a ride will clear my head a bit," Maggie said as she turned to pick out a horse.

"If you haven't ridden in a while, it will sure give you a pain that will take your mind off the other troubles," Luke laughed.

Maggie met Luis where the horses were tethered, and immediately fell in love with the buckskin.

"Miss O'Brien, this is not the horse for you. It threw Captain Luke like a rodeo bronc just yesterday. None of the other men want to ride him either," Luis tried to talk her out of her choice.

"Nonsense, Sergeant, He likes me," She said as the horse nuzzled her hand while she held his head, "I want this one, and that is final."

Luis just thought of how much trouble he was going to be in when Luke found out that he had saddled the buckskin for her, but he was not one to argue with a woman either, especially a red headed one.

"I've got an older saddle with an undercut swell that will help you stay on longer," Luis told her as he picked up an old breaking saddle and tossed it onto the buckskin.

The horse didn't flinch when the heavy saddle hit his back, and Maggie continued to talk sweet to him while Luis finished getting him ready.

Julie came around the corner and called to her, "Maggie, I've got to put this mike on you before you ride out."

Luis just kept his mouth shut, but he was thinking that riding out wasn't going to be the first thing that Maggie O'Brien was going to do when she stepped into that saddle.

The women worked quickly, and soon Maggie was wired and ready for the buckskin. She put her left foot into the stirrup and swung gracefully into the saddle while Luis held the reins on the big horse.

The buckskin just stood silently and relaxed as Maggie climbed aboard, "See Luis, I told you that he was gentle."

About that time, the horse exploded into his best imitation of a wild west bronco with a series of leaps and bone jarring, stiff legged landings. He turned and sunfished for all he was worth to shake his rider, but Maggie stuck on his back like a burr. Out through the tents he crow hopped, and straight into the area where Luke and the others were waiting for her. Maggie had lost her hat on the first jump, and was using her right hand to wear the horse out with the end of his reins like they were a quirt, and with every bite of the leather on his rump, the contrary animal tried to find a new way to toss the woman into the mesquite.

The early morning sun made her hair look like it was on fire, and Luke just stared in dumbfounded amazement at the show that Maggie O'Brien was putting on, while the others were whooping and hollering for her to stick on the horse's back that their friend and leader couldn't ride.

Finally, the horse was worn out to the point that he made a couple of more crow hops and then broke into a trot as Maggie rode him back to where the men watched in amazement.

She reined the sweating, lathered up animal in alongside Lucky, and said to Luke, "He just was a little spirited, is all."

Luke looked at her for a second, "Uh, huh," Was all he could say as he handed her the hat. It was going to be a while before he lived this one down.

Of course, Julie Meyers had everything recorded, including the prim and proper Maggie O'Brien giving that animal a muleskinner cussing as she rode him like a cougar on the back of her next meal.

CHAPTER 22

Jeb jumped from the Chinook into the middle of the sixty man security detail on the sloping flight deck of the damaged carrier. A Navy Lieutenant met them and escorted him and ten of the security force to the bridge where they were met by Captain Horatio Spires.

"Governor Atkins, welcome aboard, sir," Spires gave him a salute.

"How bad is it Captain, and what can we do to help?" was the first thing that Jeb asked.

"We've moved the dissenters forward, Governor, but we need to get them off this ship. Can you arrange for transportation for five hundred sailors and Marines?" Spires asked.

Jeb turned to Amos, "Make that happen Captain."

"I understand that Admiral Smith was killed and Admiral Stokes was wounded in the attack," Jeb said.

"Well, it was during the initial explosion, a Marine Captain ran in and shot both men before we could subdue him," Spires said, "He shot at me and missed while we wrestled for his gun."

"Is he still alive?" Jeb asked.

"We thought it best to place him under guard in restraints away from the other men," Spires replied.

"First of all, can you get the remaining aircraft off the ship?" Jeb asked.

"If the pilots would fly them, but they have been reluctant to take part in any of the war plans against Texas," He replied.

"I understand. May I make a ship wide announcement, Captain?" Jeb asked.

"Certainly sir, the phone is hanging right there. I'll get their attention," He said as he walked to the ship's phone and picked it up. "Now hear this, now hear this. This is Captain Spires speaking. The Governor of the State of Texas is going to address the crew."

He handed the phone to Jeb, "This is Governor Jebediah Atkins of the Nation State of Texas. I would like to welcome all of you to relocate your allegiance to Texas and our cause, but understand that some of you will not. Right now, I have two announcements: Number one is that from right now Captain Spires is now Admiral Spires of the Texas Navy, and is in charge of this carrier group. Number two, I need all available flight crews and pilots to get the air worthy planes off this ship and over to Fort Dyess. We have help on the way to fight the fire and help with damage control, so everyone do the jobs that you were trained to do, and we'll have her seaworthy again in no time. That is all."

Jeb hung the phone up and turned to the new Admiral, "You will need to make a announcement to the rest of the fleet, sir. Heightened security levels might be in order. Now what do we need to do to get these planes off her?"

"They are already pumping ballast into the starboard tanks to level the deck. Three elevators are still functional, and we still have the catapults. There are forty-five fixed wing fighters that are flight capable, so, assuming the pilots will fly for Texas, we can have them off in a couple of hours," Spires told him.

"I've got a seasoned Navy pilot here with me, Admiral. How about giving him one of those fighters so he can fly cover with the boys from Dyess?" Jeb asked.

Amos looked astonished that he was going to do the one thing that he loved more than breathing, and that was to fly a combat mission.

"Captain Whitehorse can have the first one up, Governor. We have heard of his combat reputation, and I know that the men will be proud to fly with him," Spires said with a smile.

"Thank you Jeb…Admiral! I appreciate this more than you know," Amos gushed his thanks.

"Just don't get yourself shot down, and that's an order. Now I've got to find Tex and get off the ship, but Admiral Spires, I am leaving a detachment of our best for your protection. I also want that Marine Captain that killed Admiral Smith to be transferred immediately to one of the destroyers and hung from that thing that you fly your signal flags from," Jeb told him.

"The yardarm, sir?" Spires looked like he was in shock.

"That's the one. Admiral, we threw politically correct out of Texas when we seceded a few days ago. We have three witnesses that saw him kill Admiral Smith so there is no doubt of his guilt. I want him hung immediately, and then paraded past every ship out here as an example," Jeb replied coldly.

Spires turned to the XO and relayed the order. "it will be taken care of immediately, Governor."

"Good, now I've got to get ashore and take care of some government business. Amos, I'll see you back at the Hive," Jeb shook hands all around and started to followed Tex Peterson to a waiting Chinook.

"Are you sure that is wise, Jeb?" Amos asked with a worried look on his face.

Jeb turned back to Amos and gave him a hidden wink, "Call me from Dyess after you finish up down here, and make sure to stop by Captain Moffett's camp and check on Miss O'Brien on your way back in,"

"Yes, sir!" Amos replied to Jeb's back.

CHAPTER 23

Maggie O'Brien rode next to Luke as the troop started their day patrol to the southwest of the camp. Sergeant Gonzales had half of the men with him to search for the two men that Rodriguez had reported killed, and Luke was taking the others further south to see if they could locate the stragglers from the first firefight. Sergeant Leonard drove the HumVee with Julie Meyers and her equipment, but he felt more like he was her captive because of all the attention that she showed him.

Thirty of Colonel Jenkins' troop had been left at the camp as a security team, but Luke knew that the Islamists preferred to work against unfortified and un armed encampments and civilians. With the heavy casualties that they sustained and the loss of their leader, he figured that it would be a few more days before they had their nerve built back up. In the meantime, the colonel wanted them hazed and kept moving to reduce the impact on the ranches and civilians in the area.

Two hours into the patrol, Charlie rode up abreast of Luke and told him that the Colonel was on the radio. Luke turned and rode back to the Hummer while old Charlie fell in alongside Maggie with a big smile.

"Captain Moffett here, sir." Luke spoke into the mike.

"Captain...Luke, I've got some bad news. John Post didn't make it. I was with him last night when he went home. I'm sorry to have to break it to you," Jenkins said.

"Damn...sorry Pastor...er, Colonel. I'm sure going to miss him. Is Mary Louise all right?" he asked.

"Well, she has a big church family and their children. Your wife was at the hospital with her last night. She says that she is going to the house and will wait for you to get home. She told me to tell you that she knows that you aren't cooking, if that means anything," The colonel told him, "There is also a video circulating about you hanging a terrorist last night. Did you know it was sent out?"

"No Sir, but I'm standing next to the young lady that did it," Luke told him.

"I don't think that it will cause us any public relations problems, but make sure that all of her reports come to me first from here on out." Jenkins said.

"I'll take care of it sir. I would like to talk to Mary if you can arrange it…maybe later tonight or tomorrow whenever we get back," Luke replied.

"Carry on Captain. I've got the Apaches headed for the base camp just in case you need them," Jenkins closed.

"Roger that, and Thank you sir," Luke handed the mike back to Leonard.

"Well, young lady, you heard what the man said, so I expect you to follow that to the letter. Is that understood?" Luke sternly told Julie.

"Yes sir, I'm sorry about your friend," She replied, looking like she might cry at any moment.

"I appreciate that, youngster. John and I go way back, and the best part of us is in this land. He was ready to go, and that is something that you can't say about everyone. I just wish it wasn't at the hands of that sadistic S.O.B. that we hung last night," He told her.

Luke climbed back on Lucky and rode back to the head of the column. Charlie saw the look in his eyes first and reached over to pat him on the shoulder.

"John didn't make it, did he?" he asked softly with a tear starting down his weathered cheek.

"Tell the men, Charlie, John died last night and went to heaven," Luke told him.

Maggie reached across and took Luke's hand, "I'm so sorry for John's death. We met briefly at the funeral in Myrtle Beach."

"I'm kind of envious right now. Old John has got his new look on, and I'm stuck in the middle of the desert with a bunch of old guys and a red haired reporter," Luke managed a smile, "Well, enough sniveling, let's go find us some terrorists!"

Maggie just smiled and patted Luke's hand as she straightened herself in the saddle and gave the buckskin a little nudge with her heels to get him moving.

The next sound that they heard was like a swarm of bees flying by their heads and two horses screaming in pain. The rein in Maggie's right hand fell free of the bit as a round cut it clean and then struck Luke's saddle swell. He quickly reached for her good rein and headed Lucky and the buckskin for a shallow wash at a dead run. The rest of the men were already there except for two that had their horses shot out from under them.

"Give them some cover!" Luke yelled loudly as slid from Lucky's back and jerked the .308 out of the scabbard, "Get down and let the horse go, Maggie. Hug the ground!"

He made his way quickly to a point where he could just see over the rise and down to where the enemy fire was coming from. Looking through the Leupold, Luke saw a black spot at five hundred yards in the mesquite just behind a reoccurring puff of dust from the muzzle blast of a big rifle. He watched for the target to make three more shots and noticed that every time he fired, a little more black was visible. Luke held the cross hairs two inches above the small black target and waited for the dust as his finger tightened slowly on the Timney trigger. There was the puff followed instantly by the jump of Luke's rifle, and the black covered head snapped up into full view with a crimson mist floating in a halo around it.

As soon as the sniper was eliminated, the rest of the force started moving toward the wash, and were readily visible to the men who delivered a devastating fire, but from a yardage that was at the limit for the 5.56mm round. Suddenly, the advancing enemy turned and started firing behind them at an unseen force.

"Hold your fire, men!" Luke shouted down the line, "We've got some friendlies in the back of them!"

Luke managed to pick off two more before the rest threw up their hands in a gesture of surrender, and right beyond them came the troop led by Sergeant Gonzales riding at a full gallop straight up to the enemy.

Luke whistled for Lucky and swung into the saddle, "Hold this rifle for me Maggie, I'll be right back."

Leonard drove up and dropped Julie off with her camera before tearing off down the slight hill with the other riders in pursuit. As Luke reached the enemy prisoners, he pulled his 1911 from the holster and moved Lucky in alongside of Luis and his men.

"Nice work Sergeant, how many do we have?" He asked.

"It looks like twenty two, sir, counting several wounded back there in the brush. I think that you found Rodriguez's Barrett by the way. Some guy with not much head left is laying on it over there," Luis pointed behind him, "There are also two more Hummers hiding in that wash over yonder, but nobody is around them."

"Send some men over to retrieve the vehicles, and I want these men stripped and searched. If they won't comply, just shoot them. It probably wouldn't hurt to gather all of the weapons and stack them here, either," Luke told him, "Leonard, call the Colonel and get someone out here to pick up these prisoners, and retrieve that Barrett while you are at it."

Luke rode back to where he left the newswomen to give them a report. Julie was filming the battle field while Maggie provided the commentary.

"Those fellas are going to be naked in a few minutes. You might want to cut that short," He said to Julie, "We don't want to offend your viewers with pictures of nasty bodies, do we."

"I guess not, Captain Moffett. I'm sorry if putting that film on the internet got you in trouble," Julie said to him.

"It certainly sent a message. I didn't like killing that man anymore than I liked killing those down there, but there comes a time when it is the necessary thing to do," Luke told her, "Maggie, there is one little thing that you can do for me."

"Certainly Luke, what is it?" she responded.

"Walk out here where you can be seen from down there and wave my rifle over your head," Luke said with a grin.

"Well, okay, but why?" she asked.

"When one of them thinks he is going to be shot by a woman, he believes he will go to hell. It might make them a little more pliable…if you know what I mean," Luke smiled, "Now I am going to go back down there and tell a little white lie. When you see me point up here, just wave that rifle like you've won a turkey shoot."

"Okay, I guess. What's a turkey shoot?" she asked.

"Something good, you know, like you felt when you were cussin' that ornery buckskin this morning. That was plum beautiful by the way, I haven't heard that kind of cussin' since before I got saved," Luke was laughing.

Maggie's face almost matched the color of her hair, and she just shook her head in agreement. Julie was laughing so hard that she couldn't hold the camera.

"Jules, tell me that you didn't record me this morning!" Maggie said to her as Luke galloped off to where Luis had the prisoners stripped.

"I cannot tell a lie, Maggie. You'd better start waving that rifle," Julie replied.

Luke dismounted in front of the men that had been taken prisoner and asked if anyone of them could speak English.

"We all speak English," One young man volunteered.

"Okay, listen up. I want you to look up at that hill over there," pointing to Maggie, who was waving the rifle over her head, "That is a red headed killer lady, and she was the one that smoked a few of you bastards during the fight. If I have the slightest bit of trouble out of you, she is going to kill every last one and send you to hell. Is that understood?"

"We understand, Infidel, but if we get the chance, we will kill you and hang your head on a pole," The first man said defiantly.

Luke's .45 came out of his holster as if by reflex, and all of the men, prisoners and guards, were stunned when he fired it point blank into the forehead of the prisoner, scattering blood and gray matter over five of the men behind him.

"Does anyone else want to cut my head off?" he shouted as the naked lifeless body fell limply to the ground.

None of the prisoners made eye contact with him as he waited for a response with the still smoking 1911 in his hand.

"Luke, Luke, put the pistol up. We've got this," Luis had moved in front of him, "Colonel Jenkins is sending some men and transportation for the prisoners."

"John died last night Luis, and these animals killed him. I guess my trigger is wound up a little bit, but I probably shouldn't have killed that man," He said looking at the corpse whose head was still steaming in the cold morning air.

"Any of us would have done the same, all things considered. I'll take care of this bunch if you want to make tonight's bivouac with your guys. Charlie lost his horse so he can drive one of those Hummers, and I'll bring the other one after they pick these savages up. My old butt is hurting from all of the riding that we've been doing," Luis told him.

"Thanks Luis. Get all of their weapons loaded in Charlie's Hummer, and we'll head out. Stay in radio contact so we can get back if you need help," Luke told him, "Once they've been checked for weapons, give them back their clothes."

Luke rode back to where Maggie and Julie were waiting, not knowing that Julie had filmed the shooting of the terrorist a few minutes earlier. Luis called Charlie over as Luke rode away.

"Charlie, Luke wants you to take one of the captured Hummers and go with them to the night campsite. Listen, I've seen this before when men like Luke kind of lose it during the stress of battle. We need to keep an eye on him," Luis said.

"We were all friends of John Post," Charlie replied, "But what Luke did here was murder, pure and simple. You need to Call Colonel Jenkins and let him know."

"I'll call him as soon as the prisoners are taken care of," Luis promised.

CHAPTER 24

"Mister President…Sir, what do I tell the Chinese regarding their oil fields in Texas?" The Secretary of State, Julian Crump asked for the third time.

The President acted preoccupied, "What? The Chinese? Yes, the Texas holdings…I understand. Well, you will have to ask Durrah about that."

"Sir? The Chinese have a delegation that has been waiting two days for an audience with you. They are implying that they will side with Texas militarily if we continue to prohibit them from working their fields down there," He objected, "I don't think that this is the time to really piss off the Chinese with them holding several trillion dollars of our debt, do you?"

"You worry too much Julian. Durrah has everything under control, don't you Durrah?" the President said with an angry look on his face.

He was not used to being questioned in front of the other cabinet members like this, and the scowl on his face had grown darker as the Secretary had talked.

"We do have a plan to meet with the delegation this afternoon, Julian. Now, I need an update about what happened with the meeting this morning that allowed three people to be killed," She coldly addressed the query to the Secretary of Defense, Michael Swain.

"Well, we still have investigators working the case, but initially it would seem that General Doggett broke under the pressure of you putting two foreign generals in charge of the Joint Chiefs, Durrah. How he smuggled the firearm in is still a mystery, but they have tightened security to prevent another incident. I don't know if you are aware, but a video was posted on the internet last night that shows a bunch of cowboys hanging one of our desert fighters, as you have named them, from a windmill in west Texas. This is presumably the same bunch that attacked and killed the United Nations checkpoint guards down on Interstate 10 a few days ago, and routed the two companies of desert fighters two days ago. The attack on the Governor's stronghold was not successful, and we've lost track of his whereabouts," Swain briefed her in an equally cold tone.

What he withheld from the meeting was the fact that they had intercepted an encrypted Russian signal from the Gulf of Mexico, and his people were working feverishly to break the encryption.

Durrah sat in stony silence for about two minutes, glaring around the table as if looking for victims. Finally she spoke.

"Does anyone have some good news for the President?" she shouted.

Dwight Hatcher, the head of the Department of Homeland Security, a dull looking, long faced man that also had known ties to the Muslim Brotherhood, spoke up, "I am happy to report that we have not lost nearly as many officers as we had previously thought due to the violence associated with our firearms confiscation program. In the last five days, we have had less than five hundred killed across the country, largely due to the fact that after the first two days, we couldn't get many officers that would take part in the raids. The downside is that we believe that there may be two hundred thousand well-armed militia on the move right now, with at least fifty thousand already in Texas. That is in addition to their Texas Guard. We can't be certain beyond speculation because our field agents keep disappearing."

"This is absolutely inexcusable!" Durrah was standing and shouting at the crowded room. If there had been any doubt as to who was running the country that doubt had now vanished.

The President just sat and looked at his hands that were folded in front of him. Durrah came around the table, took him by the arm, and they exited the room together.

Michael Swain stood up and made a brief announcement, "I've got to meet with what is left of our Joint Chiefs and come up with a plan that will put us back on top. Any suggestions will be greatly appreciated."

With that, he left the room and headed for his office. The events of the last few days had drained him, but even more of a concern to him was the mental condition of the man that was supposed to be leading the country. Swain considered himself neither Republican nor Democrat, but cherished a middle of the road position that allowed him to work both sides of the fence when it came to policy. Now, faced with the task of defending the country with the drastically reduced effectiveness of the armed forces, he felt like the captain of a sinking ship after all of the rats had left. For the first time in a career that was by all accounts less than stellar, Michael Swain was considering his rather bleak appearing options.

Meanwhile, halfway across the continent, another meeting was taking place under a cloak of secrecy that felt for all of the world like a party to those in attendance. On a ranch close to San Antonio, picked for the historical significance, a group of powerful men from the legislative and judicial branches of the Texas state government had gathered to confer on Jebediah Atkins the title of Provincial President of the Republic of Texas.

Tom Hastings was the first to shake his hand after the proclamation had been read.

"Congratulations, Mr. President!" he exclaimed loudly so that the entire room would hear, "This is an exciting time in Texas history."

"Thank you, Tom," Jeb replied, "I need to hurry this along just in case word of this meeting has leaked to our enemies. As we are at war with the Government of the United States of America, I am requesting that you all grant me special powers to prosecute this war with the help of our military and not too much bureaucratic oversight."

Applause rang through the room as the members unanimously agreed to the new president's request, not realizing that they would soon be looking back on this decision as possibly the worst one that could have been made to mark the birth of the fledgling nation.

"Mr. President, we have a ten man detail of Texas Rangers that will be traveling as your personal body guards. They have been handpicked from the tactical group and will act as your Secret Service detail until after the war," Tom told him.

"Well, I doubt that I need protection, but we can always use some more tactical people. Now there is the matter of a Vice President, gentlemen, and I would like for Tom Hastings to fill that position, with your approval of course," Jeb replied.

"Absolutely, Mister President!" came the resounding response.

"Great, well I need to get back to 'the Hive' as we call it. If transportation has been arranged, we need to conclude this meeting," Jeb said as he stood.

The newly appointed President, Jebediah Atkins, left the building with many pats on the back and handshakes until the Texas Rangers intercepted the group as they left the building, and escorted him to a waiting convoy of black SUVs that would carry them to the ranch airport for the flight back to Big Bend. Security had been heavy for the meeting, and the Texas Air Guard had cleared the skies to make certain that no harm would come to the new leader of the Texas Republic.

CHAPTER 25

"Miss O'Brien, Captain Moffett says to get your gear ready for a trip to the command center to meet with President Atkins. They have a chopper coming for you and Miss Meyers in about twenty minutes," Charlie announced at the tent flap.

"Certainly Charlie. Can you find Julie for me? I think she will be close to Sergeant Leonard," Maggie responded.

"Yes ma'am," Charlie replied.

Maggie left the tent and walked to the remuda where Luke was saddling Lucky.

"I just heard that Julie and I are going to meet the new President, Luke," She said.

"Good morning, Maggie. I got the call a few minutes ago. Colonel Jenkins is coming out here to talk to the men about me shooting that fella yesterday, and you are going to fly out for a meeting with our new President," Luke answered.

"Luke, I wish that I could say that this has been an enjoyable couple of days, but the men have been really sweet to us. I hope that we can all spend some time together when the war is over," Maggie shook his hand and walked away.

"Well, Lucky, I sure feel a little low right now. It looks like you might be my last friend out here," Luke finished tightening the cinch, and Lucky followed him back to the cook fire.

"Elroy, have you seen Sergeant Leonard this morning?" Luke asked as he got his breakfast.

"Yes, sir. He is over by the hummer with a long face. It appears that he might be a mite sweet on that little girl of Maggie's," Elroy said with a laugh.

"Well...head on down there and tell him to get his gear packed. I'm sending him back to the Colonel, er, President along with the reporters. He won't be worth a spit to us after they leave anyway," Luke ordered.

"Yes, sir Captain!" came the response as Elroy left to relay the command.

The sound of the Huey coming in flanked by two Apaches caused everyone to migrate to the makeshift landing area behind the camp. The two Apaches flew to the higher ground of the butte top so that they could observe the surrounding terrain for hostile activity.

Colonel Jenkins jumped from the door of the Huey that sat with the rotors turning as it waited for its outgoing passengers.

"Hello, Captain Moffett," He said loudly for the benefit of the men as he saluted Luke, "I've brought a gift from Mary. She said that you had left it behind and would probably need it."

Jenkins handed Luke a package wrapped in brown paper with a note attached.

"Thank you sir," Luke replied.

"It's going to be all right, Luke. Trust in God," The Colonel smiled and moved to speak to Maggie as they boarded the chopper along with Sergeant Leonard.

Luke gathered the men in the mess tent and waited for much anticipated speech with a growing sourness in his stomach. They didn't have long to wait as Jenkins came in right behind them and moved to the front of the room.

"Jasper, how about some of your world famous coffee?" he asked first, "Men, I'll get right to the point. Two days ago you fellows hung a terrorist that you believed responsible for the death of Captain Post. Now I know that you all were acting under the direction of Captain Moffett, and so he alone must bear the consequences of his decision. I watched the video of the hanging, and I have spoken to General Clarke in detail about it. While the needless taking of a human life cannot be abided by any God fearing man or woman, we need to realize that Texas is now a sovereign nation, and it has its own laws separate from the United States. The new President of this Republic has issued a declaration that all rustlers, rapists, murderers, horse thieves, and persons acting as a threat to this Republic can be summarily executed if they cannot be brought to trial in an expeditious manner. Further to this end, he dictates that no Islamic Terrorist that is engaged in an act of war against the Republic will be granted quarter while engaged in said act of war. Are there any questions before I proceed?"

The men just sat looking at the floor or around the room depending on their embarrassment at having spoken out against Luke for shooting the Muslim prisoner.

"Now did anyone of you hear that fellow yesterday make any threatening remarks before Captain Moffett shot him?" Jenkins asked as he looked around the room.

First one and then another of the men shook their heads in the affirmative before Charlie spoke up.

"Colonel that Muslim threatened to kill Luke and hang his head on a pole," Charlie said.

"Do you think that he would have done it, considering what they did to Captain Post?" Jenkins asked.

"Yes, sir, I believe that he would have," Charlie replied.

"Then I rule the shooting justified!" Jenkins exclaimed, "Now I am not asking you men to be executioners. If the enemy surrenders and is no longer a threat, call for a team to pick them up, but as long as they fight, these need to be killed to the last man. Am I clear on that?"

A hearty "YES SIR!" rang out in the tent.

"Very well, you are dismissed. Jasper is it too late to get a bite to eat? My stomach is cutting a hole in my backbone," Jenkins laughed as he turned to the new business at hand.

Luke came in and got a cup of coffee before sitting down across from the Colonel who was working on his second helping of fried potatoes, ham, and eggs.

"If you don't mind me asking, sir, where are they taking these prisoners that we've rounded up?" he asked.

Jenkins looked across the table and answered, "We've been ordered to load them in rail cars down in Alpine for shipment to a prison camp that has been set up in a pretty remote area to the west of us. There are quite a few prisoners too. Surprisingly, not many are U.S. troops. Most are United Nations and a few like the ones that you've encountered. I'm not sure what the plans are past that, but it would be a pretty good bet that we won't be sending the Islamists home. As you well know, war is a brutal thing, Luke, and I have reservations about what is happening, but the only way to eradicate Islam is to kill the fighters off to the last man or woman…kind of Old Testament like."

"I still feel bad about shooting that one yesterday," Luke responded.

"It means that you've still got a conscience, Luke, don't lose it," Jenkins said, "I have a feeling that the package Mary sent will help with that."

"Yes, sir," Luke replied and left the tent.

CHAPTER 26

Maggie O'Brien's headphones crackled shortly after the helicopter was airborne.

"Is everything okay back there Maggie?" Amos' voice was in her ear.

"Why Captain…Whitehorse? Captain Whitehorse, we've got to stop meeting like this!" Maggie exclaimed, trying not to laugh.

"I just wanted to make this run so I could apologize for the last one. I promise that there will be no bags on your heads this trip!" Amos told her.

"And where exactly is this trip to, Captain?" Maggie asked.

"You can call me Amos, and I can't tell you on the intercom…just in case someone is listening," Amos replied, "Hey Leonard, it's good to see you again."

"Yes, sir, Captain Whitehorse. I'm glad to be on this flight," Jackson Leonard answered without taking his eyes off Julie, who appeared just as smitten with him.

"Are we safe flying in this helicopter, Amos? I mean, the last time I flew with you somebody did try to shoot us down," Maggie asked sarcastically.

"Safe enough, I guess. We've got our Apache escorts behind us, and three Texas Guard F-16s overhead. The trip won't be that long this time, and our landing site is very secure," Amos answered.

He had just gotten that statement out of his mouth when several small arms rounds banged off the fuselage like angry bees.

"Hey boys, I'm picking up some small arms from the deck. Can you check it out for us?" Amos called the Apaches.

No sooner had he made the request the Apaches were in a dive for the area where the attack was believed to have come from.

"Everybody okay back there? Nobody hurt, I hope?" Amos asked.

"We're fine Amos; just get us out of here!" Maggie exclaimed.

"Roger that, Maggie. We'll be out of range in a second," Amos responded as he climbed steeply to gained altitude.

Amos heard his radio, "Angel One this is Shadow One. We've got about one hundred and fifty troops down here with some heavy armor. Can you drop down and give us a hand?"

"Shadow One, We are on the way! Angel One out."

Seconds later three F-16s screamed past the Huey on their way to the fight, leaving Amos feeling slightly vulnerable as his escort left him. A movement to his right got his attention as Maggie climbed into the second seat next to him.

"You don't mind do you, Amos? She asked as she put the co-pilot headset on.

"Not at all, Maggie. Buckle up! Miss Meyers, have you got that camera rolling yet?" Amos asked.

Julie had strapped herself in next to the side door with Leonard's help, and was busy trying to pick up some of the action from the high altitude.

"I do, but I can't make much out," Was the reply.

"I think that we can fix that," Amos said.

He threw the old Huey into a steep right-handed bank, and the chopper fell like a stone toward the fighting below. He could hear Julie screaming in his phones and saw Maggie white knuckled with her mouth open in terror next to him. As soon as they were close enough to film the melee below, Amos righted the Huey and brought it head on toward the column of the enemy troops that were trying to flee the deadly assault from the F-16s and the Apache Helicopters and their Hellfire missiles.

"Sergeant Leonard, would you mind manning the door gun, please?" Amos asked with a grin.

"Yes, Sir," Came the reply followed by the ragged burst of the 7.62mm GAU-17A machine gun in the door.

"Julie, those boys didn't leave us much to shoot at, so there won't be any retakes. Are you ready?" Amos asked.

"I am if you don't throw me out," Came the reply.

"There is one personnel carrier down there directly in front of us. He's trying to get to the cover of that deep wash, and our boys have missed him. Get it in your view finder," Amos told her.

He put the chopper in a shallow dive to come behind the fleeing vehicle before unleashing two rockets from the LAU-61rocket launcher that was mounted below the nose of the Huey. The rockets flew straight up the back of the personnel carrier and raised a fireball that Amos had to climb over.

"Good shooting there Whitehorse!" the radio crackled, "That must have been their ammo supply."

"Somebody had to clean up your mess!" Amos responded good naturedly, "That is going to cost you a beer the next time we get together."

"I can't get a copy on you, Amos. You're breaking up," was the response.

"Yeah, yeah," Amos replied with a grin.

The rest of the flight was uneventful with Maggie doing a voice over on the footage that Julie had shot of the action. Amos called for a team to scout for survivors before the opportunity to make small talk presented itself.

Maggie held the microphone close to Amos, "Captain Whitehorse, can you tell our viewers what they are seeing in this footage?"

"Certainly Miss O'Brien, they are seeing the demise of a group of foreign fighters infiltrating the nation of Texas to do us harm. We don't play well with others down here in this great country, and the world is finding that out," Amos replied.

"Thank you Captain Whitehorse. This is Maggie O'Brien reporting from deep within the Republic of Texas," Maggie signed off and handed the camera back to Julie.

"So, Amos Whitehorse, after having the crap scared out of us, is there going to be a place for girl to get a drink where we are going?" Maggie asked with a mischievous smile.

"I would be happy to show you to the lounge area of our bunker, Maggie. It's certainly not fancy, but for an underground stress reliever, it is on par with your run of the mill Irish pub," Amos replied with a laugh.

Maggie laughed, "If we have time after meeting President Atkins, I'll take you up on it, but first I want a hot shower and a change of clothes!"

"I'm sure that can be arranged. Let me check in so they'll know we're coming," Amos replied.

Twenty minutes later, Amos sat the Huey down in a secluded wash to the south of "the Hive" and loaded his passengers into a vehicle driven by Manny Hernandez. Another pilot saluted in passing and boarded the aircraft as soon as it was vacated.

"Hi Amos!" Manny greeted him.

"Hello Manny. I'm surprised to see you pulling this duty. Do you remember Maggie O'Brien and Julie Meyers?' Amos replied, and this is Sergeant Leonard, one of the men that helped get the President out of trouble when this started.

"It's only been a few days. I could not forget such beautiful women if it had been years. Hello ladies," He replied, "Sergeant, good to meet you."

"We probably looked different with our hoods on," Julie said sarcastically.

"Okay then, let's go meet the boss," Manny changed the subject.

Amos sat in the front of the big Ford SUV with Manny so they could talk on the short drive to the hidden entry of the 'Hive'.

"Why are you pulling this detail, Manny? What's going on with Jeb?" He asked.

"Things have changed, Amos. I'm out as far as security goes, and you had better not call him 'Jeb' to his face. He is now 'Mister President' or 'President Atkins', and he has his own security surrounding him twenty four seven," Manny replied in a whisper.

"I've known him for years, and that does not sound like Jebediah Atkins to me," Amos said.

"Maybe so…maybe not, but I know that things are different now," Manny replied.

The rest of the bumpy ride was made in silence as the Ford climbed the side of a wash and headed directly toward the sheer wall of one of the many mountains in the Big Bend area. Suddenly, just as it seemed that they would impact the cliff face, a well disguised door shot up, and the vehicle drove into a large garage ringed with armed security in full combat gear and skull masks that were definitely not Texas Guardsmen.

"Step out of the vehicle and keep your hands where we can see them!" came a command through a loud speaker overhead.

The occupants of the vehicle all got out slowly as they were directed and were searched with metal detector wands individually before being allowed to produce identification.

"Is this really necessary?" Amos asked, "We are here because the President ordered us here, and you damned sure know who this woman is, unless you've been under a rock for the last four years."

"We know who you are, Captain Whitehorse. We are doing our job to protect the President," A tall man with a skull mask on his face addressed him while two others trained their weapons on him.

"I don't intimidate easily friend, so unless you are prepared to use deadly force on me, I'm boarding that elevator with my party," Amos glared back at him for three full seconds before turning his back and walking toward the elevator doors.

"Stand down and let them pass," He heard the order given behind him, and the hair on his neck relaxed a bit.

Amos felt a hand slide around his arm as Maggie stepped in close beside him, followed by Leonard with Julie holding on to his arm for dear life, and Manny who kept an eye on their rear. Only when the doors slid shut did the group exhale with audible sounds of relief.

"I told you things had changed, Amos. Do you believe me now?" Manny said.

"You're talking to an old ex-Navy fighter jock, Manny. I know how to kiss up to the brass. Trust me, everything will be fine," He replied while secretly doubting his own words.

"The last time I heard 'trust me', I ended up running nearly naked through a cactus patch to get away from my wife's father before we got married," Manny replied.

"Well, this time you've got your clothes on," Amos responded.

The elevator doors opened into the cavernous command center almost thirty stories underground. Standing beside the doors on both sides were two Texas Department of Public Safety Special Operations personnel that had been assigned to protect President Jebediah Atkins. After submitting to another search, Amos and his troupe were ushered into Jeb's office at the other end of the room where they found him sitting at his desk with his back to the door. They stood quietly waiting for the President to finish his call, and to recognize their presence for what seemed like ten minutes before he finally turned around.

"Ah…Amos, it's good to have you back down here with us. I understand that things heated up over the carrier after I left. Maggie O'Brien, I would recognize you anywhere, and I am so happy that you've accepted my invitation along with your friend," Jeb greeted them.

"Julie Meyers, Mister President," Julie stepped forward and offered her hand.

"It's a pleasure Miss Meyers. Hello Sergeant Leonard, I didn't get the chance to thank you properly for helping me out of a tight spot out there, but the promotion to Sergeant should help," Jeb said, "How is Rodriguez?"

"He is fine, Mister President. We left him at camp, sir," Leonard replied.

"Very good. Maggie, I have a business proposition for you that we can discuss after you freshen up, so if you would follow Sergeant Hernandez, he will show you to your quarters. Amos, stick around for a minute, and let me catch you up on the enormity of the things that have been happening over the past two days," He dismissed them while waving Amos to a large overstuffed chair that had been positioned perfectly to put a visitor at a height lower than the presidential desk chair,

"It looks like we may have Washington and that buffoon Onbekend over a barrel, so to speak. Based on that radio transmission from the Russian sub, I had one of our diplomats open a channel of communications with the Kremlin, and it looks very positive for us. The Chinese are tired of trying to work around the State Department, and they are making overtures also in hopes of getting their oil shipped. The governors of the two Mexican states, Chihuahua and Coahuila are talking softly about seceding from Mexico and aligning themselves with us. That will require a military intervention, but should not pose much of a problem. Besides, I've wanted to bust President Fuentes' chops since they took our Marine a while back.

It also looks like a sure thing that Colorado, Oklahoma, New Mexico, Wyoming, and Kansas may join us as states in a new sovereign nation, which is almost as good as piecing the old republic back together."

"Man oh man, Jeb…er, Mister President, things are certainly moving fast, aren't they?" Amos responded to the bombshell news.

"In this office, you can call me Jeb, Amos. We go a long way back, and I consider you a close friend, but outside we have to respect the office," Atkins answered.

"Tell me something, Jeb, what is going on with Washington? There haven't been any bombings in two days that I know of, just the Muslim problem that is slowly being contained," Amos replied.

"My intelligence teams are reporting that the Joint Chiefs' ranks have suffered devastating losses in the past week, and now Durrah is worried about the real possibility that the Russians sunk that sub, although she doesn't know for certain. They can't possibly fight a war against the American people and Russia, especially since most of the armed forces are refusing to fight against fellow Americans. With the pressure of public opinion from the outside world, and the mounting hostility between Russia, China, and Washington, it is almost a certainty that the President will back off and give us the truce we've been asking openly for. Also there is the small matter of the leverage that we hold with that carrier group safely in port. I think we may have won this thing in less than a month!" Jeb replied, "The Muslim eradication program is doing well also. We've gotten reports of hundreds of Muslims crossing the border into Arkansas and boarding the transport systems that we've set up with the empty cargo vessels. All of the mosques in Houston have been destroyed, and the Guard is blowing them up in the surrounding country as they find them.

"That mounted patrol where I picked up Maggie told me that all of their prisoners were being loaded on trains in Alpine. Where are they going?" Amos asked.

"Those people are a different story, Amos. If we turn them loose, they will find a way to attack and kill again. The only solution will be to executed them expeditiously," Jeb told him, "On a happier note, I've got a plum assignment for you…if you want it. We want Maggie O'Brien to be the face of our national news program, and I would like for you to fly her around Texas to cover for the world what is happening in our new country,"

"I think that I can force myself to do that, Mister President. When do we start?" Amos replied with a smile.

"Two things first; Maggie has to accept the assignment, and we have to wait for your new chopper to get here," Jeb laughed, "Now I've got work to do. Go clean up, and we'll talk later this evening."

"Yes, sir, and thanks," Amos said, but the President was already on his next phone call.

Amos left the office and walked slowly across the command center that was a bee hive of activity and awash with light from several dozen large screen displays. The DPS guard was standing by the elevator as he pressed the up button and did not acknowledge his presence, but stood in stony silence as they watched the activity in the room. Things had certainly changed in the past couple of days, but he couldn't figure out whether it was for the better or not.

Amos' room was on the dignitary level of the command bunker, one floor above the command center itself. This area offered the best protection from any above ground attack, and it also was closed to any personnel operating in a lesser pay grade. As he exited the elevator, Manny was waiting outside of the door.

"I'm not supposed to be here, but here is my room number," He said as he slipped a piece of paper in Amos' hand while brushing past to get on the elevator.

It was only after getting into his room that Amos looked at the paper and memorized the number before burning the note and flushing it down the toilet. Right now, his first priority was getting a hot shower and a fresh uniform. The possibility of having a beer with Maggie O'Brien was the foremost thing on his mind; Manny would have to wait until evening.

CHAPTER 27

After Colonel Jenkins' speech, Luke walked back to his tent with the package that Mary had sent to him. Inside a carefully folded leather oilskin was Luke's old bible with a note from his wife.

"Luke, the answers that you need are in this book. I'll be at the house when all of this is over. Love, Mary," The note read.

Luke slipped off the cot and onto his knees beside it for the next ten minutes as he sought the solace that only came when he was in prayer. His moment of reflection was short lived with the arrival of Nathan Jenkins outside of the tent.

"Luke, can we talk?" Jenkins asked in a low voice outside of the tent.

"Of course Colonel, come on in," Luke replied.

"I didn't mean to interrupt you, but there is a team coming in that will need some space. This is a top secret ops unit so everything needs to be kept quiet about their activities," Jenkins informed him.

"Is this Maggie O'Brien's father and his team?" Luke asked.

Colonel Jenkins was taken aback for a minute, "It would be better if she did not find out that they were here, Luke."

"She is already suspicious, but I can keep my mouth shut, sir," Luke replied, "Besides, we'll probably not see her again out here once she has talked to the President."

"They'll be in after dark this evening, so get them a place to sleep and some food. I'm not sure how long they'll be around, but tell the men to stay out of their way," Jenkins added, "…and Luke, try not to let this get to you. War always passes, and then we go back to our lives. This will be over soon enough."

"Thank you, sir. Mary sent my bible out here to keep me focused, and I'll make sure that they're taken care of," Luke stood until the Colonel had left the tent.

The men were still gathered around the cook tent when Shaun O'Brien led his men in from the dark. To a man they were all stunned by the look that these professional soldiers had about them. Each man was wearing the latest in body armor, and carried the newest model spec ops equipment down to their suppressed Springfield M-14s, but it was the coldness of the eyes that made the goose bumps rise on the arms of the older men. They had seen this before in the long-range recon troops that had floated in and out of almost every theater of operations that these old men had been in, but never as up close and personal as in the confined space of the crowded mess tent.

"I'm looking for Captain Moffett," The leader of the ops team spoke loudly.

He was a big man, much older than the men that were in his group, but it was readily apparent that the control of these mercenaries was all his.

"You've found him, sir," Luke spoke up from the end table where he had been nursing a cup of coffee.

O'Brien moved to the table and offered his hand. Luke stood and looked the man over while he shook his hand.

"I can see where Maggie got her eyes from, but thank God her mother must have supplied the looks!" he said with a grin.

"I've got several ex-wives that I could go to for insults, Captain. Have you got a place for my men?" Shaun said with a smile that matched his firm handshake.

"We have everything arranged, Mister O'Brien, but have the men fill up on some food first before you turn in," Luke responded as he gazed around the tent looking for someone that he hoped would be with this crew.

"Call me Shaun. If you are looking for Michael Tucker, he is making a perimeter check. His instincts are buzzing tonight," O'Brien said.

"I knew he was alive when Maggie said that she thought you were on the plane with her!" Luke exclaimed, "Praise the Lord!"

"I should have known better than to open my mouth during that flight, but she is my little girl, and I put her through a lot. Did she act upset?" he asked.

"No, I think more relief than anything. She has a lot of spunk," Luke told him.

"Yes she does," He answered.

They were interrupted by two men coming through the entrance. One was a tall heavyset bull of a man that at six feet two inches and two hundred and eighty pounds looked out of place among the rest of the group, and the other was Michael Tucker. He caught Luke's grin and made a beeline for the table. When he reached Luke he bypassed the outstretched hand and gave the older man a bear hug.

"Good to see you, Luke," he said, "I'm sorry that we had to disappear like that."

"Dang boy! It's good to see you too! How is Hanna and little Emily" Luke asked as he wiped tears from his eyes.

"They are still home. Hanna is expecting another baby in about a month, and Emily is anxious for a little brother," Tuck answered, "Oh, by the way, this is Terry McFadden, a gun runner from Tennessee. Actually we think of Terry as more of our procurement expert than gun runner."

The big man offered his hand to Luke who took it with a smile.

"Pleased to meet you Terry," Luke told him.

"Likewise, sir," He replied.

"Speaking of procurement, we've got a couple of extra Hummers that were only used by a little old terrorist a couple of times," Luke answered with a laugh.

"There is something that I could use, Luke," Tuck stated, "how about a good rifle?"

"I've got just the thing, Tuck. It's in my tent," Luke told him, "You fellas get some grub in you, and then we'll ease over there so you can look at it."

"Will do, Luke. It sure is good seeing you again. By the way, how is John Post these days? Hanna wanted me to be sure and say hi to those folks. They treated us like royalty," Tuck said.

"John didn't make it, Tuck. One of these Islamists tried to cut his head off a couple of days back, and John lost too much blood to recover," Luke told him.

"I hope you were able to even the score a bit," Terry replied.

"I hung the bastard on the windmill overnight, but it didn't bring my friend back," Luke told him.

Terry just looked at the old man that stood before him and thought about how much hardness a soft look could cover.

"I'm sorry about your friend, Captain Moffett," He said to Luke, "We have all lost something in this one."

Tuck just stood looking at the floor with the expressionless face that he put on when things got tough. Luke patted his shoulder, "Go get something to eat, Tuck. We'll talk later."

Shaun O'Brien came over to the table with a plate and two cups of black coffee. He slid one across to Luke.

"Why thank you Mr. O'Brien," Luke said as he took the cup and held it between both hands for the warmth.

"Call me Shaun, Luke. I need your help with an assignment that we are on. There is an Imam somewhere close by this area that is stirring up these jihadists to attack us. My men and I are going to take him out of the picture, but first we have to find him. Have you an idea where he might be?" O'Brien asked.

"Well, we had a run in with a bunch that we stumbled on two days ago that looked like they might be fresh. We killed most of them, but some prisoners were sent to Alpine. That would probably be a good place to start," Luke told him, "I should probably add that it is most likely those will be executed straight away, so you'd better hurry."

"I'll get a call in to our handler this evening. Did I say that you had two extra Hummers that we can use?" O'Brien asked.

"Yes, Sir, and a pot full of weapons if you need them," Luke replied.

"Very good. We'll be pulling out before daylight so if I don't get the chance, thanks for taking care of Maggie during that firefight," Shaun told him.

"Well, we couldn't be the bunch of old geezers that lost the most popular news anchor on the planet, now could we?" Luke grinned and shook the big man's hand.

"I guess not," O'Brien laughed, "By the way, Luke, if you see Maggie, don't tell her that I am here. I'd like to do that myself when this is over."

"Of course. I won't say a word," Luke replied.

Later that evening, Luke heard boots outside of the tent. "Come on in, Tuck."

"You've got pretty good hearing for a 'geezer'," Tuck laughed.

"Some things work better with age, and some things don't. My hearing is one that does, you can guess at what doesn't. Your surprise is on the other bunk," Luke motioned to John's bunk.

"Well if this doesn't beat everything! I thought for sure that rifle was gone forever," Tuck exclaimed as he pulled the custom Remington from its case.

"Otis gave that to me after your funeral," Luke laughed, "I kind of think he might have known you'd be back for it."

"I don't know who all was in on that, but after we killed those cartel folks, it was pretty apparent that Hanna and I were going to have a target on us for a long time. As it is, we still have to keep the cover up. No one knows that I'm here but the team and you," Tuck told him.

"And it will stay that way, Tuck, but you have to promise to tell that little girl about her uncle Luke from time to time," Luke replied.

"She will think you're Pecos Bill when I get through," Tuck laughed, "I've got to go. Thanks for keeping this old girl clean for me."

"She bailed us out a couple of times already. I hate it that I'm going to have to use that McMillan now," Luke said as he shook the young man's hand.

"I hope we can get together after this, Luke. Hanna will be tickled that I got to see you. She worries about not being able to tell Kathryn and her sisters that we are alive, but the danger to the kids is too real for us to take any chances. Well, hey, take care of yourself, and we'll have a party in a short while," Tuck finished and headed out.

"Keep your head down, Tuck," Luke bid him farewell.

At least this time his heart felt a whole lot better with the manner that his friend left. Luke just wished that he could have a do over with John and the others that had died in the last week. Sleep was late in coming to him as he spent most of the night reflecting on his life and some of the misadventures that had come on him. It was just as his thought started making no sense, and sleep weighed heavy on him that the sound of gunfire from the perimeter sentries startle him out of the bunk.

Luke grabbed for his boots and hat, stopping only to pick up an AK that he had saved from the captured weapons, along with two extra thirty round mags, and ran out of the tent straight into Luis Gonzales who was coming to get him.

"What's going on Luis?" Luke asked while trying to pull on his boots with one free hand.

"One of those young fellas thought he saw some movement down the hill from us and cut loose with a couple of bursts," Luis answered.

The shooting had stopped and the camp was covered in an eerie silence. Shaun O'Brien came up to the two men in a semi-crouch and an AR in his hand.

"I've got the men in the brush, Luke. We'll know in a minute if it was a coyote or an attack," He said.

"Luis, put everyone on alert and have them take up defensive positions. Get somebody to check the horses and move them closer to the camp center. Let's play it safe," Luke ordered.

Fifteen minutes had passed without even the hoot of an owl to break the tension, something that seemed strange and ominous to Luke, when two shadowy figures hailed the camp from a patch of brush and cactus on the western side.

"Friendlies coming in...hold your fire men," The shadows called.

Two men stepped out into the light that was being shown in their direction, and Luke could see Tuck and Terry dragging a weight behind them. Shaun ran over to investigate followed closely by Luis and Luke.

"We caught him sneaking this sack of grenades in down there, and I'll bet there are about twenty more laying low in the wash," Tuck told Shaun, tossing a heavy bag at his feet.

"Is he dead?" Luke asked.

"Naw, he's just being shy," Terry replied while kicking the prone body with his boot toe.

The figure on the ground moaned slightly before he regained full consciousness, and then turned over on his back. His face and arms had hundreds of cactus spines visible, and Luke was sure that the rest of his body had received the same treatment. Now his eyes opened wide in terror as he realized, probably for the first time, that he was in big trouble.

"How many of you are down there?" Shaun squatted down and asked in a low tone.

The man just lay there and shook in pain and fear.

"Well, he doesn't look Mexican, but let Sergeant Gonzales have a run at him. Let's see if he will talk before you use more extreme measures," Luke spoke.

Luis stood over the shaking figure and asked in Spanish, "¿Cuántos de ustedes están allí?"

The man looked at Luis for a few seconds and then said, "Bastante!"

"Well?" Luke asked.

"Sergeant Gonzales asked him how many there were, and he told him 'Enough!'" O'Brien spoke, "I speak fluent Spanish also. Tie him up and gag him, Tuck. I want to question him after we kill the rest of them,"

"Do you think he is a Muslim?" Luke asked.

"Probably cartel, but we won't know that or what they are doing out here until we interrogate him," O'Brien answered.

The rest of the ops team checked in without seeing anything beyond the man that Tuck and Terry McFadden had captured below the camp.

"Have you got sentries posted on top of the butte, Luke?" Tuck asked.

"We posted two men up there after I hung that fella a couple of nights ago, but not tonight," Luke answered knowing that he had made a tactical mistake.

Sergeant Luis Gonzales spoke up, "I'll take two men up and that sack of grenades. If they are scaling that south side of the butte, perhaps we can make it a little tougher for them to get up."

"I would send ten men up, preferably ten of the younger hands…no offense, and I'll take my men up also," O'Brien spoke up.

"Grab Rodriguez and take him with you Luis. As angry as he is, he will be an asset if you have to fight," Luke ordered, "The rest of us will guard the main camp, and I'll have Jasper turn the mess tent into a hospital."

Luke watched the men disappear into the blackness for a second before getting to the radio and putting a call into Colonel Jenkins. Quickly assured of gunship backup within the next hour, Luke checked his perimeter guards and waited for the fireworks to begin. He didn't have long to wait either. Ten minutes after O'Brien left the camp for the top of the butte, the distinct sound of O'Brien's Ak-47 firing broke the cold silence of the desert night followed closely by the booming of grenades.

Grabbing his signal flare gun, Luke fired an illumination flare out over the wash directly below the camp. In that instant of light, several enemy troops were caught by surprise, quickly drawing fire from the camp defenders. The ones that were not hit drew back into the mesquite as the light faded.

The gunfire from the top of the butte had intensified, and Luke realized that they were going to need more light if they were to have a hope of holding off a frontal assault before help arrived. They still had about two hours before dawn, and it was a pitch black night with no moonlight. Before the flare had died out, he had seen a pile of dead wood and mesquite directly below the camp that had been pushed up out of the wash when some clearing had been done the past year. If he could get that thing burning, it was just possible that they would be able to keep the enemy at bay until the Apaches arrived.

Luke looked around quickly and saw two five-gallon jerry cans of gasoline that they had for the generator. He quickly ran to his tent and grabbed a riot gun that was had belonged to John Post. John had told him that it was loaded with a round called Dragon's Breath and was supposed to shoot a flame several hundred feet from the muzzle. Armed with the shotgun, his 1911 .45ACP, and the two jerry cans of gas, Luke struggled down the steep hillside about seventy five yards to the pile of debris that he had seen. He could hear movement coming toward him from the other side, but the enemy was just as blind as he was.

Luke set the cans as far up on the pile as he could and turned to climb back up just as several shots rang out from a very few yards below him. Almost instantly, the men above returned fire using the muzzle blasts as approximate targets, and Luke dove for the rough ground that was barren of cover in hopes that he didn't get hit by friendly or unfriendly fire. It was while he was lying there that he realized just how hard it was going to be to hit those cans from up on top of the slope where his men were hunkered down. Instead, he pulled his sidearm and emptied the magazine at where he thought the cans were, being rewarded with the sound of at least two of the rounds striking metal.

Un-slinging the shotgun from his shoulder, Luke crawled up the incline until he was about fifty feet from the pile. Small arms fire was hitting the general area where he was laying as the enemy fired randomly towards his apparent position. Turning over on his back, he fired one of the Dragon's Breath rounds in the general direction of the pile, and all hell broke loose. Luke didn't know which event surprised him more, the long tongue of fire that erupted from the shotgun barrel, the explosion of ten gallons of gasoline igniting into a huge fireball that looked like an atomic bomb going off, or the heat from the fireball burning off his eyebrows and scorching his face.

He wasn't the only one taken by surprise by the blast and resulting fireball. On the opposite side of the pile were three of the enemy that had been much closer to the pile than Luke had, One was on fire and trying to beat the fire out with his hands while running in circles and screaming. The other two had their hands over their eyes and had dropped their weapons, an act that didn't save them from the debilitating fire that rained down from the camp now that they could be seen.

"Get up here Luke!" Jasper called down to him.

"On the way!" he answered and started making his way up the hill.

He made an effort to climb the steep incline with some speed, but it felt like his legs were made of rubber. Bullets were now whizzing past his head and throwing up dirt above and beside him as his men tried to keep the shooters below pinned down. Finally, he reached the spot where Charlie was directing fire down the hill, and threw himself over the slight berm to relative safety.

"Glad you made it Luke," Charlie whispered.

"Me to Charlie…me too," Luke just lay there out of breath for a minute.

The firing was getting more intense up on the butte, but there was something else making noise in the distance that sounded like faint thunder. Luke realized that the support helicopters were on the way and made his way to the radio. After a short call to the lead chopper, Luke swapped his shotgun for a rifle and headed for O'Brien's position at a trot up the steep dark trail that lead to the top of the butte.

"Luke, get your head down!" a voice came from his left as he crested the slope.

He squatted quickly and tried to make out the shape of whoever called to him.

"Who is it?" he asked in a whisper.

"Tuck. Our team has night vision, so I've got your men back here with me. Shaun is on the edge of the drop over there picking off those boys when they show themselves. So far, we seem to be holding them, but there are probably a hundred or more. That guy at the camp was supposed to be a diversion," Tuck answered.

"We figured that out," Luke said dryly, "Help is on the way, and I've told them to light up the south side of this rock if you want to get over there."

"Okay, but keep these youngsters of yours back until we get some light. A couple almost fell off the other side already," Tuck laughed.

The sound of the Apaches coming in at attack speed around the east end of the butte was music to their ears. Suddenly the world beneath the butte top was lit up in a brilliant flash followed by the sound of Shaun's team picking off targets as fast as they could fire.

"Come on men, we can't let those boys have all of the fun," Luke urged the 39th forward toward the edge.

The Apache pilots made a turn and came back below the butte with their guns making a ripping sound as they destroyed target after target, including two armored personnel carriers that had been hidden in the brush. Suddenly the gunfire from below stopped as the remaining enemy tried desperately to melt into the desert scrub to no avail. The first rays of dawn in the crisp, cold morning air lit up the tableau below the butte and made it impossible to move unnoticed.

Tuck was picking off multiple targets with the Remington, while Rodriguez made shots out past twelve hundred yards with the McMillan, and then it was over. Twenty-two men threw down their weapons and came toward them with their hands raised over their heads. The Apache pilots circled the soon to be prisoners until Luke could take them into custody.

Shaun O'Brien walked over and said, "I need to interrogate these prisoners before they get sent off, Luke. There is something strange about them, and we need to know where they came in from. My suspicion is that they are Mexican military trying to put a sneak on us and grab some territory. You might want to have somebody check this side of the border for armor if that is the case."

"I'll call Colonel Jenkins if you want to send your guys down there. My men will stay out of your way," Luke replied.

"Okay, I'll go back with you and pick up those Hummers. We can drive down there and save time. As soon as we finish with those, I'm going to try and catch up with the ones that are still alive in Alpine," O'Brien told him.

Luke followed Shaun off the butte and back to camp after having the patrol keep watch on the prisoners until Shaun and his team could take over. A night of no sleep and maximum adrenalin flow had left him drained, and the first-degree burns on his face needed some salve, other than that, he was anxious to saddle Lucky and put some distance between the camp and his patrol.

CHAPTER 28

President Onbekend sat in the Oval Office behind the Resolute desk and glared across the White House lawn at the crowd that had been building at the fence since early morning despite the cold and the threat of snow. There had been rumors of a protest against the martial law edict, but he had expressly ordered that no protestors were to be allowed into the capitol. Now it looked as if there were several thousand people with signs gathering in a kind of silence, just standing and staring back at the window of his office as if they could see him. He turned and buzzed for his chief of security, long-time Secret Service agent Arnold Chase.

"I want to know how all of these people have gotten this close to the White House against my explicit instruction to the contrary!" he growled at Arnold when the latter entered the room.

"Mr. President, we passed the word to the D.C. Police to block all access to this part of Washington, but somehow these protestors started showing up about two hours ago, just after daybreak," Chase answered, "So far they have been peaceful, and we've been told that there is a caravan of traffic fifty miles long headed in this direction. The Virginia State Police are just waving them through."

"Make certain that Marine One is standing by. I'm going to fly up to Andrews this afternoon and check on the new clubhouse. Make certain also that the first lady doesn't know where I am," President Onbekend ordered.

"Yes, sir. I have already ordered extra security personnel until after this protest is over," He answered.

"I want these protesters dispersed immediately! We are not going to wait for this to build out of hand. I've declared martial law for God's sake. Doesn't that mean anything to you people?" the President practically screamed at Arnold Chase, "If the park police won't do their jobs, send your people out there, and start arresting some of these Tea Party extremists. If that fails, I want the military called in to secure the city. Is that understood?"

"I understand, sir. We'll take care of it immediately," Arnold replied and started for the door.

"One other thing, Chase. If anyone of these people climbs that fence, use deadly force to repel them, and I don't care if you fire into the crowd outside either," the President said as he dismissed him.

"I understand, sir," Arnold headed for the door with a bead of nervous sweat gathering on his forehead.

Once outside, Arnold Chase summoned his senior agent and apprised them of the President's orders.

"You've got to be kidding me!" one of the men gasped.

"I'm afraid not, Jones, he is deadly serious about breaking up that protest," Chase replied, "Find out why D.C. Metro has let this go on and get back to me. The rest of you get everything in place to carry out the order. God help us, if He will, but I'm afraid we may be looking at this administration's birds coming home to roost. Oh, and will one of you mention to the First Lady that the President is planning a golf outing this afternoon?"

"I'd be happy to take care of that detail personally, sir," Jones replied, "I love it when she throws those screaming fits that she does."

All of the men laughed at the image Jones had painted for them, causing some staffers to look in their direction out of curiosity, and then they scurried off to handle the business at hand.

Durrah Jowles sat in the war room briefing in place of the President and listened to each of the members of the Joint Chiefs give their weak assessments of the situation with Texas. Several of the junior staff members were conspicuously absent as was the secretary of defense. The under secretary looked frightened when it came her turn to report in her boss' place.

Durrah went straight for the jugular. "I want to know where Secretary Swain is and why he is not in this meeting!" She shouted at the red-faced woman.

"I honestly don't know, Ma'am. I called his phone this morning, but there was no answer," She replied.

Durrah turned to one of her guards, "Find him!"

With a nod of his head, the security guard headed for the door while talking into his headset.

"Now, can anyone tell me why we haven't got a plan to take the Permian oil fields on the President's desk yet?" Durrah asked the entire room in a menacing tone.

"The Chinese have sent word through our State Department that if we do not stop our activities close to their oil fields, they are going to bring a naval battle group into the Gulf to protect their interest," USMC General Leslie Hamms, a last minute replacement for General Doggett answered, "We decided to back off on our efforts to secure the oil fields for that reason first, number two because world opinion is against us, and number three, for the fact that Texas is holding an entire carrier group hostage.

Durrah sat in a stony silence and just glared around the room at anyone stupid enough to meet her gaze.

"Very well, If we can't bomb close to the oil fields, then I want the southern portion of that state devastated by tomorrow morning, starting with the Alamo. Grind that symbol of Texas independence into dust, and destroy the city with it! I also order that you use a tactical weapon on that infidel governor's command center, and hit the residences of every last one of his cabinet members. Is that clear enough?" She shouted.

"We need the President to authorize every one of these actions, Ma'am," General Hamms told her.

"You have his authorization, General, and if those targets are not obliterated by tomorrow morning at this time, you will be out of a job!" Durrah answered and then stormed out of the room.

General Hamms sat for a minute and remembered what had happened to his friend General Wayne.

"You all have your orders. I want all of the planning wrapped up and on my desk by sixteen hundred hours. This is in strictest confidence; not a word spoken outside of this room," He addressed those in attendance, including Marine Corps Commandant General Murray Slokum, and then walked briskly to the door.

Deep in the mountain below the Big Bend National Park, President Jebediah Atkins welcomed Maggie O'Brien and Julie Meyers into this office.

"Miss O'Brien, Miss Meyers, I'm so glad that you could come to our humble command center," He greeted them jovially.

"Thank you for the invitation, Mister President," Maggie replied, "Tell me, are we going to be reporting on any of the activities down here?"

"I'm afraid that won't be possible, but I do have something along those lines that I would like to discuss with you. Please have a seat," He motioned for the women to take seats across from his desk.

"Texas needs a good national news program to keep its citizens informed, and I wanted to offer you the position of News Director for the Republic of Texas News Network. What do you think?" he said with a big smile.

"Wow, I mean this is quite a surprise, sir. Is there a little time to reflect on the offer, and can I keep my number one camera woman with me?" Maggie matched Jeb's smile.

"Certainly to the second question and just a little time to the first one. I have a new news chopper coming in tomorrow and your pilot is on standby for the first assignment," he answered, "Of course you will have all of the latest gadgetry at your disposal, and a very secure base of operations until the war is over."

"Let me ask a couple of questions then, how much leeway will I have to report the news, and will the government censor my broadcasts?" Maggie asked.

"You will be in control of the news, although I would expect that my office would be kept informed prior any report that might put us in a bad light. Censorship would only be for security purposes to protect our troops, etcetera," Jeb answered.

Maggie stole a look at Julie who was grinning from ear to ear before she answered.

"Mister President, you have a news crew!" and gave a big handshake to the President of the Republic of Texas across the table.

"Excellent!" he responded, "I'll have the contracts drawn up in the morning. Now go enjoy your evening as much as you can while down here. I recommend the restaurant up on level twenty seven if you are in the mood to celebrate, and I will see you bright and early in the morning."

"Thank you very much, sir. We will be looking forward to getting started," Maggie said as she headed for the door.

Julie was like a little kid once they had left the office and walked across the buzzing command center to the elevators where they were met by two stoic DPS guards.

"Hi guys," Julie said as they walked between them but got no response.

"Julie, I think you would poke a bear with a stick just to get a rise from him!" Maggie admonished after the door closed behind them.

"Those guys are just big teddy bears, you'll see," Julie laughed, "Now let's go find the boys and get something to eat. I'm about starved to death."

"Don't play matchmaker with me, Miss Meyers. I'm only interested in Captain Whitehorse on a professional basis," Maggie replied with a blush.

The elevator doors opened two floors up, and who got in but Amos Whitehorse.

"Well, if this isn't a coincidence!" he said.

"Isn't it though," Julie replied with a big grin, "Do you know where Jake is staying, Captain?"

"Hello Amos," Maggie said with the blush making her face hot.

"Hey Maggie, guess who is going to fly your news chopper tomorrow?" Amos said with a grin, "Julie, Jake is on level twenty five with the other troops. We'll have to have him paged."

"We were just going to dinner, Captain Whitehorse. Won't you join us?" Julie asked mischievously.

"I would love to. We can have Sergeant Leonard paged from the restaurant," He replied without taking his eyes off Maggie.

Julie just gave her a wink behind his back as the doors opened on level twenty seven, which only served to intensify the blushing.

There is something to be said for a dinner that consists of a sixteen ounce fire grilled, medium raw Porterhouse steak, loaded baked potato, and fresh grilled vegetables washed down with the libation of your choice. In this case the table drank a copious quantity of Lone Star beer in celebration of the Republic, with the exception of Amos Whitehorse who had several sweet teas under his belt by evening's end.

"Why Captain Whitehorse," Julie slurred slightly, "I didn't take you for a tea drinker."

"I just prefer tea to beer, Julie, especially when I'm flying tomorrow," Amos smiled as he answered, "As a matter of fact, I need to go check out this new bird that we have for Maggie to buzz around in. I'd hate to crash it on my first time out."

Maggie smiled a smile that Amos felt like he was going to get lost in and giggled drunkenly, "I'd hate for you to crash it too, especially if I'm going to be in it, Captain Whitehorse."

Amos leaned over to give her a handshake and was taken completely by surprise when Maggie pulled him toward her and kissed him goodnight.

"Well…I…uh…better go check on the chopper," He mumbled.

"Goodnight Amos," she replied with another smile.

Amos walked unsteadily to the elevator and turned to see her eyes still on him as the doors closed. His hand went into his jacket pocket for the note that Manny had slipped him before he remembered that he had burned it. With shaking fingers, he pushed the button for the 24th floor. It had been a long time since any woman had that effect on him, but something about the way Manny had passed off the note told him that now was not the time to lose his focus over a pretty smile.

The corridor was empty as he made his way down the hall to room 2410 and knocked softly. Manny answered the door without taking the safety chain off and peering through the crack.

"Amigo," He said with a relieved sound.

"You were expecting trouble, Manny?" Amos asked.

"I'm not sure, but there are some troubling things in the air. We need to get outside where it is safe to talk. I'm sure that there are cameras and microphones everywhere in this facility, and what I want to tell you needs to be between us," Manny told him.

"Every exit is under heavy guard, Manny. How do you propose that we get outside?" Amos asked.

"Come on, and I'll show you," Manny went to the door and peaked into the hallway, "Come on."

"Right behind you," Amos followed him out of the room and down to the stairwell.

"The stair wells do not have any monitoring devices that I know of. We need to get down to the command center level without being seen," Manny explained.

They climbed down the six flights of stairs to the thirtieth level below ground just outside of the command center and the DPS guards. The stairs continued for another one-half flight with a door at the bottom. Manny went down to the door.

"There are two more levels of structure below this one that are not on the plans. My cousin Alberto was in charge of the excavation, and he told me about this. I didn't think anything about it until I talked to him this afternoon. We need to get through this door," Manny explained while quickly picking the lock.

"Is it alarmed?" Amos asked while looking up at the next floor.

"Probably not, none of the other doors are. Besides, no one knows that it leads anywhere," Manny said as he slipped through the door into the dark hallway behind.

As Amos came through and shut the door quietly behind him, he heard footsteps in the stairwell. The men froze in place as someone twisted the door handle to check the lock, and then left.

"That was close, Manny. Where to now?" Amos asked.

"At the end of this hallway is another stairs that leads down. At the bottom there is a false panel that my cousin installed that opens into an old quicksilver mine shaft that they came across while digging. My family's smuggling business keeps all of us looking for ways to sneak around, you understand," Manny chuckled nervously.

"Shine your flashlight into one of these rooms, Manny," Amos said as he noticed that the doors had small windows in them.

Manny did as he was asked, and they suddenly realized that they were looking into a very secure maximum-security prison cell!

"I've got a very bad feeling about this, Manny. Let's get to that mine shaft and get out of here!" Amos whispered.

"It's over here," He indicated with his light.

Once inside of the dark stairwell, the two men went down to the last floor and crawled into the recess under the last set of stairs. Manny ran his hands around the concrete block and found the release for the panel which slid open into the old shaft with very little effort. Once inside the mine, they pushed the panel quietly back in place and breathed a sigh of relief.

"Now how do we get back inside?" Amos asked him.

"Unfortunately, the same way that we got out, unless we can think of something better," Manny told him.

"I was afraid that you were going to say that," Amos replied, "Let's get outside in the fresh air."

"Watch where you step. Snakes use these old mines to hibernate in," Manny warned.

"Now that is awfully reassuring, first an underground prison and now snakes," Amos answered.

"I see a little light up ahead," Manny told him, "I think it is the moon."

They made their way slowly out of the mine and into the desert several hundred feet below the main entrance to the compound.

"I think you need to tell me why we risked getting into serious trouble just now," Amos said.

"My cousin Alfredo heard something, maybe just a whisper of something that sounded an awful lot like somehow Mexico is going to try to take over Texas again," Manny told him.

"If that is true, then we need to tell Jeb immediately!" Amos answered.

"I do not think that would be such a good idea, Senor Amos. The President's name was also mentioned in that whisper," Manny continued.

"Are you accusing President Atkins of selling out Texas? I've known him for fifteen years, and he would never do anything like that!" Amos argued.

"I'm not saying he would, and I'm not saying he wouldn't. I'm just telling you what was whispered to me. Have you noticed the increased security since we got hit just after you both flew out of here? Did you notice that the only real damage was to the ranger station and motel down in the crater? Don't you think the timing of that attack was just a little bit suspicious?" Manny pushed back.

"Come to think of it, I never heard of you guys finding the spy," Amos told him.

"It might have been because one of you two is the traitor," Manny replied.

"Now wait a minute. That's the second time you've questioned me. I'm just about ready to kick your Mexican…" Amos started.

"I'd be real careful where you go with that now, Amos. There is something not right with all of this, and we could both be in big danger if anyone finds out that we know about that secret prison or any kind of rumor of a plot against Texas," Manny stopped him.

"You are absolutely right, Manny. I apologize for losing my temper," Amos said.

"And I apologize for thinking about shooting you," Manny slid the derringer back into his pocket, "I think that I can get us back in without having to go through that mine again, but we will have to climb."

"You were going to shoot me?" Amos was dumb founded.

"It's a Mexican tradition. You'll get used to it if you stay down here long enough," Manny laughed.

They climbed quietly up the rough mountainside past the main entrance un-noticed, and Manny found the large air intake screen that covered the main airshaft servicing the mountain retreat. Working quietly with only a Leatherman tool that Manny had in his pocket, they removed the screen and climbed into the ducting. Manny pulled the screen back into place behind them, and they started slowly through the three-foot square duct intent on finding an opening inside of the "Hive" without being detected. About two hundred feet in, there was a large air return that serviced the top level of the installation. Manny quickly worked the clips that held the screen and filter in place and the men dropped out into the hallway un-noticed.

"Easy as pie, Amos," Manny said as he reattached the vent cover.

"I'm going back out and look at the new helicopter before I go back in. Do you want to join me? It will be the perfect cover," Amos said

"Good idea, but first we need to get into that bathroom over there and clean up a bit. That duct was pretty dusty," Manny said as he slapped a dust storm off his shirt.

They spent the next ten minutes shaking the dust off and getting presentable before walking out into the empty hallway and down to the guarded exit that led to the hanger. As they stepped through the door, they were stopped by the special ops guard that Amos had seen earlier that day.

"Where are you two going?" one of the men asked.

"I'm the pilot for the new news helicopter, and I'm going to look her over before we take it out in the morning," Amos replied nonchalantly.

"It's sitting over in the second bay. One of us will have to escort you through here, President Atkins' orders," The guard told them.

"I understand. We can't be too careful with all of the folks in Washington trying to kill us," Amos told him.

The guard just gave him a nod and led the way to the new helicopter that was sitting in a well-lit section of the large hanger and parking deck. Amos was impressed to say the least.

"Man oh man, a Twin Star AS355. What a sweet ride!" he said to Manny, "And just look at that paint job. They've got her all fixed up to resemble the Texas flag!"

"She is certainly something to look at, Captain Whitehorse." Manny used his military title in the presence of the soldier.

"I'm going to get in the pilot's seat, if you don't mind, friend. If there is a problem, call the President and tell him that Amos Whitehorse is up here," Amos told him.

"It's all right Captain Whitehorse; we were told that you would be up tonight. I'll just wait here until you are finished checking it out," He answered.

The next thirty minutes were spent in running through the checklist and flight manuals for the helicopter until Amos was certain that he would have no issues with getting it off the ground safely. He and Manny finished up and headed back to the first level entrance under the watchful eye of their guard. Once inside, they headed back to their respective rooms and a night of fitful sleep. Amos tossed and turned as his mind conjured up images of a medieval fortress complete with dungeon.

CHAPTER 29

Five o'clock came too early, but Amos worked through his morning exercises and hit the shower before dressing and heading up to the restaurant/cafeteria for breakfast. He had a seven o'clock with Jeb and then a preflight before they would make the first news run for Republic of Texas News Network, the new organization that Maggie would head up.

He was pleasantly surprised to see Maggie and Julie already in line before him in the otherwise almost empty restaurant.

"Hello ladies," Amos greeted them jovially.

"Hi Amos. Can you dial it back a bit? My head is splitting," Maggie protested.

"Mine too, but hi back," Julie said with a big grin.

"Well, I hope the headache won't keep you from flying today. I've seen the new bird, and she is a beauty!" Amos told them.

"Some greasy eggs, bacon, and coffee will fix me right up," Maggie promised, and had the server load her tray with the fore mentioned items.

"Just a little juice and dry toast for me," Julie told them.

"Well, I'm thinking steak and eggs with a big helping of fried potatoes, biscuits, and strong coffee," Amos laughed at the women's queasiness.

He led them to a seat overlooking a living mural that depicted the beach off Padre Island in the summer.

"Well Ladies, last night will go down in history as a legendary good time. What do you think?" Amos asked.

"I think that I may have had too much to drink, and possibly got a little too forward with you, Amos. I do hope that we can put that behind us," Maggie told him.

Amos looked at Julie as she gave him a hidden wink, and then reached over and patted the back of Maggie's hand, which she didn't withdraw.

"I understand how these things can happen, Maggie. Of course we can put it behind us…if you want to," He told her with a smile, "Now eat up, we've got a briefing before we can escape the bonds of earth this morning, and I for one, am anxious to get some air under me."

The rest of the breakfast was spent dancing around the events of the night before, and Amos was very careful not to mention visiting Manny Hernandez after leaving the dinner table. They instead made small talk, and then made their way down to the command center for the meeting with the President.

"Good Morning Mister President!" Amos said loudly as they were ushered into the office by one of Jeb's many armed security people.

"Good Morning, Captain Whitehorse…ladies. Have a seat please, what I have to tell you will just take a few minutes, and then you can go cover the war," Atkins replied, "First of all let me tell you how excited I am that Maggie O'Brien is going to be running the Republic of Texas News Network, and I would like for you to fly to several towns like Alpine, Marfa, Fort Stockton, and Pecos to name a few. Interview the people and get a feel for how the war and Texas Independence is affecting them. All news feeds will come back here to our studio for editing before going "live", and I'm sure that you can see the prudence in that."

Amos and Maggie exchanged discreet glances but held their opinions in. Julie also was silent as if on a hidden queue from Maggie. It was obvious after only a minute that this effort was going to be a huge propaganda machine for Texas, and any news that didn't solidify the sentiments of the people to the Republic's way of thinking would be censored. Atkins rambled on for about five more minutes before releasing them.

"Amos, can you stick around for a second, please. The ladies can find their way to the helicopter," he said.

"Certainly, Mister President. What can I do for you?" Amos answered as simply as nerves would allow.

"Did you see Sergeant Hernandez last night after your dinner?" Jeb asked coldly.

"Why yes I did. He wanted to see the new helicopter so I took him up with me. It is a really beautiful beast," Amos tried to sound nonchalant.

"I want you to stay away from Hernandez from here on. That will have to be an order, I'm afraid. My men have him under investigation for treason," Jeb stated bluntly.

"Oh my God! You have got to be kidding me. You mean that I spent time with a traitor that could have killed me last night? Why didn't you tell me yesterday?" Amos feigned surprise.

"I apologize for that, Amos. Look, we've been friends for at least fifteen years now, and I want to keep our friendship intact. Just keep away from Hernandez and report back to me if you hear anything that we can use on him," He finished.

"Absolutely, I will Jeb…absolutely I will," Amos reassured him

"Well, go give Maggie a safe ride in that new hot rod of a helicopter, and report back to me when you return," Atkins dismissed him with a wave of his hand.

Amos made his way to the garage area and found that the Twin Star had been rolled out to the landing pad just outside of the doors. He quickly made his way around the chopper doing a visual inspection before boarding and starting his pre-flight checklist.

"Why hello again ladies. Are we ready to take her for a spin?" he asked for the benefit of the security that was hovering outside of the open cabin door.

Maggie just looked at him with slightly bloodshot eyes, and Julie simply nodded, which made Amos wonder what was wrong. Well, a lot was wrong, but besides the crap in Jeb's office, something was obviously up. He reached out and closed the door with a wave to one of the skull-masked security, and started the engines whining. It would take several minutes to warm the turbines and get the bird ready for flight, so Amos just kept his silence until they could build rpms and leave the "Hive" behind them for a few hours.

Finally they were airborne, but Amos motioned them to remove the headphones before talking.

"Okay, what in the hell is going on?" he shouted.

Maggie looked back at Julie who was pointing to the pile of equipment in the back of the rear compartment.

"Your friend is hiding in the back of the helicopter!" Maggie yelled at him.

About that time, Manny Hernandez climbed out from under all of Julie's equipment and into one of the rear seats, "Amos, they were going to kill me! I had to escape, and this is the only thing that I could think of."

"Amos, what is going on?" Maggie screamed over the noise of the turbines.

"We've got to put down somewhere so Manny can get away. I'll tell you then. Put you headsets back on, and let's act normal. Be careful because I'm sure we are being monitored," Amos replied.

Julie just continued to stare at Manny with a frightened look on her face as Amos pushed the throttles up and headed the garishly painted bird to the border town of Presidio at one hundred and twenty miles an hour.

"Well, ladies," Amos spoke over the intercom, "we will make our first stop in Presidio down on the border, and then hop up to Alpine. If Julie can shoot some pictures 'outside' of the chopper while we are making our landing approach, it might give the viewers a feel for this kind of reporting."

"I think that President Atkins will be happy with the small town approach to this report. We'll try it just as you've suggested, Captain," Maggie said for effect.

Julie just stuck her tongue out and kept her eyes on Manny while she prepped her equipment.

Amos kept the chopper down low and below radar as he maneuvered through the hills and mountains of the border area until they reached Presidio. He then made a beeline for O'Reilly Street and a few of the more popular stores where he hoped for a crowd to hide Manny in.

"News One, where are you planning on landing?" came a voice in his headset.

"Shadow One, I've got a vacant lot down here in the shopping district that we can fit in. Why don't you wait for us at the airport up on sixty seven, over?" Amos replied.

"News One, my orders are not to let you out of my sight, over."

"Well, hover up there if you want, we'll only be a couple of hours, over and out," Amos cut the switch.

He headed the chopper for the vacant lot across from a Family Dollar store and signaled Julie to start the camera rolling. The big chopper settled in the slot with little room to spare, and certainly not enough room for the others that Amos forgot would be following them. He exited the aircraft and walked around to Julie's side with his fingers on his lips. Their shadow buzzed by overhead and was out of sight behind the skyline of the building, but he knew they would be back in a matter of seconds.

"Manny, get out and make a run for that parts store, pronto!" he ordered.

Manny hit the ground at a dead run and disappeared through the front door of the auto parts building just as Shadow One came buzzing back over the roof tops. Amos gave them a big wave and signaled Maggie to get out of the bird, and for Julie to film her doing so. Everything fell into place after that, and Maggie spent the next hour walking from one store to the next talking to the shoppers. Amos stayed with the chopper and made sure it would be ready for the run to Alpine and their next stop.

"Shadow One this is News One, over," Amos called when they were back aboard.

"Go ahead News One."

"We are headed for Alpine, over," Amos reported. As he throttled the turbines up and eased out of the vacant lot.

"Roger News One, we are right behind you, over."

"Figured you would be," Amos switched the headset to intercom only,

"Next stop Alpine, Maggie. Not much there, but the folks are friendly. I'm thinking that the University would be a good place, plus there are a couple of good restaurants nearby. You do have an expense account don't you?"

"We need to talk, Amos!" Maggie gave him the 'look'.

"Wait until we are out of the chopper," Amos replied, "We'll be setting down at the Alpine-Casparis Airport just a little ways form Sul-Ross University. There is some outstanding scenery that we will be passing over if Julie wants to include that in the story."

The flight to Alpine took just a little over an hour with the turbines screaming and the security team having trouble keeping up. Amos just gave a grin every time the pilot complained about his airspeed, but he didn't respond. As they approached the town of Alpine on the east end, Amos noticed the long line of rail cars that were sitting on the track just out of town.

He made a little turn toward them, and the radio crackled, "News One, do not change course. That area is off limits, over."

"Nonsense Shadow One, we are a news chopper. Nothing is off limits, just censorable, over," Amos replied.

He swung the chopper sharply in the direction of the train, and what looked to be a tent city directly south of it.

"Start the film rolling Julie. Maggie, are you seeing this?" Amos shouted and pointed.

"Get us down there, Amos. You fly for me not those security bozos!" Maggie exclaimed.

"Yes, Ma'am, Boss!" Amos replied and headed for the train.

"News One, you are not to land here. That is an order!"

"Shadow One, you are breaking up, over," Amos switched off the radio.

He made one lap of the train, and Maggie got a good look at the gallows that had been erected out of sight of the main highway. Julie was busy filming, and it hadn't sunk in exactly what they were seeing. Amos start to set down, but suddenly found the security chopper directly in his way with guns pointed directly at them. He made an evasive move with a hard bank to the right, and then dropped the AS355 directly to the ground, pulling up at the last second for a rough, but safe landing. Maggie and Julie beat him from the aircraft and started filming the scene before them as the other chopper tried to raise a dust storm to throw them off.

Suddenly, right in front of them, as if materializing out of the dust, stood three men in Texas Guard Camouflage. The leader of the group took one look at Maggie, and then up at the security force that was descending on them. He raised his hand toward the chopper, and the men with him directed a deadly volley of fire at the pilot, and those that were visible in the side door. The aircraft pitched forward and spun out of control as the dead pilot slumped over the controls. In a matter of seconds, it had crashed nose first two hundred yards from the news chopper in a ball of fire.

Maggie didn't turn at the sound of the explosion; instead, she seemed mesmerized by the figure that was approaching her at a run. Her hand went to her mouth in shock as she realized who they were.

"Daddy? Daddy is that you?" she cried out and ran toward him.

"Hey Maggie, are you all right?" Shaun asked as he wrapped his arms around his baby girl.

I'm fine, but you have got a lot of explaining to do, starting with why you are here," Maggie sobbed.

"Ever the news woman aren't you, Maggie? Well, this is a story that you will have to wait for. We are still trying to unravel the pieces, and we missed a big one here. They executed the prisoners before we could question them and buried them out there," O'Brien pointed to the south.

Maggie wiped her eyes and looked around, "Michael Tucker? Oh my God, you're alive too? Is Hanna with you?"

"No Maggie, They are at home for safe keeping. It's just me this time. I'm sorry that we had to leave that way, but the situation was not resolvable otherwise," Tuck answered as he walked over and got a hug from an old friend.

"Hey, I hate to interrupt this party, but you guys shot down a security team belonging to the President of the Republic of Texas. I think he is going to be a little upset at that, don't you?" Amos spoke up.

"And you would be?" Shaun asked.

"He's Captain Amos Whitehorse, my pilot," Maggie told him with a smile.

"Whitehorse? I've heard of you. You were a hot shot fighter jock before your wife died, and the bottle took over, weren't you?' he asked.

Amos looked at him in amazement, "How did you know that? I haven't told anyone except Jeb Atkins about my past in fifteen years."

"Daddy is what they call a 'spook', Amos. He knows a lot of things that he shouldn't," Maggie shot her father the 'look'.

"All right, enough pleasantries. What was the radio frequency that you were operating on, Captain?" O'Brien asked, and what was their call sign?"

"They were Shadow One, and our frequency was 123.0250, standard helicopter. Why?' Amos asked.

"Come over to our vehicles," Shaun told them, "McFadden, can you mimic a distress call from the bird so that it will sound like they crashed due to engine failure?"

"Absolutely, sir. I just need the frequency and the call sign. The letters are burnt beyond recognition though," Terry answered.

"Just use Shadow One and 123.050. They'll think that there was no time to switch to an emergency frequency. Amos, I need you to fire the news chopper up and get this crew in the air. We'll make the call from them to you that they are going in hard. You will fly back here and report as if this was a real crash, and that you all were surprised by it. Understood?" O'Brien told them.

Tuck came up as he finished, "Shaun, one of those men got thrown out during impact and is dead on the other side of that bird. He's a Russian, by the look of his face and tattoos, Spetznaz most likely."

"Well, this is what we are getting paid for. Little did I know that my daughter would provide us with the key to solving the case," O'Brien replied, "Get going. Fly to the airport and signal us with a double click on the mike key when you get there. Remember that these men were your friends, and you are rushing back here to help. Can you do this?"

"Piece of cake!" Amos replied and headed for the news chopper.

"I'll see you at the college after you report this, Maggie. We'll meet in the museum," Shaun gave her another hug and walked off.

"Come on Julie, we've got work to do!" Maggie called as she got back in the chopper.

The plan went off without a hitch, and within thirty minutes, Amos was calling in a May Day for a downed aircraft. He followed that with a transmission by secure channel to Jeb's direct line and told him what had happened.

"We lost sight of them when they made a turn towards a group of rail cars east of Alpine, Sir. I got a call that they had engine failure as we were landing at the Alpine airport so we hurried back over, but there were no survivors," Amos told him.

"Have you got the film?" Jeb asked.

"Julie was shooting the approach to the airport for the story when we got the call. I told her to keep recording, so there is a record," He replied.

"Very good, Amos. Bring the ladies back and well regroup tomorrow," Jeb told him.

"Sir, if I might. They are having a very difficult time of this. I'd like permission to stay here tonight, and come in tomorrow. We can still finish the report with a stop in Marathon on the way back," Amos told him.

"Very well, but I need you to stay close to the wreckage as my liaison until we get some guard troops in there to clean it up . I most expressly do not want the local authorities to get their hands on those bodies. Is that understood?" His tone was brusque.

"Absolutely, Sir. I'll stand by here and redirect any local inquiries straight to your aides," Amos answered while breathing a sigh of relief.

"Very good Amos. I can always count on you to come through in a pinch, can't I?" Atkins told him.

"Yes, Sir, you can. I'll see you tomorrow afternoon with the crew," Amos replied, but the line had already gone dead.

Two hours later, the cleanup crew had secured the crash site, but not before Tuck had stripped the body that was not burned for any identifying items, including pictures of his tattoos. Amos flew Maggie and Julie back to the airport and secured the news chopper before ordering a taxi to take them to the museum at Sol-Ross University for a meeting with her father. Amos filled them in with as much as Manny had told him the night before, including the prison that they had found. When they met with Shaun and Tuck, Maggie relayed that information to them.

"I wish that you didn't have to go back down there, Maggie, but if we are going to stop this transition of Texas back to Mexico, President Atkins must be kept unaware of our suspicions," Shaun told her, "Amos, I'm relying on you to protect Maggie and Julie, and to get them out safely when the time comes. Can you do that for me? We are also going to have to get into that prison. Can you guide us back through the mine to the false door? You wouldn't have to go in."

"I can do all of that Mr. O'Brien, especially taking care of Maggie," Amos responded enthusiastically.

"There's no need to suck up to me, Amos. Maggie makes all of her own decisions where men are concerned, and I haven't agreed with any of them up to this point. You might just surprise me, and call me Shaun," Shaun told him.

Maggie kept quiet as her father spoke but didn't take her eyes off Amos, as if looking for a response.

Amos chewed on that for a minute before speaking, "Shaun, there is a man that can be an asset to the operation. We smuggled him out this morning and dropped him in Presidio. His name is Manny Hernandez, and up to yesterday was a Texas Guard Sergeant that had security clearances for all of the areas of the 'Hive' as they call it."

"My men and I will leave immediately for Presidio. If he is there, we'll find him. You find a place to stay here, and work a normal routine tomorrow, especially after you get back in Atkins' presence. We'll get word in when we are ready to move. Remember, we have until Texas is recognized as a sovereign nation before our time runs out, so plan accordingly," Shaun told them.

Maggie gave him a hug, "Stay safe, Daddy. I want to spend some time with you after this is over."

"We will, I promise. Now we have to get moving before one of Atkins' men sees us together," He replied.

Shaun O'Brien and Michael Tucker left the museum separately and met Terry McFadden in the parking lot where he was standing next to a new Plum Crazy Purple Dodge Challenger with a 392 hemi and heavy suspension.

"I thought we decided on something low key?" Tuck said.

"I thought you would like something a little faster than the Hummer for this trip, sir," He said with a grin, "This is the only color that they had in that dealership."

"Just don't get us killed along the way, McFadden. There will be opportunity for that later," O'Brien told him as he let Tuck in the back seat and took the shotgun position, "Weapons?"

"In the trunk, sir. Also under your seat both in the front and back," Terry replied.

"Let's get the show on the road then," O'Brien said as he buckled his seat belt.

The hemi fired up with a growl, and Terry eased slowly out of the college parking lot. His driving skills were the reason that he was on the team, and now he was going to earn his pay.

After Julie and Maggie shot some footage with people in the museum and around the college for about an hour after her father left, Amos called for a taxi to take them to the Hampton Inn on the far end of town. He figured that there was less chance of an encounter with any of the Texas Guard down there that might have questions about the accident. Once they checked in and Maggie signed autographs for the staff that recognized her, they went back into town to find some food, since they hadn't eaten since early morning. The cabby suggested Los Jalapenos Café for some Mexican food and beer. Julie took one look at the seedy outside and decided to wait in the cab.

"Believe me, Senorita, the food is good, and in the fall when the weather is cold like it is, there are no flies to worry about," The cabby told her with a grin.

"Okay, I'm coming with you guys, but I don't have to eat," She replied.

Once inside with the delicious smells coming from the kitchen assailing her nostrils, she and Maggie ordered the chicken mole and a round of Corona beer and limes. Amos stuck with sweet tea and a hamburger with everything on it, including jalapenos.

"Amos, does it bother you that we are drinking in front of you?" Maggie asked.

"Why no, I drank enough to float a battleship after my wife died. Your father had some good intel on that. My drinking ruined my Navy career, and I was washed out and washed up. Jeb Atkins found me flying a cargo helicopter in Kuwait for a bunch of mercenaries out of South Carolina. We hit it off and became friends. Not long afterward, I realized how much I was drinking and decided to stop, which I did with a lot of encouragement from Jeb. Things got better for me after I came home to Texas. I was hired to pilot oil field engineers for a large outfit out of Houston, ran into Jeb again when he ran for office, and the rest is history…as they say," He told them.

"How long were you married, Amos?" Julie asked.

"Three years. She was killed in a car accident while I was stationed on a carrier in the Mediterranean back in 1998. We didn't have any kids, and her parents didn't like the idea of their only child married to a fighter jock. I haven't seen them since the funeral. Hey, listen to me talk. How about some background on you, Miss Julie?" he asked with a grin.

"Not much to tell really, I'm from New York City, went to school at Fredonia State, and have been a camera woman for the last five years, mostly following Maggie around. We met while I was vacationing in Myrtle Beach, and, like you said, 'the rest is history'," She replied smiling.

"Julie is being modest, Amos. She has a gift for finding the right angle to shoot a story from," Maggie told him.

"What about you, Maggie? We all know the Maggie O'Brien that charms her viewers on the Vanguard program every night, but what else is there to know?" Amos asked.

"Well, a girl has to have some mystique surrounding her, but I will tell you a little bit about me. I was raised mostly by my mother since dear old dad was busy with his CIA job most of my developmental years. We did have some great times when he was around though. He taught me how to hunt and fish, ride a horse, which most of my friends just think they know how to do, and he taught me to be wary of entanglements that might seem good at first, but are harmful in the long run. I've only had a couple of serious relationships, but always nagging me was the question, 'what would Daddy think of this one?', and most of the time it ends right there. I suppose that I want what every girl wants, a knight in shining armor, a home to come back to, kids, and maybe a little church close by that we would visit. We used to go when I was little, but not so much since I was a teen. Well, Amos, that's all you get with one beer," Maggie said with a laugh.

The food arrived before Amos could respond, and the next half of an hour was spent eating. One thing that he noticed was that Maggie switched to sweet tea after one beer, and that brought a smile to his face. Later that evening, he and Maggie sat by the fireplace in the lobby of the Hampton while Julie stayed in the room that she and Maggie shared, fiddling with her camera gear. They talked about small things mostly; very careful to not say anything that could be recorded and used against them. When they went to their separate rooms a little after midnight, both of them knew in their hearts that they were going to be together for a good while…if they survived the next few days.

CHAPTER 30

At exactly fourteen hundred hours, General Leslie Hamms sat at his desk and waited while the others sent the envelopes by way of their aides that contained the information that he had ordered. He had always been a man of action, and firmly believed the oath that he and his men had taken to defend the Constitution of the United States against all enemies foreign and domestic, was not something to be taken lightly. Now he was faced with a monumental decision that could not only end his career, but most probably would cost him his life. He picked up the phone and rang the Commandant of the Marine Corps, four star General Murray Slokum.

"Plan Charlie Hotel is a go for sixteen hundred hours," He spoke cryptically and hung up the phone.

Now the waiting started, which was always the worst part of any exercise. In the back of Hamms' mind was the nagging question about how the American people would respond to the action that was about to be taken. Well, it was decided, and he would have to bear the brunt of the criticism after it was over. Now to brief the President on the action that his advisor had ordered. Hamms made his way to the Oval Office and waited to be called in with ten other officers and dignitaries.

Outside of the White House and well back into the common areas of the Capitol grounds, over a half of a million people had gathered since daybreak in the freezing cold and blustery weather. Except for the sound of thousands singing the 'Battle Hymn of the Republic', the large throng was orderly. Vanguard news was broadcasting pictures of tens of thousands still on their way into the city, and the traffic jam on the Interstate exceeding fifty miles in length. The other news agencies were playing down the participation in the protest by showing close ups of small groups and under reporting the overall size of the crowd. Much less coverage was given on the huge number that were on their way in and being helped by the Virginia Highway Patrol and the local DC Police departments, including the Park Police who either joined the protest or simply walked off the job.

In the Oval Office President Onbekend glared at the protestors lining the fence and growled at his Secret Service head Arnold Chase "Why hasn't this crowd been dispersed? I specifically ordered you to handle this mob earlier in the day. I want to know why you've refused that order."

Since the snowfall and wind gusts had grounded the flight of Marine One and showed no sign of letting up, the President had been in a very foul mood.

"Sir, the crowd is just too large to control without military assistance. Since they are not violent, we just thought it better to let them congregate," Chase replied nervously.

"Consider yourself relieved from your position immediately. I'll handle this myself," The President ordered.

"Gladly, Sir," and Arnold left the room.

"Get me General Hamms immediately!" he barked an order into the phone.

The door to the Oval office opened almost instantly, and the general was ushered into the room where he stood at attention in the front of the Resolute desk.

"General Hamms, how many Marines can you muster in the next hour?" the President asked.

"At least two hundred, maybe more. I would have to ask the Commandant for an exact number sir. May I ask why?" Hamms replied.

"I want those demonstrators dispersed, and I want it done as soon as you can get the manpower to do it. Bring in Army troops if need be, but clean Washington of these trouble makers, and clean it tonight. Is that understood?" President Onbekend shouted in his frustration.

"I'll take care of it immediately sir!" Hamms replied.

If there was ever any doubt in his heart about God's ability to bring a plan together, those doubts had all fled by the time he closed the door behind him. His next call was to Commandant Slokum.

"Murray, there has been a change in plans. The President has ordered me to have all available personnel mustered at the White House within the hour to chase off those demonstrators. Can you believe it?" Hamms shared the news excitedly.

"This is probably going to be the most unbelievable part of this night's activities, Les. I'll have all available personnel in their combat gear at the White House in less than an hour. Is there anything else that you need?" Slokum asked.

"Come to think of it, how about bringing the Marine Corps Band with you. I have a special project in mind for them," Hamms replied.

"Consider it done, and may the Almighty help us tonight."

"Amen, Murray, amen!" Hamms replied.

Now for the next step in the plan, and that was to call an emergency meeting of the Joint Chiefs and the President's cabinet in the war room. General Hamms called his aides together and had them start spreading the word, beginning with Durrah Jowles.

At exactly fifteen thirty hours, Hamms stood to address the Joint Chiefs, Durrah Jowles, and the various cabinet members that had been in the White House area when the meeting was announced.

"I have called for this emergency session of the Joint Chiefs and our distinguished cabinet members because it is important for you all to be here when the plan that was outlined yesterday in regard to using tactical weaponry on Texas citizenry is discussed. This afternoon at approximately fourteen hundred hours, the President of the United States ordered me to take military action on the protestors that have been gathering in Washington, DC since early this morning. I would like at this time for the television screens to be turned on and Vanguard News selected so that we can witness the response to that order," General Hamms addressed the group.

The televisions were now showing the demonstrators moving back away from the fence in response to over two hundred Marines dressed in battle gear and carrying their rifles, moving between the crowd and the fence.

"Keep your eyes fixed on the crowd, folks. This is going to get interesting," Hamms told them.

Inside of the fence, there moved another group of Marines, this time in dress blues and winter wear carrying an array of musical instruments. As soon as they were positioned facing the crowd, the armed troops were marched double time to the front of the White House entrance, and the band struck up 'the Battle Hymn of the Republic' to which the crowd first started cheering, and then started to sing along.

Commandant Slokum excused himself from the room and went to meet his Marines at the front door where they were being blocked by a detachment of Secret Service.

"You men need to surrender your weapons and stand down. These Marines are here at my behest," Slokum told the agents.

The Captain in charge of the Marine detachment ordered his men to lock and load. The sound of the bolts of two hundred rifles being worked, made the Secret Servicemen toss their firearms to the floor of the entry way and stand back as the Marines entered the building at a run.

As they came past the security station which was now unmanned, they broke off into groups of fifty, one group tasked with arresting the President, one with arresting the cabinet, and two groups that would head to the rotunda to seize control of the Congress and Senate as soon as the White House was under military control.

Back in the War Room, Durrah Jowles was on her feet screaming obscenities at General Hamms and demanding that she be allowed to leave the room.

"I'm sorry, but that is not going to be possible for a little while. In the meantime, I want all cell phones tossed on the top of the table in the front of you, and I mean all!" he replied.

The sound of many boots running in cadence echoed down the hallway, getting louder with each second. Hamms went to the door and ordered the Secret Service agents outside to place their weapons on the floor and step back. One of his aides gathered the weaponry and moved them out of the reach of anyone that might be foolish enough to take on the Marine Corps.

The young captain came at a run with his men and ordered them to halt right in the front of General Hamms.

"Captain Evers, Sir. What are our orders?" he saluted crisply.

Hamms returned the salute and replied. "Arrest everyone in this room and secure the room. Post a dozen men on both sides of these doors. Shoot anyone who resists. Is that clear?"

"Perfectly Sir!" Captain Evers shouted and turned to direct his men.

"By the way, Captain, where is Commandant Slokum?" Hamms asked.

"He's with the President Sir!" Evers answered with another shout.

Hamms turned to the dumbfounded Secret Service agents, "You men and women are relieved of duty. Please leave the premises immediately!"

They all nodded in the affirmative and hustled down the hallways leading to the exit with a good deal of relief showing on their faces.

Hamms' phone rang, "Les, we've wrapped up the action in the Oval Office, what do you want to do with the President?" Slokum asked.

"Take him to his quarters and place the entire family under house arrest. The charge is treason and collusion with the enemy. We'll let the lawyers gin that up, as they will. Post a guard on all exits. No one enters or leaves without yours or my express permission. Have you sent the troops to the Rotunda yet?" Hamms asked.

"We should have word from there in about twenty minutes. I had to call in some favors, but we had a company of Army Rangers in the area, and they are conducting the preliminaries over there. I don't expect any trouble that they can't handle," Slokum responded.

"Very good, Murray. I'm going to call Vanguard News and a few others to give them a heads up. As of right now the war is over!"

Amos was up early the next morning and saw that the number of people in the hotel lobby was significantly more than what they had expected when he, Maggie, and Julie had checked in the night before. Somebody had leaked word that Maggie was here, and it looked like half the town had turned out for an autograph. Amos went to the desk, and settled their bill before using the house phone to call Maggie's room.

"Good morning, Maggie. How close are you to being ready to leave?" he asked.

"We were just coming down to breakfast, Amos, why?" she answered.

I'm calling for a taxi to meet us around the end of the building away from the highway. You've got a lobby full of autograph seekers down here, and I'm sure that at least two of Jeb's men are in the mix," Amos told her.

"Call as soon as the cab is here, and we'll meet you outside," Maggie told him.

Amos called the taxi and waited in the lobby for it to come into the parking lot. As soon as he saw it on the road, he called Maggie.

"Aren't you Maggie O'Brien's pilot?" someone called out from the crush in the lobby area.

"Yes. I am, but I have to check on our helicopter and then come back for Miss O'Brien. She'll be down for breakfast in about ten minutes," He called as he slipped outside.

The taxi was just pulling in the parking lot, and he flagged it before it could get to the front door.

"Drive around the other end and pick my friends up down there," he directed.

The cab had no sooner pulled up to the end of the building than Maggie and Julie ran out of the end door and jumped into the back.

"Let's get out of here! There's and extra twenty in it if you beat everyone else to the airport," Amos told him.

"Yes, sir. Have the ladies slump down, and they'll think you're alone in here," the cabbie told them.

They drove out of the parking lot and headed toward downtown Alpine with no one in pursuit. At least their luck was holding so far. Amos just hoped that they could get the chopper prepped and airborne before Maggie's admirers learned of her escape. Except for the surprise of the morning, everything else went smoothly with no interruptions as Amos got his preflight finished and the helicopter engines started. As soon as they could, he radioed the tower and announced his departure and flight plans for the day. It wasn't until he was airborne that Maggie looked down and saw a group of military vehicles coming directly to the paddock where the chopper had been parked overnight.

"Something's up, Maggie. We just have to keep with the day's schedule and act natural when we face Jeb this afternoon. I think that we'll have a little change of plans about where we are going to stop next. What do you think?" Amos told her.

"Well, we seem to be under suspicion anyway. I'd just as soon get some sightseeing in. Where do you want to go?" She asked

"I think that Julie would get a kick out of Marfa. It's an artsy community in exactly the opposite direction from where we are supposed to be heading. We can spend an hour or so there for the film, and then head straight back down to the border around Big Bend Ranch. If what we have heard is true, I would expect to see evidence of Mexican forces gathering along the southern edge of the Chisos mountains below the 'Hive'," He told them.

"You're driving, Amos. Let's go see Marfa!" Maggie laughed. Julie just rolled her eyes.

Marfa was an eye opener for Julie. Seeing the old Volvo drivers and hippie types walking the streets of the city showed her just how out of touch with reality people could get when they restricted their ability for reasonable thought and discussion. Out of the dozen or so people that they questioned about Texas independence and statehood, hardly any had a clear knowledge of what it meant, or they espoused ideologies that were even more left wing than most of the left wing that she had met in Washington, DC. They agreed to wrap up the interviews quickly and fly down along the border for a late afternoon arrival at the 'Hive' and the meeting with President Jebediah Atkins.

"I had a Border Patrol officer tell me that they wished they could build a fence around Marfa," Amos told them with a laugh after they were airborne again.

"I can see the point after being there," Julie replied, "Texas certainly doesn't seem like the anything goes, wide open conservative stronghold that I always envisioned."

"It's not, but it is big enough that you can certainly separate yourself from the foolish when the urge arises," Amos told her.

They flew in silence until they could make out the Rio Grande River in the distance.

"We'll pick up the river close to a little village called Castolon, and then follow the border for about thirty miles before turning up toward the 'Hive'. Julie, can you shoot footage of this part of the river on a different memory card or something in case there is anything down there that we shouldn't know about?" Amos asked.

"Sure, just give me a few seconds to set it up, and I'll make you a personal copy," She replied.

Maggie turned to him and asked, "Is this going to be dangerous, Amos? I mean, we are in a brightly painted helicopter. It's not like we are going to be able to hide."

"Well, I haven't been officially told to stay away from the border, so let's give it a shot. If we draw fire, I'll skedaddle out of there," He replied.

They passed over Castolon and Amos pulled the throttles back until their airspeed was about one hundred knots. He stayed on the Texas side of the border with just enough elevation that they could see into Mexico. It didn't take long to find what they suspected would be there. In one area where an old road crossed the river, hundreds of vehicles with the markings of the Mexican Army and several hundred Mexican troops were camped. Other than a wave from some of the men, nothing adverse happened when the brightly painted news chopper flew past. Amos sped up and gained some altitude to get them over the canyon country, and their view into Mexico improved by several miles. It looked as if the entire Mexican Army was in position to invade Texas, but they were just sitting idle.

"It looks like Manny was right after all," Maggie said, "President Atkins has sold out the people of Texas."

"Not only them, but New Mexico, Colorado, Oklahoma, and Wyoming. They were all part of the original parcel that Mexico lost to Texas in 1836 under the Treaties of Velasco. Now it looks like they are going to take it back," Amos replied, "Let's get back to the Hive and see what all of the fuss about us leaving Alpine was about."

When they landed outside of the 'Hive' entrance, the chopper was surrounded with Jebediah Atkins' security troops, and right in the middle was the President of the Texas Republic himself.

"Where have you been?" he almost screamed at Amos when they got out.

"Filming the documentary that you sent us out to do, sir," Amos tried his best to look puzzled, "What is going on?"

"The war is over! There has been a military coup in Washington, and President Onbekend is under house arrest!" Jeb exclaimed, "Hurry up. There is no time to lose if we are going to make an announcement from our news group."

Amos shot Maggie a look as they followed Jeb back into the command center under the watchful eyes of the security team. Maggie and Julie were hustled into the newsroom, but Jeb motioned for Amos to follow him to the office.

"Sir, when did all of this happen, and what does it mean for Texas?" Amos asked as soon as the door closed behind them.

"Well, it started a couple of hours ago, but the announcement wasn't made public until about five pm our time, so six o'clock back there. We will need to make sure that there will be no more attacks directed at us, but I suspect the Muslims within our borders will still be waging jihad until they are wiped out. I'm going to be very busy for the next couple of days negotiating with Washington, and whoever is in power. We need our nation status recognized as soon as possible," Jeb told him, "By the way, Amos did anything unusual happen when you picked up Maggie in Cozumel?"

"I don't know about unusual, but someone tried to keep her from leaving there. That security team that you flew in with us saved the day though," Amos answered.

"Security team?" Jeb just looked across the desk for a second, "What are you talking about? That was just a ruse to flush a spy inside of our group."

Amos realized that he had put his foot directly into his big mouth but the cat was already out of the bag, so to speak, "Those spec ops guys that work for Shaun O'Brien, Maggie's father."

Jeb's complexion turned pale, and it looked like he threw up in his mouth. He just sat there staring at Amos, swallowing hard to recover his composure.

"How did Maggie react to her father being on the plane?" he finally asked.

"Well, she and Julie had bags over their heads for the entire flight, so she never found out," Amos lied.

"Where did you drop them off?" Jeb asked with a shaking voice.

"We dropped them near the Texas Guard compound where Maggie imbedded with Captain Luke Moffett. I don't know where they went after that," Amos lied again.

"I see. Well, stay close to the base for the next couple of days and rest up. I'll probably have to fly out of here for meetings, so keep your schedule open," Jeb dismissed him.

"What about flying Maggie around?" Amos asked as he stood to leave.

"She is no longer your concern," Jeb replied in a brusque tone that made it an order.

Amos was stunned as he suddenly realized that he had put Maggie and Julie in grave danger by mentioning the presence of her father to Jeb. Instead of replying, he just nodded in the affirmative and left the room flanked by two of Jeb's handpicked security. When he got to the elevator, they got on with him.

"You guys going up?" he quipped.

"Our orders are to escort you to your room, Captain," Was the reply from the largest of the two, "The President wants you to have around the clock protection, so when you leave the room, we will go everywhere with you."

"That's great, guys, that…is…great. I feel much better just knowing that you two have got my back," Amos said with a straight face.

CHAPTER 31

"Captain Luke, Colonel Jenkins is on the radio. He says it's urgent," Luis ran to the mess tent to convey the message to Luke.

"I'm on the way, Luis. Did he say what it's about?" Luke asked as they jogged back to the Hummer that had the radio onboard.

"No, just that he needed to talk right away," Luis answered.

Luke reached into the vehicle and got the mike, "Go ahead for Captain Moffett."

"Luke, Jenkins here. The war is over! I repeat the war is over!" Nathan Jenkins shouted into the radio.

"Are you sure, Colonel? I mean, it's been such a short one," Luke was dumb founded.

"It's over Luke. I want you to spread the word to the men. I've got choppers coming in the morning to pick up my soldiers and trailers to pick up your horses. You're coming home!" Jenkins replied.

"What about Texas, sir. Are we a state?" Luke asked.

"We haven't heard anything about that yet. All I know is that the order has been given to stand down and disband," He replied.

"Copy that, sir. I'll pass the word and get the men ready," Luke hung up the mike, "Well Luis, assemble the men in the mess tent. Let's give them the good news."

"We made it, Luke. It's a shame that John isn't here though," Luis answered.

"Yep, I'm going to miss him, but someday we'll see John Post again," Luke agreed.

The next two hours were like a huge camp meeting as the old timers mixed with the youngsters and sang, danced, and joked as the stress of war melted off them. Luke finally broke up the group at eight that evening and ordered them to pack up and get ready to leave in the morning. Rodriguez came to Luke's table where he sat drinking a last cup of coffee after the mess tent cleared out.

"Captain Moffett, can I have a minute of your time?" he asked.

"Sure, Rodriguez, Have a seat," Luke answered motioning to a chair, "What is it?"

"You know when Leonard and I were with the Governor in the desert?" Rodriguez started, "I still have that pack that we were carrying with the grenades and all. I also have the governor's cell phone that he dropped during one of our encounters with the enemy. I meant to get it back to him, but completely forgot until I found it again this morning. Can you turn it in for me?"

Luke looked at him and replied, "I guess that I can do that as long as I get the grenades too."

"They're just outside. I'll go get them for you," Rodriguez answered and ducked out of the tent to retrieve the items, "I felt bad about the phone, but I didn't want anybody to think that I stole it."

"Nobody will, I promise," Luke answered, "President Atkins will probably give you a commendation for retrieving it. Now go get some sleep. You men have busy day tomorrow."

"Yes, sir," He answered and left Luke sitting alone in the mess tent.

Luke placed the two grenades on the table in front of him and then picked up the phone. He turned it over a couple of times in his hand before deciding, "What the hell," and turned the phone on. There was enough battery to power the thing up, so he waited until all of the notifications were finished before pressing the text message retrieval app. Luke stared at the last message for several long minutes before turning the phone off and leaving the tent. He needed some air to clear his head, and he needed to talk to the Geezer patrol in private.

Charlie and Jasper were coming around one of the common fires that the men kept burning outside of their tents when Luke asked them to muster just the original patrol and Rodriguez in the mess tent. He then walked to the HumVee and made a call to Colonel Jenkins on the radio.

"Jenkins here Luke, go ahead," He answered.

"Colonel, can we go to a secure channel?" Luke responded.

"Sure," Jenkins sounded puzzled, "head up two."

Luke turned the selector to the new settings and waited to see if the channel was clear.

"Captain Moffett for Colonel Jenkins, over," He called.

"Go ahead Luke. I think we are alone here. What's going on?" came the response.

"Sir, I've just been handed a cell phone that President Atkins lost during the first couple of days of the war. I think that you need to come to camp with the equipment tomorrow," Luke told him.

"Luke, we are really busy up here trying to get all of the paperwork and stuff organized. Is this that important?" he asked.

"Life and death, sir," Was all Luke would tell him.

"I'll be there at first light," Jenkins ended the transmission.

Luke headed for the mess tent to address the patrol. When he walked through the entry, a hush fell over the men who were all intrigued by this second meeting of the night.

"Men," Luke cleared his throat, "I've come into some information that might be of interest to you all, so I am just going to lay it out for you to chew on. President Atkins is in cahoots with Mexico's President Fuentes to give the Republic of Texas back to Mexico once we have sovereignty."

The uproar in the tent was deafening for at least five minutes after Luke made the announcement.

"Quiet down, fellas, I feel the same way as ya'll. If we go home now, we are going to become Mexican citizens as soon as the announcement is made. I'm for heading south and seeing if there is anything that a bunch of Geezers can do to slow this thing down a bit. Is anybody with me?" Luke asked.

The uproar was deafening again so Luke let them vent for a few more minutes.

"Okay men, In the morning, have your mounts saddled, and we'll trailer down to Terlingua. I've got a feeling that we'll meet some friends down there that might be able to help. Sergeants Gonzales and Rodriguez, if you will stay behind, I might need your help," Luke dismissed them and returned to the HumVee and the radio.

"Luis, do you have any way to reach O'Brien and his men? I know they had a radio in one of those Hummers that we gave them," Luke asked.

"I think I might have an idea, I 'accidentally' overheard one of them calling another station. Their call sign was 'Dark Knight Two'," Luis responded.

"Perfect, Luis, see if you can raise them on that call sign. If you do, tell them only that we are having a Geezer reunion in Terlingua tomorrow to celebrate the end of the war. Oh, and tell them to dress appropriately," Luis finished.

"Yes, Sir Luke," Luis turned and started calling.

"Sergeant Rodriguez, I'd like to borrow that McMillan that you've got in your tent. I promise that you'll get it back if we make it," Luke told him.

"Sir, if it's all the same to you, I'd like to tag along with you old farts…you know, just to make sure that you don't damage my rifle. Besides, Leonard is down there, and he is kind of like family to me,"

Luke laughed, "Done! Find us enough ammo and supplies for a couple of days out, and see if there might be a heavy machine gun that we can borrow from one of those young fellas."

"Yes, sir!" Rodriguez replied excitedly and left.

Now there was nothing left for Luke to do but to go back to his tent and pray.

Charlie and Jasper had coffee and breakfast ready at five am when Luke came into the mess tent. He was surprised to see all of the patrol already sitting down.

"Good morning, Captain Luke!" Luis greeted him, "None of us could sleep after last night, so we decided to get an early start."

"Where are all of the youngsters?" Luke asked.

"Still in their sacks, I suppose. You know how kids are," Luis replied.

Luke greeted each man in turn with a wave or a handshake, and then made his way to the coffee, and a big portion of beef and potatoes the boys had fried up.

"I'm not going to miss much about this war, except the food, fellas," He told them, "Maybe you can open a little place back home and give the Wagon Wheel a little competition when we get back."

"We enjoy meeting over there too much to do that Luke, but we sure appreciate the complement," Jasper told him.

The atmosphere in the tent was charged with excitement as the men talked in hushed tones between themselves. Luke finished eating, and was into this third warm up on coffee when he heard the sound of a helicopters reverberating off the walls of the butte.

"Time to go men," He called and strode out into the brisk December air.

Two Chinook helicopters sat down below the camp followed closely by two Apaches that made a wide circle, and then laded behind the Chinooks. Luke saw a big man jump from the first chopper and knew that Colonel Nathan Jenkins had arrived. Just as he was getting ready to run to the HumVee, Rodriguez pulled it up beside him, and they bounced down the hill to welcome the Colonel who was jogging up the road that led to the camp. As soon as they picked him up, Luke handed him the cell phone that had belonged to President Atkins. Jenkins turned it on and read the last text message that Atkins had received from President Fuentes of Mexico.

It said simply, "Viva la revolucion! Viva Atzlan!"

Jenkins just stared at the phone for several minutes in silence, "Luke, it looks like you have stumbled on something that might save Texas."

"Well, Sergeant Rodriguez deserves all of the credit for the find. I just called it in. Since we are no longer at war, my men and I are going down to Terlingua for a sort of reunion. We sure could use those transport trailers to shorten the trip," Luke said.

"Certainly, I brought them out here to get you men home, but if you are headed for the border, so be it. I'm going to step outside and make a quick call to Andy Clarke and kind of feel him out on this," Jenkins told them.

"Andy?" Rodriguez asked and raised his eyebrows after Jenkins have gotten out.

Luke laughed. "General Clarke is his brother-in-law."

Both men had a chuckle over that revelation and waited for the next fifteen minutes while Colonel Jenkins conversed with the highest-ranking soldier in the Texas Guard. The door to the hummer finally opened and the colonel stood outside while he gave Luke the news.

"The General is as surprised and outraged as we are, Luke. He's going to call Washington and talk to whoever is in charge of the country now, we think it is still General Hamms, but it might not be this morning. Andy went to West Point with Hamms so we might get a delay on the resolution to grant nation status to Texas. If you have a contact that can help us down in Terlingua, I'm to take my men and gunships down to back you up until the reinforcements arrive."

"Sergeant Luis called last night and got a message to the spec ops team that came in with Maggie O'Brien. As a matter of fact, the head of that bunch is an old CIA spook by the same name. He never did tell me why they were here, but I think they were sent in here to find Governor Kincaid. The last that I heard from them, they were on the way to Alpine to question some of the prisoners that we sent down. I just figured that if President Atkins is planning on selling us out, we will need those men to help raid his fortress that he built down there and smoke him out, but I hear it is impregnable," Luke told him.

"Well, the Titanic was 'unsinkable' but that didn't stop a very determined iceberg now did it?" Jenkins laughed, "Besides, the battle always belongs to the Lord; all we're supposed to do is prepare for it."

"For a few minutes, I forgot that you were a pastor, Pastor. I'm glad you're going to lead the charge," Luke chuckled.

"People are going to talk about this for a long time, Luke. Let's give them something to shout about when the topic comes up," Jenkins answered.

Both men in the Hummer gave him a hearty "Yes, Sir!"

Michael Tucker hit pay dirt in the third place that they asked about Emmanuel Hernandez. The store manager thought it was odd that a man matching the description that Tuck gave him had stopped in that morning to buy a change of clothes, especially since he was wearing Texas Guard MultiCams.

"Bingo, Shaun!" Tuck exclaimed when he got back to the charger, "He was here yesterday buying some new clothes. The manager said to look for a Mexican, five feet three inches tall with a yellow shirt, jeans, and a new black hat."

"That shouldn't be difficult at all," Terry McFadden said sarcastically.

"Well, we've got five men down here. Get everybody spread out and start searching close to the border. I have all ideas that if Mr. Hernandez hasn't made a run for it yet, he soon will," Shaun told them, "If he gets over there, we probably won't be able to find him in all of that housing. I'm going to check the local motels. Maybe one of us will get lucky."

Three hours later, Shaun O'Brien pulled up in front of the Three Palms Inn in a very modest part of town. Shaun rang the bell on the desk and waited for almost five minutes for a sleepy eyed desk clerk to come from the back of the office to the answer the bell.

"Yes, what can I do for you?" he asked.

"I'm looking for Emmanuel Hernandez and I was told that he had a room here," Shaun lied.

"I can't give out information on our guests, you understand," The clerk stated.

Shaun pulled a twenty-dollar bill out and slid it across the table, "He's a friend of mine."

"Of course, we can make an exception for friends of our guests," He responded and pulled the bill across the counter, "Mr. Hernandez is in room number 112."

"Thank you very much," Shaun told him and went outside.

He had just gotten to the room when the door opened, and Manny Hernandez bolted out. So much for paying the desk clerk,. Manny must have paid him more for the warning.

"Manny, wait a minute. Amos Whitehorse sent me!" Shaun shouted, "We need your help."

Manny stopped and turned around cautiously, "Who are you?"

"I'm Shaun O'Brien. We ran into Amos yesterday in Alpine, and he sent us down here to find you. We need your help getting into Atkins' fortress," O'Brien told him.

"Why in the world would I want to go back in there?" Manny asked.

"Because you know that we have to stop President Atkins from handing Texas over to Mexico," O'Brien replied.

"This immediately brings to mind the 'what do you mean "we" white man?' joke. Okay, I'm in. Now what's the next move?" he asked.

"We pick up the rest of the team and head for Terlingua. The cavalry is meeting us there," O'Brien told him.

"I hope that is all that will meet us there! You don't think that Atkins' men have stopped looking for me, do you?" Manny asked nervously.

"Probably not, but then again, they won't expect to find us with you. We need to hurry," O'Brien told him.

The strange looking convoy of two HumVees and a purple Dodge Charger raced along route 170 from Presidio to Terlingua, following the Rio Grande River with no signs of any patrol units that might be looking for Manny Hernandez until they were about three miles from Lajitas on the desolate southern corner of the Big Bend Ranch. Ahead of them were several military vehicles arranged to block the road from both direction, and over a dozen troops in Texas Guard uniforms standing by the trucks.

"Well, our luck just changed," Tuck said to O'Brien.

"We'll see shortly, Tuck. Arm up and sit tight," He answered.

Terry McFadden drove up to the roadblock and didn't wait to be questioned, "Let us through. We have Emmanuel Hernandez in custody!"

"I need to see some ID, sir," The young soldier told him.

"Terry handed out the fake ID that he had secured and held his breath. Tuck started to pull the suppressed Berretta from under his leg when the soldier handed the ID back through the window.

"Go on through, and we'll follow you in," he told Terry, "There's no need for us to be out here now since you got him."

"You heard that the war is officially over haven't you, son" O'Brien leaned over and spoke to the guard.

"Why, no sir, we haven't!" he answered excitedly.

"Last night the military over threw the President of the United States and ended it. You all can head on home since General Clarke has disbanded the Guard since last night," O'Brien said convincingly.

The soldier ran over to the rest of the men and started talking in an animated fashion. Shaun gave the nod to Terry who eased the Dodge through the roadblock, followed closely by the two Hummers behind them, waving and blowing the horn as if in celebration.

"Nice touch, Terry. Now quit playing and let's put some distance between us and them," Tuck told him.

The Dodge picked up speed with a growl of the hemi, and they were soon out of sight of the checkpoint and nearing the rendezvous at Terlingua as planned.

When they reached the airport, Colonel Jenkins was waiting on them with Luke and the men of the Geezer patrol in addition to the regulars of the 39th that he'd brought with them.

"Mr. O'Brien, "he called as he walked over to Shaun as they got out of the car, "Colonel Nathan Jenkins, Texas Guard."

"Nice to meet you Colonel. Hello again Luke, I'm glad you could make it for the party," Shaun called out. Has anyone seen or heard from Maggie O'Brien since yesterday?"

"We haven't seen Maggie since Captain Whitehorse picked her up a couple of days back," Luke told him.

They walked into the small terminal building and almost immediately saw that a special news broadcast from the Republic of Texas News was playing on a small TV screen in the passenger waiting area.

"…we repeat again, the war with the United States has ended thanks to the efforts of President Atkins. As soon as the details can be worked out, Texas will be a free and independent nation once again! In other news, well-known TV newscaster and a recent addition to the Republic of Texas News Network staff, Maggie O'Brien is missing and presumed dead. Her pilot, Captain Amos Whitehorse has been detained as a suspect in her disappearance and the disappearance of her camerawoman, Julie Meyers. Captain Whitehorse flew back from a documentary shoot yesterday evening with the two women missing from the Republic of Texas News helicopter," The reporter droned on with other news, but Shaun turned and walked out of the terminal.

Manny Hernandez followed him outside, "Amos would never do anything to hurt Maggie. I know it!"

"I know it too, Manny. If Maggie is still alive, she is in that 'Hive' of yours, and I have to find a way to get her out. Got any ideas?" Shaun asked.

"I can get you back inside, but to get back out, we would need a pretty big diversion," Manny told him.

"Let's get the ops team involved here along with Colonel Jenkins. I want to put a plan together for this evening if we can work out the details," Shaun told him.

The men grouped together over a set of maps that Jenkins had brought with him showing the basic layout of the Hive from the outside. Michael Tucker looked over the different approaches, committing them to memory.

Manny gave them the details from his security knowledge, "There is a big door about three hundred feet up that south slope at the end of an access road. It is very heavy and it probably would take a direct hit with something big to come down. The biggest problem is that you won't be able to see it readily. Above the door is an air intake shaft that Amos and I used to sneak back into the building after sneaking out through the old quicksilver mine down below. If they have not discovered that we did, a team could sneak back in there and come in behind the security in the hanger bay."

"Tell me what is below that command center," Shaun ordered.

"Well, we didn't really have a chance to find out much, except that the first floor under the command center is a maximum security prison. The bottom may be also. There were no lights on, and it is darker than pitch down there," Manny told him.

"What about Amos?" Tuck asked, "Where do you think they are holding him?"

"He is either being held in his room which is two floors above the command center, or he is in one of those cells."

"Tuck, what are you thinking?" Shaun asked.

"I think that you and I go in with Manny, Terry rigs the mine for a quick departure, and the rest of our team makes a try for the air duct. If they can open the door, Colonel Jenkins' Apaches send in a couple of missiles and some heavy fire to keep those Spetznaz in place. If we can find Amos and the ladies, we bring them back out into the mine tunnel to Terry, and then you and I go back in for Atkins," Tuck told him.

"Well, our handler said that you had a knack. Now I know what he meant," Shaun slapped him on the back, "All right men, you've heard the plan. Colonel, do you have any problems with it?"

"Not a one, except that there are lots of good people in there that believe that they are fighting for a new nation. What about them?" he asked.

"See if General Clarke can put some people to work hacking the communications in that fortress. I know that everything is probably security hardened, but if you can get in, you can warn the folks inside," Shaun told him.

"Will do. We've got about three hours until dark. It is going to be hard to get to that mine entrance without being spotted in the daylight, and very difficult to navigate the terrain in the dark," Jenkins told him.

Shaun thought about it for a minute, and then pointed to Luke and the patrol that were unloading their horses and gear.

"A few men on horseback wouldn't raise much suspicion out here would they?" he asked.

"Not at all, especially with the announcement that the war was over. What did you have in mind?" Jenkins asked.

"I need for Captain Moffett and several horses to take us up there in the next few minutes. We'll be in a good place to sneak into the mine by dark," Shaun told him. "Let's say that we enter the mine at nineteen hundred hours. The diversion starts at nineteen thirty hours, and if they don't succeed by nineteen forty hours, you do your best to blow the doors off that hanger."

"I'll take care of it. You'll probably need the mules also for supplies," He replied and walked off.

"Hey boss, I don't think that I can ride one of those things very well. Truth of it is, I've always been a little bit afraid of horses," Terry told Shaun.

"We'll work something out, Terry. Get some explosives ready for the mine if that will take your mind off the horses," O'Brien told him, "We'll have to leave our body armor behind also if we are going to fool anybody that gets close to us."

In the end, Luke suggested that Terry ride one of the more docile mules that he would lead, and they would pack the equipment on the other. It was going to be a hard ride through the mountainous terrain to get in place in three short hours, but Shaun O'Brien had the determination of a worried father pressing on him. He kicked himself mentally for pressing Maggie to return to Atkins yesterday, knowing that she would be okay right now if he hadn't.

Tuck seemed to know what was going through his mind because he rode up close and told him, "Maggie wouldn't have stayed even if you had insisted. She's a reporter in every sense of the word, Shaun, plus her head is almost as hard as yours."

"Possibly, Tuck, but I still worry about her. What I can't figure out is why would Atkins tell the world that she is dead if he is holding her prisoner?" Shaun replied.

"Only one thing comes to mind for me, and that is he knows that we are on to his plan, and the announcement is meant to be bait. Since Captain Whitehorse was arrested, it is possibly that he told Atkins about Maggie's father being in the area," Tuck told him.

"Change of plans, Tuck. Manny, is there any cover once we get close to the mine?" Shaun asked as he pulled up his horse.

"Rocks possibly. The terrain is very rough there, but any spotters will see us long before nightfall," Manny replied.

"Luke, I need for you to take Terry on in close to the mine as if you are sightseeing. Cache the explosives as close to the mine entrance as possible without being seen, and then wait for us. Manny, Tuck, and I will high tail it back to the airport and pick up the Charger. If we drive up road 118, we can get close to the mountain, and nobody will suspect an attack from a purple car. It will mean a four mile run in the dark, but it has to be done," Shaun told them.

"Good luck to you then," Luke told him.

"Same to you. Just make out like you're camping," Tuck replied.

The ride back to the airport was without incident, and the men hastily explained the change in plans to Colonel Jenkins before heading out in the Dodge up the twisting back road that would connect them with road 118. It was just gathering twilight when Shaun pulled the car off the road in the cover of a large rock outcropping. He briefly surveyed the terrain in the direction that the mine lay in for any signs of movement, but only saw the faint glimmer of a small fire about four miles away.

"The boys have got a signal fire for us. We've got our work cut out if we are going to cover that distance across this terrain in an hour," He said.

Tuck had his rifle out of the case, and Manny had picked up an AK-47 along with a few magazines. After shouldering their packs, the three headed out at a fast paced walk toward the firelight.

Down at the fire, Luke was being questioned by four rough looking men in Texas Guard uniforms that had a distinctive Baltic accent. Terry was trying his best to look like a tourist, but his eyes were searching for any type of weapon to even the odds a bit.

"I'm telling you, friend, my client here heard that the war was over, and asked me to bring him up to the park for a couple of days. We didn't pack heavy because he intends to stay at the Big Bend Resort tomorrow after we rough it tonight. I'm just doing what I'm paid to do," Luke told the biggest of the group.

"Where is your friend from?" the leader pointed at Terry who appeared to be shivering with fear.

"I'm from Lafayette, Tennessee, and I would really like to be back there right now," He muttered.

"What if we don't believe you?" the man questioned again.

"I suppose that is your right, but I am a citizen of the Republic of Texas, and if you don't believe me then you can kiss my…" Luke didn't finish because the man's head jerked sideways from the impact of a 9mm bullet from Shaun's suppressed Beretta.

The other three were quickly dispatched in similar fashion before Shaun and his team stepped out into the ring of light from the small campfire.

"Did you miss us?" he asked Terry.

"It sure took you long enough, boss. I thought I was going to have to take them out myself with a rock or something," Terry laughed.

"Shaun, if you are going into that mine, you need to be very watchful for rattlers. There are apt to be a bunch of them denned up in there, and it didn't get that cold today," Luke warned him.

"Thanks, Luke. I'm going to let Manny lead so he can get bitten first," Shaun laughed.

Tuck looked down at his boots, "I wish I had some of those Chinese made snake boots on right now."

"Come on men, it's the two legged snakes that we need to be concerned with," Shaun chided them.

The three disappeared into the small mine entrance, and Terry got busy rigging the cave mouth to blow, just in case they were followed out. Manny led the way with all three of the men using their flashlights to look for snakes until they came to the section of false wall. Manny reached for the release carefully and tripped it with just a small clicking sound. They stepped through into the darkened hole under the stairs and crawled out into the stairwell one at a time.

"Where are we now, Manny?" Shaun asked.

"We should be on the bottom level of the fortress," He replied, "I think that this one is a prison too."

Tuck shinned his light into one after another of the small, locked cells before something caught his eye.

"Guys, over here!" He exclaimed in a whisper, "There is someone in this one!"

They all took turns trying to get a good look through the filthy glass view port of the door, but could only see a small form that appeared to be curled up on the bunk.

"We need to get this open, Manny. Do you know where the master control is located?" Shaun asked.

"No, I didn't even know that this was a prison until Amos and I came through here," He replied.

Tuck shined his light down the hallway and then took off at a jog toward the other end. In less than a minute, there was the sound of multiple door locks releasing, and Tuck came running back to the cell.

"Guard station at the end," He explained slightly out of breath.

They opened the cell and went in, hoping that the smell was not an indication of the condition of the prisoner. Shaun reached out his hand and gently rolled the form over onto its back.

"Holy Mother of God!" Manny exclaimed, crossing himself.

Looking up at them from the emaciated and bearded face were the sunken eyes of Arnold Kincaid, the missing governor of Texas!

"Governor Kincaid, we are friends. I want you to go with this young man who will take you to safety. Can you understand me?" Shaun asked gently.

"Yes," He said weakly and stretched his hand for help in sitting up.

"Tuck, if you can get the Governor out through the mine, we will wait for you on this level. Make it fast though," Shaun told him, "Remember, we can't call in for medical support until we get everyone out."

"I'm on it. Come on Governor. Let me help you get out of here," Tuck told him as he half carried the frail man out of the cell toward freedom.

"Manny, you take that side, and I'll take this one. Search each cell for anyone else that might be down here," Shaun told him.

They went from cell to cell looking into each one, but that level had held only one prisoner. Tuck came back ten minutes later and reset the locks on the prison doors to keep an alarm from being raised.

"Let's hope that they don't pick tonight to do a bed check down here," Shaun said as they made their way slowly up the stairs to the next level.

The next level proved to be empty of prisoners, so Shaun had Manny lead them quietly up the stairs past the command floor to the level where Amos' room was. Tuck slowly cracked the door and looked up the hallway. Standing in front of the room on either side of the door were two of Atkins Spetznaz mercenaries. Tuck very quietly eased his arm into the hallway and fired two rounds from the suppressed Berretta into the heads of the men.

Amos heard the bodies drop with a slight thud on the other side of the door and was just getting ready to check when he heard a knock.

"Who is it?" He asked.

"Open up, Amos, it's us!" Tuck whispered loudly.

Amos opened the door and they quickly dragged the two dead guards inside.

"Man, am I glad to see you guys!" Amos exclaimed.

Shaun didn't mince words, "Where is Maggie and Julie, Amos? Atkins is broadcasting that you killed them."

"I did no such thing! They were here last night because I brought them back with me. Atkins had me in the office, and I let it slip that they weren't the only ones that I brought back from Cozumel. Hell, I thought you were working for him!" Amos replied defensively.

"Where would he be keeping them if they are alive?" Shaun asked.

"Their room is two floors up, but I didn't get the number. If they are there, there will be a guard," He said.

"Tuck, take Manny, and check for a guarded room. We'll wait here for you," Shaun told them, "While we wait, tell me what happened after you flew out of Alpine."

"Well, we had some of Atkins men try to intercept us at the airport, so we decided to fly to Marfa and then make a run down to the border below here to see if there were any troops gathering." Amos said, "Boy, were there! It looked like the entire Mexican army was sitting on the other side just waiting for an invitation. We came in after that, and I was escorted to see Atkins. That was the last time I saw Maggie or Julie."

"I think that maybe Atkins is holding Maggie hostage knowing that I'd come for her. With what you told him about the Cozumel trip, he has pieced together that we were hired to find out what had happened to Governor Kincaid. When that news leaks out, he is finished, and will probably hang for treason," Shaun told him, "Right now he has the upper hand because he thinks that his secret hasn't gotten out, but boy is he in for a big surprise!"

"Did you ever find out what happened to the Governor?" Amos asked.

"He was down below the whole time," Shaun told him.

"I've known Jeb for fifteen years, and I would never have believed him capable of selling us out like this. What could have happened to him?" he asked.

"Who knows? War changes people sometimes, especially if they aren't wrapped up tight to begin with. Maybe the lure of money and power got the best of him. Whatever the cause, Jeb Atkins must be stopped tonight!" Shaun replied.

Tuck and Manny came into the room.

"They aren't up there, Shaun. Where to next?" Tuck asked.

"If they aren't there, they are being held in the command center. Any idea how we can get in there, Manny?" Shaun asked.

There is only the main door off the stair well or the elevator and both are guarded," Manny told him, "You know this guy is about Tuck's size, and there is not much blood on his shirt. Why not let Tuck take the elevator, and we wait by the door. He can make a distraction, and we'll rush the guard. There are two more at the office across the room, and the rest of the people in there are military consultants."

"It might work, Tuck. You can go in and shout 'The War is over!' That should cause some concern and give us time to slip in," Shaun told him.

"Okay, but we have about five minutes before they blow the doors upstairs so that isn't going to sell very well, and we need to come up with a plan to get us out after we grab the girls," Tuck told him as he hurried to exchange his clothes with those of the dead guard.

"Let me get Maggie and Julie out," Amos volunteered.

"If we can get Jeb away from them, assuming that he has them in there, you will need to work fast. Have you ever used one of these before?" Shaun handed him the Berretta.

"Not that one, but I can shoot," He replied.

"Don't hesitate if you get a shot," Shaun admonished, "Okay, Tuck, take the elevator down. Yell, 'We're under attack!' or something original. That should throw them off long enough for us to get through the stairwell door"

Tuck ran down the hallway and punched the button for the elevator, which was twenty floors above him. True to his built in clock, a massive vibration was felt at exactly nineteen thirty hours followed by a series of smaller thumps that carried down the three hundred feet depth of the fortress.

The elevator doors finally opened and Tuck stepped into a crowd of frightened Texas Guard aides and soldiers that were seeking the safety of the lower level. When they stopped at the command center, the elevator full of people emptied to shouts of "We are under attack!" from multiple mouths, a fact that was already apparent on the faces of the men and women crowded around the command table. Tuck burst into the room without even a glance being given to his presence and started moving to the opposite end of the command center where an office with shuttered windows was located. The presence of two guards, presumably Spetznaz, marked it as the place where Jebediah Atkins was holed up, hopefully with the women. When he was slightly alongside the guards, one of them turned his head in Tuck's direction, and then he dropped silently to the floor, as did his partner. Shaun had shot each one behind the ear, but no one in the large room full of panicked people seemed to notice.

Shaun nodded to Amos, and then motioned towards the door with a move of his head. Amos took that as his cue for action, although he wasn't sure just what that action was going to entail. He stepped over the bodies lying at the door and knocked.

"Mr. President, Mr. President, its Amos, sir. We are under attack and being overrun. You need to come with me so we can get to safety," He called through the door.

Shaun and Tuck drew themselves up close to the outside wall of the office as the door opened just a crack and the barrel of a 1911 Colt protruded.

"Amos, how did you get here, where are my guards?" Jeb called out.

"They are dead, sir. We need to get out of here right now or we will be too!" Amos was certain the last statement was true.

"I was wrong about you Amos. There are two hostages in here that will help us get away. Can you get us out?" Jeb sounded frightened for the first time that Amos could remember.

"Absolutely, sir, but we have to leave now!" Amos prodded him.

"I'm coming out," Jeb told him and withdrew the pistol.

Amos stepped back as Jeb stepped out behind Maggie and Julie who had their hands zip tied behind them and gags in their mouths. Maggie was wide eyed when she saw Amos, but didn't make a move to resist. As soon as they were clear of the door, Shaun hit Jeb behind the head with the flat of the Berretta, knocking him unconscious, while Amos put his arms around Maggie for a second before cutting the restraints on both women.

"Well, you said that you wanted a knight in shining armor, didn't you?" Amos grinned.

Julie replied with her characteristic wit, "My Hero!"

"Come on, we've got to go!" Shaun ordered as he and Tuck grabbed Atkins by the arms, and then dragged him to the stairs.

Manny and Amos led the women out behind them with no one paying any attention. In the background they heard a transmission that said, "The war is over, and President Atkins is planning on selling Texas to Mexico"

Once on the lower level, Tuck ran ahead to call in a helicopter to take them out, and also check on the Governor, who had seemed to be on his last legs. Amos and Manny took the women through the narrow opening and out of the cave, being cautious for snakes, and Shaun brought Jeb Atkins with him after pushing the false wall back into place, dragging the disoriented man by his right arm.

Terry McFadden met them a few yards inside of the cave entrance and started to help with Jeb when the man suddenly made a move against the startled Shaun O'Brien and pushed him into

Terry. As he made the move to get O'Brien off balance, Jeb also grabbed for the Berretta that was in his enemy's hand. He fired two shots at the men in rapid succession, and then ran back into the mine in the direction of the false wall.

"I'm hit boss. The bastard shot me in the chest," Terry gasped as he started sliding to the ground.

"Help is on the way, McFadden. Stay with me," Shaun told him as his own blood trickled from a shoulder wound.

Tuck came running back as the two emerged from the mine.

"What happened, Shaun?" he asked as he helped carry the two hundred and eighty pound Terry to safety.

"Atkins got the drop on me, Tuck. He got my gun and shot us. I've got to go back in there after him," Shaun told him.

Tuck just looked at him a minute before replying, "Not tonight old friend, not tonight."

Luke had taken the detonator for the explosive charges in the cave mouth from Terry's hand and now pushed the plunger. The entrance spit out a blast of dirt and dust as the expertly placed explosives brought the roof down to seal the mine permanently.

"That was for John," He said quietly.

Inside of the mine, a desperate Jebediah Atkins ran in the pitch dark right past the location of the false door and further down the old mine tunnel than he should have. Suddenly his feet were no longer on solid rock, but over a twenty-foot deep vertical shaft. The wind was knocked out of him when he hit the bottom, and a searing pain rocketed through his body as his left leg and arm snapped with the crunch of broken bones.

The next things that he was aware of were the slight buzzing noises that seemed to be coming from all around him. Jeb laid the Beretta pistol down, and then struggled to reach his unbroken right hand into his pants pocket for a Bic lighter that he carried. He rolled the striker several times before the small fire shot out of the end, and then he held the lighter up so that he could see where he was. As Jeb's eye became accustom to the dim light, he made out the shapes of the dozens of rattlesnakes that shared the deep hole with him. His screams of fear and pain went unanswered in the cold darkness of the pit three hundred and fifty feet below the top floor of his fortress until the soft pop of the Beretta silenced all but the buzzing of the snakes.

EPILOGUE

"Well, Luke, I didn't think that I'd be having coffee with an honest to gosh Texas hero on Christmas Eve. What are the odds?" Jerry told him.

Around the tables of the Wagon Wheel Restaurant, men applauded Luke Moffet as he walked in for an early cup of coffee and a plate of bacon and eggs.

"Good morning everybody," Luke replied to the accolades, "I sure didn't think that I was going to be eating here on the day before Christmas either, or ever again for that matter."

The Vanguard News channel was buzzing with the news that Governor Kincaid was now recovering in an unnamed facility, and Tom Hastings was acting as the interim Governor of Texas until his return to office. There was also a report about Maggie O'Brien, a former reporter of Vanguard News getting married in a special Christmas Eve ceremony in Gardendale, Texas.

"You goin' to that Luke?" Charlie asked loudly over the talking.

"Yep, this is one wedding that I wouldn't miss," Luke replied.

"That little girl sure could ride, couldn't she?" Jasper spoke up.

Everyone in the restaurant laughed at that remark as the ones that had been present to witness her tame the buckskin had been telling how it had tossed Luke in three jumps. Luke laughed along with them, but didn't mention what he had heard coming out of her mouth.

"Hey everybody, there's some kind of special news coming on!" someone called out to quiet the crowd.

"We interrupt our normal programming to bring a special report from the White House. General Leslie Hamms is about to make a statement," A reporter for Vanguard News announced.

The camera view switched to the press briefing room and General Hamms entered flanked by two civilians.

"I want to make a brief statement to the American people this morning on the eve of Christmas. While the military is going to maintain control of Washington until the people of this country can decide on a new President and their representatives in elections scheduled for next month, I am ordering an end to martial law, and also ordering the pull back of all troops engaged in related enforcement, effective immediately. I am encouraged by talks that we held yesterday with almost all of the various states governors, and we have been assured that the states will assume the responsibility for law enforcement as we start the healing process across our land.

In answer to the question that is foremost on most minds: No, we are not going to pursue any military interdiction in Texas. The root cause of the problems there has been dealt with. At this time we are negotiating the return of the George H.W. Bush carrier group, and have offered a full amnesty to any officers and men that may have participated in turning over United States Government property during this brief conflict. I feel like Texas secession is a matter for Texians to deal with, and we will not interfere with that decision except to say that Mexico will not be involved in any activity within what is for now the state of Texas. That is all."

"Well, I didn't think that we'd get off that easy," Jerry said loudly.

"We lost a lot of good men because of the greed and poor leadership of a few shortsighted individuals both here and in Washington. I wouldn't exactly call that getting off easy, Jerry," Luke replied.

The rest of the breakfast was quiet as the patrons reflected on what Luke had just said. When he finished, Luke got up silently and walked to the door.

"I now pronounce you husband and wife. Amos, you may kiss the bride!" Pastor Nathan Jenkins declared with a smile.

Amos gave Maggie a kiss to the applause of the church full of guests and well-wishers, and then the couple exited the church through a cloud of birdseed and well wishes. Their chauffer drove them around the back in a new F350 Ford crew cab that had been decorated for the occasion by Julie, Jackson Leonard, and Maximillian Rodriguez for a small reception in their honor that had been thrown together by the ladies of the church on short notice. When Julie caught the bouquet, she gave the frightened looking Jake Leonard a big smile.

Shaun O'Brien came over to his daughter who gave him a very tender hug, trying not to touch the shoulder that had the bullet hole in it. Shaun did his best to hug back with the arm that was not in a sling, but had less luck keeping the tears from leaking out of his eyes.

"Well, Maggie, I may not have made many of your other big moments, but this is one that I wouldn't have missed even if I was dead!" He told her, "Amos, you take care of my little girl."

"Yes, sir, Shaun. You know that I will," Amos shook his good hand with a big grin on his face, "By the way, have you any news about Terry?"

"Tuck stayed with him last night until he passed. They are going to send him back to Tennessee for burial. He was a good man and gave his life for a good cause," Shaun replied somberly, "I have to go now, they are holding a flight for the team, but I want you to know that if you need anything, you can reach me through that number that I gave you. Merry Christmas, you two."

Maggie hugged him again, and Amos shook his hand. Shaun O'Brien made a hasty round to shake the hands of those that he'd met on this assignment, and to press a gift into the hand of Pastor Jenkins.

"That's our queue also, Honey," Amos said to Maggie and they started for the back door, and the truck that Rodriguez had kept waiting for them.

"What did Daddy mean by reaching him? I don't have his number, so how did you get his number?" Maggie pressed.

"Well, I was going to tell you a little later because it is sort of a wedding present from Shaun, but there is a group in Key Largo that needs a pilot for a seaplane that they use for their business, and your dad has something to do with that business," Amos told her, "Anyway, we are using the plane for an all expense paid trip to Barbados! How about that?"

"You do have an idea what my father does for a living, don't you?" Maggie gave him the raised eyebrow look.

"I'm sure it is something exciting, Maggie, but let's get to the hotel and change. We've got a flight out of here in a couple of hours, and I'd like to spend Christmas with you in the tropics!" he exclaimed.

Maggie gave him a smile and squeezed his hand, but her mind kept bringing up troubling visions of what they had seen in the past two weeks.

The black limousine pulled up at a private hanger that had received little damage during the bombardment of the week before. Sitting outside, fueled and ready for departure was the Beechcraft King Air 350i that they had flown in from Cozumel on.

"There's your plane back, and in fairly good condition I might add, and here is the bonus for the team," Henry Albright said as he handed Shaun a very thick manila envelope, "Merry Christmas."

"Thanks Henry, I appreciate the call on this one," Shaun said as he took the envelope and put it in his bag.

"Tell Tuck that I'll be down to see them in a couple of months. I've got a taste for some deep-water fishing. Did your new son-in-law take the job?" Henry asked.

"Yes, I'm sending them down on a 'honeymoon' before we tell him what the job is, although Maggie probably already knows," Shaun laughed.

"Well, I see that your men are already on board. I'll be in touch," Henry told him, "Thanks for bringing Harold back alive, Shaun. That was icing on the cake for me."

Shaun nodded before getting out of the limo and boarding the plane. As he headed for the pilot's seat, he tossed the envelope to Tuck.

"Merry Christmas! Settle with the men, Tuck, and don't forget Terry's share," He said.

"Roger that, boss. Let's go home," Tuck replied as he climbed into the co-pilot's seat and started counting the money.

The big Beechcraft throttled up and rose into the sky headed in the direction of Miami. Tuck was going to fly back to Barbados on the company plane with the new pilot, while the rest of the team went to wherever home was for Christmas.

ACKNOWLEDGEMENTS

In addition to the political climate in this great country at the time that this story was conceived, I was inspired by the indomitable spirit of the Texans that I've had the privilege of calling friends, especially the folks that live and work in the western reaches of the state

Other Books by W. W. Brock:

COUGAR!

NIGHT WIND

THUNDER RANCH

W.W. Brock